Frank Brown
Sea Apprentice

by

Frank T. Bullen

Frank Brown Sea Apprentice
by Frank T. Bullen

ISBN: 978-93-61420-38-2

Published by

DOUBLE 9 BOOKS

2/13-B, Ansari Road
Daryaganj, New Delhi – 110002
info@double9books.com
www.double9books.com
Tel. 011-40042856

ABOUT THE AUTHOR

Frank Thomas Bullen British novelist, was born on April 5, 1857, in Paddington, London, to poor parents. He attended a dame school and Westbourne School in Paddington for a few years. At the age of nine, his aunt, who was his guardian, died. He then quit school to work as an errand boy. In 1869, he went to sea and traveled all over the world in various capacities, including second mate of the Harbinger and chief mate of the Day Dawn, under Capt. John R. H. Ward jun in 1879, when she was dismasted and rendered crippled. After spending 15 years at sea since the age of 12, he later described the hardships of his early life as follows: I was beaten by a negro youngster as big as myself, and only a Frenchman intervened on my behalf. Boys in Geordie colliers or East Coast fishing smacks were frequently beaten to insanity and jumped overboard, or were killed in truly savage fashion, and all that was required to account for their absence was a line in the log stating that they had been washed or had fallen overboard.

CONTENTS

PREFACE

In order to make it plain to my readers that the following pages may be read without danger of acquiring false information about the sea, or the ways of its servants, I beg to say that every incident recorded is fact, either well authenticated by others, or personal experience of my own. About the merits of the *story* I can, of course, say nothing, but I assure my readers of the accuracy of the details and information herein contained. I have naturally used the incidents to make a story, and given fictitious names of ships, places, and people. And I am not without hope that the reading of this book may be quite profitable to parents of boys wishing to go to sea, as well as pleasurable to the boys themselves.

FRANK T. BULLEN.

R.M.S.*Omrah,*
At Sea in the Great Australian Bight,
Easter Sunday 1906.

CHAPTER I
THE CALL OF THE SEA

"My dear boy, you are only feeling what I think most British boys feel at some period of their school days, a longing for an adventurous life, no matter what the outcome of it may be. Of course you can't see one inch beyond your nose, that's not to be expected, any more than that you should consider my feelings in the matter. You want to go to sea and that's enough — for you; but, Frank, aren't your mother and father to be thought of at all? I know of course that sailors are necessary and all that, but what little I know of a sailor's life and prospects makes me feel that it is the last profession on earth that I should choose for my son, especially after I have impoverished myself to fit you to take your place in the great firm with which I have been honourably connected for the last thirty years. There will always be plenty of youngsters with unhappy homes and neglected education to take up the business of seafaring, boys who have got nothing else to look forward to ashore. But you're not one of those, are you?"

The speaker, Mr. Frank Brown, was a man who occupied a responsible position in the counting-house of a great manufacturing firm in the North of England. Steady, faithful, if humdrum, service had raised him from almost the lowest position in the office to the post he had held for the last twelve years at a salary of £500 a year. He was happily married, and had three children, two daughters aged twelve and sixteen respectively, and a son, to whom he was now speaking, who came between them, that is, he was now fourteen; a fine, healthy, and intelligent lad.

But while Mr. Brown was almost a model member of that great middle class which, in spite of what sensationalists may say, is in very truth the backbone of our country, his horizon was exceedingly limited by his particular business. Outside of it he was almost densely ignorant of the world's affairs. All his abilities, and they were undoubtedly high, had been always concentrated upon his duties at the office, and he had been repaid by a life devoid of care and external difficulties. It never even occurred to him what "going to sea" meant for his native land, namely, her existence as a nation. He did not know that there was any difference between the Navy and the Merchant service, only thought of the sailor as a picturesque, careless figure who led a life full of adventure but empty of profit to himself, a rolling stone who could never be expected to gather any moss.

And he was a perfect type of many thousands of his class, whom it is impossible not to admire, while bewailing the narrowness of their minds, the restriction of their intellectual boundaries. He had never contemplated the possibility of his son striking out an original line for himself, having in his own mind mapped out that son's career, and now when in stammering accents and blushing like a girl that son had suddenly announced his determination to "go to sea," he was filled with dismay. His mental vision showed him a hirsute semi-piratical individual reeking of strong liquors and rank tobacco, full of strange oaths and stranger eccentricities, but entirely lacking in the essential elements of "getting on," which, to tell the truth, was to Mr. Brown the chief end of man.

Now Frank junior cared for none of these latter things, because he had never thought about them. Food and clothes and home comforts came as did the sunshine and the air. From his earliest recollection he had never needed to concern himself with any of his wants, because they were supplied in good time by the care of his dear mother. A perfectly healthy young animal, and free from vice because he had led a sheltered life, he had given no trouble, but having lately taken to reading stories of adventure, principally of the sea, he had suddenly felt the call of the wild, the craving of the bird reared in the cage to escape therefrom upon seeing a wild bird fly past or upon inhaling a breath from the forest or field. This primal need held him, and so, although he hardly knew how to express himself, he stood his ground, and to his father's address only replied, "I feel I must go, Dad. I don't know why, but I feel I shan't ever do any good here. Do let me go."

And that was all they could get out of him. The tears of his mother and the expostulations of his father were equally of no use, and besides, it must be admitted that he was secretly encouraged (which was needless) by his eldest sister, who said, "I glory in you, Frank; if I was only a boy I'd go, see if I wouldn't. I wouldn't stick on this mill-horse round day after day, never getting any further forward, not I. I'm proud of you, old chap."

Many a private confabulation did these two hold together, the subject always being the glorious adventure of a sailor's life, the splendid opportunity of seeing the world and of doing the things that stay-at-homes only read about and gape over, until the boy was ready to do anything, however foolish, to gratify his craving. But, like many other boyish fancies, I think this might have worn off, if it hadn't been for a circumstance occurring accidentally just then which clinched matters.

The family went, as they usually did, to Lytham for their summer holiday, Mr. Brown chuckling at the thought that while they could enjoy the sea-air his boy would not have much chance to pursue his hobby, even though so closely in touch with the sea, from the absence of shipping. And for a little while it seemed as if in his enjoyment of bicycling, swimming, and boating, which all the family were fond of, Frank had forgotten his desire for a sailor's life, the subject being tacitly dropped.

Then one day when they were all having a pleasant sail in a small boat, a piece of carelessness on the part of the boatman caused the main sheet to jam just as a sudden puff of wind came down and heeled her over. In a moment all of them were struggling in the water, and a tragedy was imminent. But a smart little yacht ran down to them and, how they never knew, in a few minutes they were all rescued and were being swiftly carried shoreward very wet and frightened, but extremely grateful to their preserver, a hale, seaman-like man of about sixty years of age, who handled his little vessel as if she was part of himself.

On reaching the shore Mr. Brown begged their preserver, who had introduced himself as Captain Burns, retired master mariner, to visit them at their hotel that evening in order that he might be properly thanked for his great skill and opportune help. The captain accepted gaily, but made light of his services, and hoping that they would feel no ill effects from their ducking, bade them good-bye until the evening.

"What an adventure," said Mr. Brown, "and what a splendid man that Captain Burns is, to be sure, a regular old sea-dog." Then he stopped and looked at his son, who, with flushed face and sparkling eyes, was evidently enjoying to the full this episode so much to his taste.

From then until the evening the talk, however much the father and mother might try to change the subject, ran continually upon the merits of sailors, especially their resource and courage in time of danger; and the parents sighed repeatedly as they realised how the event of the day was working, in spite of themselves, against their cherished hopes.

But when the captain arrived to dinner and allowed himself to be drawn out by Frank, telling marvellous tales of adventure in foreign lands and on lonely, stormy seas, even the staid father felt his breath come short and his heart swell, and he began to enter into the feelings of his boy, who hung entranced upon every word which fell from the captain's lips.

At last, during a momentary lull in the conversation, Mr. Brown said hesitatingly, "I am afraid, captain, that your yarns, marvellously interesting as they are, will frustrate all the pains I have been taking lately to persuade my boy that he ought to give up his idea of going to sea. You seem to have magnetised him. I thought he was enthusiastic before, but I am afraid he won't listen to my reasoning at all now."

There was a dead silence for a minute or two, during which Frank looked pleadingly at his parents, and the captain was evidently embarrassed. Then the latter broke the awkward pause by saying, "If I have come athwart your wishes in any way, Mr. Brown, with regard to my young friend here, I'm very sorry. And you'll know I had no intention of so doing. But you'll know, too, that when a British boy feels the call of the sea he doesn't need any encouragement to make him persevere in his attempts to get to it, and everything told him in order to discourage him only seems to have the opposite effect. I'm sure I feel that what I've said about my experiences, although I don't deny that I am proud to have gone through them, ought to make anybody feel that any life was preferable to a sailor's. But when you come to think of it, there is something splendid in the way in which our youngsters crave to face danger and hardship in a calling which has done so much to make our good old country what it is. Goodness knows where we should be without this fine young spirit, for you know we must have sailors, or what would become of us as a nation?"

"There, there," burst in Mr. Brown hastily, "don't say any more. You convince me against what I consider my own better judgment, and I don't mind admitting that, although it has cost us many a bitter pang to bring ourselves to the idea of parting with our only son, my wife and I agreed last night that we would no longer oppose him in his wishes. But we want advice as to the best means of gratifying his wish, so that he may get the most effective start possible in the profession. I am quite ignorant of everything concerning the beginning of a sea career, but I am absolutely convinced of the necessity of starting right in any undertaking. So I shall be grateful for any advice you can give me on the matter."

"Good man," replied the captain, "you can count on me to do all I can for him. First of all I assume that he is healthy and hardy, and that his eyesight is all right as regards colour blindness; for I may as well tell you at once, that unless that is all right, it is absolutely useless for him to give another thought to a seafaring career. But we can settle that at once. Here, Frank, let me put you through your first examination."

And the captain, amidst the keenest interest on the part of the whole family, proceeded to question the boy as to the colour of everything in the room. In five minutes he professed himself perfectly satisfied that, whatever else Frank might fail in, his eyesight was all right.

Frank gave a great sigh of relief, and the captain went on to say that on the morrow he would write to several shipping firms known to him who owned sailing ships—he didn't believe in steamers for beginners—and when he had learned their terms, and what vacancies were available, he would let Mr. Brown know, and advise him further as to his choice.

After which he took his leave with a fervent handshake from Frank, who looked upon him as a sort of hero-deliverer who had come just in the nick of time to save his hopes from being thwarted. The parents, as might be expected, did not feel any such enthusiasm; yet even they were relieved, as people usually are when, after a long period of indecision, they have made up their minds to a certain course, however distasteful such a course has once appeared to them.

Three days afterwards Captain Burns again called on the Browns with a lot of correspondence from his ship-owning acquaintances, and after carefully going over the merits of each opening presented, gave his advice to accept the offer of quite a small firm in Liverpool, owning three barques of medium size, from 800 to 1200 tons, usually making very long voyages to out-of-the way parts of the world, wherever, in fact, they could get remunerative freights, no easy thing in these days of universal steamer competition.

He gave as his reason that this firm was not a limited company, but privately owned, and that the owners took a direct interest in the welfare of their servants, especially of their apprentices, whom they looked upon as their personal protégés, for whose well-being they were directly responsible. The premium they demanded was £50 for four years, half of which was returnable as wages. The requisite outfit would cost, so the captain said, about twenty pounds, and the total cost for the four years would be, or rather should be, less than £100. And if his advice were taken to accept the terms of Messrs. Chadwick & Son, Frank would within three weeks be at sea and his career begun, as they had a ship now loading for several ports in the South Sea Islands. She was a nice handy barque of about 1000 tons, only about fifteen years old, and he (the captain) knew her very well as being a most comfortable ship.

Of course, having put himself implicitly in the captain's hands, Mr. Brown had no criticisms or objections to offer, or any reasons for delay. And so the next few days were very busy ones for both him and his son, and they made many visits to Liverpool under the guidance of the captain, who seemed to know everybody and his way about everywhere. They found the owner very courteous and sympathetic, but did not see the master of the *Sealark*, as the barque was called, he being at home in Scotland on leave.

They saw the vessel though, going on board of her in the Brunswick Docks, where she lay awaiting her cargo.

Both Frank and his father were very quiet as they explored the vessel's cabin and fo'c'sle, under the guidance of the worn-out old sailor who was acting as shipkeeper, Captain Burns not being with them. Everything looked so cold, and cheerless, and forlorn. Besides, there was a smell hanging about everywhere as of decaying things or bad drainage, which made both of them feel quite faint and sick, in spite of the keen wind which was blowing across the ship, and seemed to search every corner of it.

At last Mr. Brown, unable to subdue his curiosity any longer, asked the old seaman whatever the stench could mean, Frank listening eagerly for the answer.

"Oh," replied the shipkeeper, "she's just home from the Chinchee Islands with guanner, and that stinks about as bad as anything I knows on."

"Do you mean to say, then," asked the father, "that the poor fellows who sailed this ship had to bear this horrible smell all the voyage?"

"Oh no," answered the ancient mariner, "only on the passage home, about three months and a half. And then, you see, as they had the full flavour of it while they was aloading her, they'd got so used to it they wouldn't notice it when they got to sea. It wasn't near so bad then, although it was wuss nor what it is now. But lord bless you, sir, this ain't nothin'. I ben shipmates with a cargo of creosoted sleepers out to Bonos Aires, an' the stuff was that strong our noses useter bleed when we come in the fo'c'sle. An' all the grub was flavoured with strong tar, so that when we did get some fresh grub we'd lost our taste. Didn't get it back, either, for a jolly long time. Now guanner only makes your grub a bit high-flavoured, sort of gamey, like as I'm told the gentry fancies their vittles. It all depends upon taste, and sailors ain't supposed to have any."

Turning to his son, Mr. Brown said, "My boy, this is very different from what you expected, isn't it? There isn't much romantic adventure here, only dirt, discomfort, and squalor. I'm afraid you'll repent very sorely of your decision."

"Oh no, Dad," eagerly responded Frank, "I knew I should have to rough it, everybody has to that goes to sea. And I expect she'll be very different when we get to sea and all the crew on board."

"Ah, that she will," interrupted the shipkeeper; "you wouldn't know her when once the crew's settled down to work and cleaned her up. It's no place to judge a ship in dock, when there's been nobody by her for a week or two except a shipkeeper. She gets all neglected like an empty house without a caretaker."

Frank's face shone with gratitude for the comfort, and even Mr. Brown looked less worried as he realised the truth of what the old man said. But he could not help feeling grieved to think how all the little niceties of life in which his son had been brought up would be out of the question here — the little den pointed out to him as the "half-deck," or boys' apartment, being no larger than the boot-room at home, or about six feet square, and with absolutely no fittings of any kind except the four bunks. However, he reasoned that Frank would look at these things in a different light altogether, and, stifling a sigh, he tipped the old man liberally and took his departure, saying no more to his son on the subject that day.

Next day they said good-bye to their friend Captain Burns, who promised to correspond with them, and left Lytham for home, Frank almost bursting with pride as he donned his new uniform and thought of the sensation he would make among his friends at Dewsbury. He tried hard not to be self-conscious, but it was a complete failure, for he knew how his sisters were gloating over him and saw how fondly yet sadly his mother's eyes dwelt upon her handsome boy, looking so smart and manly in his new rig.

It was all like a glorious golden dream, and if ever a boy was happy he was. He did not even begrudge the delay, though it would be ten days before he was due to join his ship, because it would give him time to enjoy his triumph while pretending that he was only anxious to get away.

What a lovely time he had, to be sure, filling the hearts of all his boy friends with black envy of his luck, as they called it, being made much of by everybody, and seeing his father and mother grow prouder of him every day as if he was a young hero. Indeed it was a good job for him that the time was short, or he would have been utterly spoiled, for every one did their best to turn his head.

But the time flew by, and at last the eventful morning arrived when he must go. He was to make the journey to Liverpool alone because business claimed his father, and his mother was not strong enough for such a trial. But that only made him feel prouder of his independence, and although he could not help feeling a lump in his throat as he stood at the carriage window and waved farewell to his parents and sisters on the platform, he speedily forgot them in boy fashion as he lolled back in his seat and assumed the air of a man while the train sped swiftly towards Liverpool.

Arriving at the Exchange Station, he skipped nimbly out upon the platform and gazed around him, somewhat bewildered at the noise and bustle, until he caught sight of the burly figure of Captain Burns, who, according to his promise, was there to meet him. They were soon in a cab, and, with Frank's chest and bag on top, threaded the crowded streets towards the dock. Neither of them said much, for although Frank had a thousand questions to ask, he was, like most boys, shy with his elders, and Captain Burns had put on the "Captain" for the occasion.

They were soon alongside the *Sealark*, which, even to Frank's inexperienced eyes, looked very different from when he had last seen her. Her sails were bent and her rigging was all in place, while quite a gang of men were busy all about her putting the complications of her gear in readiness for use at sea. They did not pause to admire her, for Captain Burns was not one of those garrulous old sailors who are such a nuisance to youngsters because they will keep talking and teaching as they call it, but getting swiftly on board and depositing Frank's luggage in the house, they sought the mate at once.

He was not a prepossessing personage, being a rough, coarsely clad man of about forty, with a voice like a bull and a scowl as if he had just taken offence at something. But he was very civil to Captain Burns, who, introducing Frank, said, "Here, Mr. Jenkins, is my young friend Frank Brown, the latest candidate for acquaintance with Sou'spaining. Try and make a man of him; he's keen enough, I know, and he's come to the right quarter for experience."

The mate nodded with a grim smile, saying, "You're about right there, sir. I'll put him through his facings all right. He'll be a reg'lar tar-pot by the time we get back."

"Now then, Frank," said Captain Burns, "this is the chief mate of the ship. Next to the captain he's your boss, and if you only do what he tells you as well as you can, and as quick as you can, and never try and skulk, he'll make a prime sailor of ye. And that's what you want to be, you know. Now go and change those fine clothes for a suit of dungaree, that blue cotton stuff, you know. Put your uniform away, for you won't want it for a long time, and make haste on deck again ready to begin work. You can't begin too soon. Now good-bye and good luck to ye, and don't forget to show willing, it's only skulkers that get into trouble at sea."

And as Frank turned away towards the house, Captain Burns said to the mate, "I think he's a bit of the right stuff, strong and healthy, and I believe he'll turn out all right. Try and bring him on for my sake, and if you succeed with him I won't forget you; you know I've got a bit of a pull at the office. So-long."

And he was gone, having done his best for our hero as he considered, but having certainly arranged for Master Frank as severe a series of surprises as ever boy had. For the mate turned away muttering, "All right, Captain Burns, if I don't put him through it won't be my fault, and if he doesn't earn his Board of Trade he can't blame me. Silly young ass, I suppose he's worried his people to death to let him be a sailor, and now he thinks he is one. Well, we'll see."

CHAPTER II
OUTWARD BOUND

About a quarter of an hour after the departure of Captain Burns, Frank emerged from the boys' house, looking and feeling desperately uncomfortable in his brand-new suit of dungaree. It was stiff and smelly and exceedingly unbecoming, and besides he had been chaffed unmercifully by the two bigger boys, who left him hardly room in the house to change, and while they smoked short pipes with all the air of veteran seamen, showed no inclination to hurry on deck as he was trying to do. They were second-voyage apprentices, and accordingly looked down upon him from a supreme height as a greenhorn, and one whom it would be at once their duty and pleasure to put through his facings, as they termed it. So he was glad to escape from them, being hot and indignant at the sudden change from quite an important member of society to one of no consequence whatever.

He stood for a moment irresolute, feeling strangely lonely, but was suddenly startled by the mate's hoarse voice in his ear, saying, "Now then, admiral, don't stand there like a Calcutta pilot, but get along and make yourself generally useless. Coil them ropes up there first thing."

Poor Frank, he could only stammer out, "I—I don't know what you mean, sir."

The mate stood for a moment as if trying to realise again how helpless a home-bred boy is on board ship for the first time, then he roared, "Williams! Johnson! where are ye? Come along and show this fellow how to coil up the running gear."

His cry brought the two youths out of the house, muttering as they came, but the joy of having some one to bully soon made them forget the annoyance they felt at having their skulk disturbed, and between them they made Frank feel that instead of being a rather smart fellow, he was just a poor imbecile who didn't know anything at all that was really worth knowing. But we must set it down to his credit that he never once wished himself back home again, in spite of his grievous disappointment.

Those two bright boys led our hero a fine dance for about an hour, until there was a sudden diversion created by the arrival of the crew, every one of whom was more or less drunk and quarrelsome. Yet none of them were so far gone as to be useless, and so amidst a series of evolutions, which to Frank were simply maddening in their complications, and in which he felt always in somebody's way, the vessel was gradually moved away from her berth and dragged by the little dock-tug out into the river, where a larger tug was in waiting to seize her and tow her out to sea.

While passing out between the pierheads, Frank could not help feeling a pang of disappointment that no one whom he knew was there to bid him farewell, for he saw quite a little body of people, mostly of a very low class he thought, shabby men, and gaudily clothed, draggled-looking women, between whom and the sailors many "so-longs" and "pleasant passages" were exchanged; but the wonder and the novelty of the whole scene was such that he had little time to feel despondent, and indeed there was no delay, the vessel gliding through without a pause on the broad bosom of the muddy Mersey.

The keen wind made him shiver, but so great was his wonder at the scene around, the numbers of vessels, from the mighty ocean steamships to the swift ferry-boats and thronging small craft of varying rigs, and the manner in which the *Sealark* threaded her way among them, that all made up a panorama which kept him almost stupid with surprise.

But he was not allowed to stand staring about him; the harsh voice of the mate shouting, "Get along there forrard, boy, and lend a hand," started him off in the direction indicated by the mate's finger, where he found everybody busy at a task which seemed to him one of most bewildering complication. Not a word that passed did he understand any more than he knew what was being done or why, and if ever anybody felt a useless fool he did.

All hands were engaged in rigging out the jibboom, a great spar that protrudes over the bowsprit from the forepart of the ship, and is secured by a number of stays, guys, and chains, which, hanging loosely about it as it was gradually hove out into its permanent place, looked to him as if the tangle could never be cleared. Everything that was said or shouted was unintelligible—for all he knew they might as well have been talking in another language, and he began to feel quite dazed as well as foolish. And everybody seemed offended with him because he did not understand, bad words were freely flung at him, for whatever he did seemed to be wrong, and altogether he became pretty miserable. For, as I have said, he was naturally a bright, smart boy, and he felt angry and hurt at his inability to understand what was said to him or to do anything that he was ordered.

At last, to his great relief, the mate said, "Here, get away aft out of this, you're only in everybody's way; go and help clear up the decks. Mr. Cope" (shouting), "set them boys clearing up decks."

This order was to the second mate, who was aft, and whose acquaintance Frank now made for the first time. This officer was young and gentlemanly, with a pleasant manner, and Frank felt a great liking for him, which quite cheered the boy up. His awkward attempts to handle a broom, and his ignorance of where to put things that had to be cleared away were looked upon leniently, and, to help matters, he found himself in company with another lad of about his own age, but more delicate-looking, who found time to exchange confidences with him, to the effect that he was also on his first voyage, felt just as stupid and helpless, and that his name was Harry Carter. This was still more cheering to Frank, and he began to move about a little more briskly until going up on the poop he was suddenly confronted by a man with a red face, a bulbous nose, and little cunning eyes, who said, "Hallo, boy, what's your name?"

Now Frank, being a boy of keen observation, felt a great dislike to this man at once, but something told him to be careful, and so he answered politely, "Frank Brown, sir. I'm an apprentice."

"Oh, you are, are you?" sneered the man. "Well, I'm your captain, I'll make a sailor of you, but if I catch you skulking or coming any of your school games here I'll make you wish you'd never been born. Now get on with your work."

And turning to the pilot, who stood looking gravely on, the captain said, "Nothin' like puttin' these youngsters in their place at the first go off, is there, pilot?"

"No, I suppose there isn't, Captain Swainson," replied the pilot, and then checked himself suddenly as if he intended to say more, but felt it best not to do so.

Undoubtedly Frank began to feel that things were not at all up to his expectations. He did not realise how vague those expectations were, but they had all been of a high order, and didn't embrace a coarse bully of a mate and a red-nosed skipper who smelt very strongly of stale drink, and who began to threaten at the first interview. However, he did the best thing he could, went on with his coiling up of ropes, and descended from the poop as quickly as possible.

Just as he was wondering what the next thing would be, he heard the mate roar, "Supper." More wonder, it was not yet dark, and could it be possible that at sea they had supper in the daytime? None of his books of adventure had told him that there are only three meals a day in the Mercantile Marine, breakfast, dinner, and supper, the latter answering to our tea at home as far as the hour is concerned.

He stood wondering, until the second mate, passing, said kindly, "Now, my lad, go and get your supper, you'll want it before to-morrow morning."

Frank murmured, "Thank you, sir," and almost mechanically went towards the house he had put his traps in, being met at the door by one of the last year's apprentices, who said, "Now then, none o' yer skulking; go to the galley and get the supper, and be quick about it." At the same time thrusting two tin quart-pots into his hands.

Frank obeyed, for fortunately he knew where the galley was, and presenting himself at its door, said to a very hideous negro he saw there, "Please, I've come for the supper for the apprentices."

"Oh ho, ha ha, he he!" gasped the nigger, "geess you're a new chum, *berry* green ain't it. Neb' mine, hold out yer pots," and Frank, doing so, saw to his amazement a modicum of tea ladled out into them like soup, from a big saucepan.

"Now take dat away," said the cook, "an' come back 'gen, I've got some scouse for ye; feed yer well fus start off; letcher down easy like, he he!"

Frank's disgust and chagrin were too great for words, but he had already learned one lesson, not to talk back, even to a loathsome negro cook who looked as if made of dirt, so he hurried off to his new home, and putting the pots on the deck, in the absence of a table, came back and fetched a tin pan of what looked like very badly made Irish stew. This he carried into the house, and then sat down on his sea-chest and looked blankly at his shipmates.

The two seniors said not a word, but producing tin plates and spoons, helped themselves to a goodly portion of "scouse" and a biscuit out of a grimy box (the biscuit looked, Frank thought, like those he used to give the dog at home), and began to eat at a great rate and in hoggish fashion. The other new-comer looked on helplessly as if unable to grasp the meaning of things, and Frank wondered if it was not some horrid dream from which he would presently awake. He was suddenly and rudely roused by the elder of the two seniors rapping him over the knuckles with his spoon and saying, "Now then, mummy's darlin', wade in and get some supper; you'll get no more till seven bells to-morrow, and besides, it's bad cattin' on an empty stumjack."

For a moment Frank found his tongue and replied, "I don't know what you mean. Is this our tea?"

What a superb joke. How the two did laugh and choke, and then when they found their breath again, the senior said scornfully, "Looky here, my soft kiddy, the sooner you wake up the better for you. This is your tea, as you call it, and as Bill and me are pretty sharp set, you and the other young nobleman had better produce your dinner service and fall to, or I'm hanged if you'll get any at all."

At this point there was a diversion caused by the other new-comer, Harry, bursting into hysterical tears. For a moment the two hardened ones suspended their eating and gazed open-mouthed at him, remembering perhaps their own experiences only a year ago, then with rude chaff and empty threats they resumed their interrupted supper. But it did Frank good. He couldn't comfort the weaker boy, but he set his teeth and determined that he wouldn't be laughed at anyhow.

So he began to hunt up his mess traps, plate, pot, pannikin, knife, fork, and spoon, and at last he found them, but with all his will power aroused he couldn't use them. He had no desire for food. So he just put them in his bunk and sat down again, wondering.

He had not sat thus for more than a minute when his comrade in misfortune became violently sick, for the ship was just beginning to curtsy to the incoming sea over the bar as she was tossed seaward head to the wind, and even had the weather been as fine as could be wished, the many strange smells and the beastly appearance of the food were enough to turn any delicate boy's stomach. It did for Frank at any rate, and almost immediately he too was vomiting in sympathy, utterly oblivious to the blows and abuse the two seniors showered upon them both with the utmost liberality.

With a last flicker of sense, but almost as much dead as alive, the two new-comers crawled into their bunks among their unpacked belongings there, and lay wallowing in unconscious misery, intensified, if possible, by the fumes of strong tobacco from the pipes of their hardened shipmates, who sententiously observed that there was nothing like bacca to kill stink.

Overdrawn, exaggerated, false, I hear people say. Well, all I reply is, ask those who know. If only boys going to sea like this could have a little training first, much of this suffering might be avoided, but for those who come to it fresh from a good home ashore, it is much worse than I can express in print. However, I am not to moralise, only to tell Frank Brown's story.

He cannot even now say what happened during the next twenty-four hours, only he sometimes wonders what the others were doing. Somebody had to work, and he feels that the plight of the chaps forward in the forecastle was worse than his, for he at any rate was left in peace, such peace as it was. Sea-sickness is horrible even in a beautifully appointed cabin with kindly attendants and all kinds of palliatives tendered gently, but in a foul den, on hard bunk boards, with nubbly portions of your outfit being ground into you at every roll of the ship, and the reek of strong tobacco and bilge-water, it is worse than horrible. And yet Frank says that even through that awful time he still hoped that he was right in choosing a sea life, still felt that it would be all right by-and-by, and I believe him, except that I believe for much of the time he was enduring only and didn't think at all.

After what seemed an age of misery, Frank awoke to find his mouth dry and horrid-tasting, his head aching as if it would split, and an all-gone feeling inside of him. And he was so terribly thirsty and cold and weak. But he was not done up entirely, not beyond making an effort, and so as soon as he had grasped the nature of his surroundings, realised a little where he was, he made that effort and managed to get out of his top bunk, falling in a heap upon the floor. He lay there for a few minutes and then struggled to his feet, holding on to anything he could clutch blindly, but with one overmastering desire for fresh air, and next to that drink.

He staggered to the door and stumbled out on deck, the keen briny breeze acting like a tonic upon his poisoned blood, and as he stood swaying there the healing of the sea came to him, the strong life-giving air revived him, and he felt better.

A voice in his ear said, "Hello, Marse Newboy, you feelin' more better. Come along a galley an I give him a drink tea."

It was the nigger cook, but to Frank he was no longer disgusting, the last twenty-four hours had educated him beyond that, and he followed gratefully, guided by the strong grip on his arm of that black sinewy hand. Arriving at the galley door, a pannikin of tea (it was tepid, sugarless, and weak) was handed to him, and as he drank he wondered if anything had ever been so refreshing. He made it last as long as he could, and then set the empty pannikin down on the coal-locker with a sigh, saying, "Thank you, cook, that *was* good."

"You quoite welcome, sar," said the cook with a flourish, and Frank turned to go, but where he did not know.

The problem was solved for him at once, for the mate came along and, with a string of bad words, demanded what he meant by skulking like this when there was obviously nothing the matter with him. Meekly Frank began to answer that he was very sorry, he hadn't been well, but the mate cut him short with, "Get along and lend a hand clearing up decks. Think you came to sea for pleasure, I s'pose, but I'll show you different 'fore I've done with ye," &c.

Frank made no reply, but crawled about and did his best, and so began his sea work, as so many thousands like him have done before under exactly similar circumstances.

He had not been long at his task before one of the senior apprentices came up to him and said, "Hello, mammy's kid, what are you doing on deck in your watch below?"

For the life of him Frank did not know what was meant, and he felt this entire ignorance of everything begin to annoy him again. But he only said civilly, "I don't understand you."

"Don't understand, don't ye?" mimicking him; "well, although you haven't done a thing but make a beastly mess in the house and sleep like a hog for twenty-four hours, you ain't expected on deck till eight bells, so you can get below again."

"Can't I stay on deck, then," pleaded Frank, "it does smell so in the room?"

"Yes it does, thanks to you and that other little beast. No, you can't stay on deck in your watch below, but you can clean up the filthy mess you've been making in the house, and you shall, so get about it as quick's the devil'll let ye."

Of course theoretically Frank should have rebelled, but he felt so low and helpless that he hadn't a kick in him, and besides he did not know what power over him his young tormentor might have, so instead of firing up he meekly replied, "Will you show me what I'm to do, and I'll try and do it?"

"Oh, I'll show ye right enough," answered the young tyrant, who led the way to the house from whence Frank had so recently emerged.

But as soon as he stepped within, the foul, fetid atmosphere of the place revived his nausea, and he staggered out again on deck crying, "I can't stand it, it makes me sick."

And yet he had seen that the other two lads were asleep in it, the one from sheer exhaustion and the other because he had got used to it. He also saw that it was in such a condition that it could only be compared to a hogsty, and even in his then mental state he could not help wondering however he would grow used to sleeping in such a hole as that.

His tormentor was about to abuse him again, but the voice of the second mate, whose watch on deck it was, sounded, calling, "Williams, where are you?" and Williams answering, "Aye, aye, sir," sped away, leaving Frank sitting on the main hatch gulping deep breaths of strong, pure air.

Now for the first time he really did repent of his decision. Apart from his physical misery, which was great, he was utterly alone and helpless, and, although he felt willing to learn, he saw no prospect of anybody taking the trouble to teach him. And he could not help contrasting the ordered comfort and loving sheltering care of the home he had left with his present condition. It was as if the bottom had fallen out of his world.

And then as he sat there he lifted his eyes and saw the great white sails towering away in all the beauty of their swelling curves towards the blue sky above them, took in with a growing sense of charm the ordered web-like arrangement of the standing and running rigging, and felt even in that miserable hour a little compensation. Indeed it might have been very much worse, a gale of wind to begin with would have added greatly to his sufferings, but the weather was quite fine and there was a nice leading wind down the Channel, so that had there but been any one to show him what to do to make himself as comfortable as circumstances would permit, he was really getting a fair send-off.

It was in the month of September, and so although the time was the second dog-watch, between six and eight in the evening, it was still light, and as the ship rolled he was able to get a glimpse of the sea with its small waves and a few distant vessels dotted about like little boats, some with a smear of black smoke above them and others showing a glint of white. He began to feel more at ease except when he thought of the den into which he would have to go presently for some additional clothes, for he was shivering with the cold.

But he sat on until he heard four double strokes on the bell, when Williams swaggering up to him said, "Now then, my boy, it's your watch on deck," and passing into the house lit a lamp and called Johnson, the other senior apprentice.

Still he sat there stupidly until Johnson coming out said, "Hello, young feller, haven't you got any more clothes to put on than that? You going to keep watch to-night in only a dungaree suit?"

That roused him, and staggering to his feet he said earnestly, "Won't you tell me what I've got to do?"

Johnson stared at him for a moment and then, his better feelings overcoming his first inclination to laugh, he replied, "All right, come aft with me to muster and then I'll give you a few wrinkles."

As he spoke, the crew, nine in number, came slouching aft, a very motley gang, and mustered about the after hatch, while the second mate from the poop called out their names, to which each one answered, "Here."

Then when all had responded the second mate said, "Relieve the wheel and look-out, that'll do the watch."

The crew dispersed, and Johnson, taking Frank by the arm, said, "Now come along and get your jacket; you won't have time to change your pants, for you'll have to take first watch on the poop with the mate."

So Frank made a bold plunge into the house and succeeded in keeping down his nausea until he had extracted his jacket. Then, at his mentor's direction, he made his way up the lee poop-ladder and stood holding to the lee mizzen rigging, awaiting what should come next.

In a few minutes the mate, who was prowling about, espied him, and coming up to him said, "Well, boy, you've made a start at last, I see." "Yes, sir," answered Frank. "All right," went on the mate, "let's have no more skulking. All you've got to do now is to keep your weather eye liftin' and learn quick. For the present your duty is to carry my orders if necessary and to keep look-out for the time, the clock is in the companion aft there, an' every half-hour you must strike that bell there, one bell for each half-hour up till four bells; one, two, three, four; and at four bells Johnson will relieve you. Then you can go down off the poop and have a caulk on the grating before the cabin, but mind, no going forward into the house and going to sleep there, or you'll drop in for it." And with this brief warning the mate resumed his prowl up and down the poop.

Frank stood at his post trying to feel the importance of being on watch, and not succeeding at all well, afraid to move about and yet wondering why he should not, and hoping desperately that he would soon be able to understand a little of what was going on. As his eyes became accustomed to the gloom, he made out the dim figure at the wheel, upon whose weather-beaten face the light from the binnacle, or illuminated compass, fell fitfully; he looked over the side and saw the glowing white foam on the parted waters, looked away from the ship and saw only blackness, for the sky had clouded over, and thought with amazement of the fact that they were sailing along in utter darkness, and yet nobody seemed to mind.

And then he thrilled to the roots of his hair as a hoarse voice sounded out of the gloom, "Green light on the port bow, sir."

"Aye, aye," gruffly responded the mate, as he strode forward to the break of the poop.

And presently Frank held his breath to see a vast lumbering shape emerge from the gloom with one gleaming light on its side. On it came until it seemed as if it would overwhelm the *Sealark*, and then, sheering just a little, passed at what seemed a terrific speed close alongside, so close indeed that the mate hurled a volley of abuse at the invisible beings on board the other vessel, and was answered in kind. It was a close shave and quite unnecessary. Frank was dreadfully alarmed, he did not know why, and had no idea how near they had been to a terrible disaster.

But fate was kind to him, although he thought he had never known two hours be so long in all his life. He managed to acquit himself of his task of striking the bell all right, and nothing else occurred during the watch.

At four bells, he saw a man come aft and relieve the wheel, and waited patiently for Johnson to come and relieve him. But Johnson came not, and at last Frank mustered up courage to go and ask the mate if he might go and call the other boy. The mate grunted assent, and Frank, groping his way down the ladder—his legs being cramped and stiff with the cold and standing still so long—succeeded in finding his relief stretched full length on the grating, snoring melodiously. It was a hard job to waken him, but at last he sat up and growled like a bear.

Just then the mate's voice roared, "Johnson," and all trace of sloth disappeared. He sprang up and rushed on the poop, where Frank, with just a trace of satisfaction, heard him get a few sea-compliments and warnings of what would happen if he didn't turn up smarter next time.

But Frank had matters of his own to attend to, and with a sense of relief, such as he had never felt to his recollection in his beautiful bed at home, curled himself up like a dog upon his hard couch and passed almost immediately into deep sleep, although he had neither pillow nor covering, and was, moreover, both cold and hungry.

He was awakened almost immediately after, he thought, by a pretty hard kick, and heard Johnson's voice saying, "Now then, it's eight bells, muster the watch," and, memory coming to his aid, he pulled himself together to take part in the same proceeding as before, the calling of names, &c.

And then realising that it was his watch below, and that he had four hours of uninterrupted sleep before him, he returned to his former corner on the grating and went fast asleep again directly. The thought of sleeping in the house made him feel quite bad, and he hastened to forget it in sleep. Several times during the watch he had dim ideas of voices and noises, but not enough to arouse him thoroughly.

The wind had changed, and the starboard, or second mate's watch, had all their work to trim and shorten sail. But Frank slept through it, although when he was aroused at eight bells—four in the morning—he was wet through, and shivering with the cold. And hungry! But that was a good sign, showing that he had quite got over his sea-sickness, and that in a very short time.

The ship was now moving about in lively fashion, and as he mounted the poop again he held on convulsively, feeling almost as if his legs were of no use to him. But he had now reached the stage of passive endurance, and although he was conscious of suffering cold, hunger, and weariness, he felt dimly that he could hang on and bear it, since others around him were faring no better.

The relief was nearer than he thought. At two bells—five o'clock—there was a cry from forrard of "Coffee," and the mate striding over to him said not unkindly, "Go an' get yer coffee, boy."

He answered with chattering teeth, "Thankye, sir," and crawling down the ladder groped his way to the house, where he found Johnson already seated with a steaming pannikin of some brown liquid in one hand and a biscuit in the other.

"There's yours," gruffly said Johnson, indicating a pot hooked on to the side of a bunk; and Frank gratefully seized it as well as a biscuit out of the box.

It was not like anything he had drunk before which he could say was at all nice, but it was boiling hot and sweet, sending quite a glow through his shaking body. The biscuit was flinty, but Frank's teeth were good, and besides he was savagely hungry, so that he really found himself enjoying this impromptu meal, and quite forgot that he was sitting in the house which had been such a place of horror to him. For the wind having changed, there was a current of pure air blowing through it, and most of its foulness had been swept away. As far as Frank was concerned, the worst of his probation was over.

By the time he had eaten his biscuit and finished his coffee he felt a different being, and when Johnson said, "You'd better get aft, it's nearly three bells," he was ready, as he felt, to face anything. So he hurried aft to his place on the poop and ventured to walk about a bit in spite of the motion of the ship, the mate saying nothing to him until four bells.

Then with a roar that startled Frank greatly the mate ordered, "Wash decks," whereupon the watch came slouching aft with bare feet and trousers rolled up, carrying brooms and buckets, and Frank, having now a good look at them for the first time, could not help feeling another pang of deep disappointment. Were these the fine romantic fellows he had read of, these miserable-looking, curiously clad ragamuffins, more disreputable in appearance than any tramps he had ever seen, and speaking, when they did speak at all, in a language that he could not understand?

It was another added to the many problems which he had to solve by himself, but the present was not a time for doing so, for he found that his mind was fully occupied by the duties of carrying water and maintaining his balance withal as the ship rolled and the wet decks seemed as slippery as glass.

But he felt glad of one thing, this business was, if very wearisome to a lad who had never worked before, easily learned, so although the buckets of water seemed to grow heavier and heavier, and the quantity of them used was enormous, he stuck to it, did his best, and felt that he was getting on. He did not like the surly grumbling way everybody spoke, for it seemed to him that his efforts might have been recognised, but he grew to regard even that as a part of the business he had to learn, and was consoled.

Meanwhile the work went steadily forward, and the decks began to assume a neatness and cleanliness which appealed to Frank, although he felt how hard a task it had been to make them so. Seven bells struck and the other watch was called to breakfast, while he, with his fellow-apprentice Johnson, busied themselves in tidying up the poop and cleaning the brasswork with oil and bath-brick, Johnson giving himself more than professional airs because it was necessary for him to teach the novice the simplest thing.

There were not wanting signs, however, that Johnson and Frank would presently be very good friends, for Johnson was only a year Frank's senior and had no one else to talk to, which, as he was a sociable lad at bottom, made him forget that superiority so dear to a boy and speak every now and then as a comrade.

While they were thus busy the captain came on deck, looking even less prepossessing than he had done the day previous. His evil eye fell upon everything like a blight. He grumbled at the helmsman, and at the boys, muttered something unintelligible about the trim of the sails, and generally made himself appear as much like the enemy of mankind as possible. Frank felt quite nervous at being near him, and when eight bells sounded and Williams came to relieve them, the pair lost not an instant in getting off the poop out of their commander's way.

But it was a sore trial for the new chum to enter that house and leave the pure sharp air outside, although he felt that he would much like a little shelter. Still he was in some small measure hardened, and the filthy hole did not seem so terrible as it had done. Only the sight of the other new apprentice, Harry Carter, made him feel a curious mixture of pity and disgust. I am not going to describe him as I have seen him and his like many times, sufficient to say that he had now been lying for two days in the midst of a heap of his belongings without the slightest attention being paid to him by anybody, except for a drink or two of water which Johnson had given him. He looked almost as if he were dying, and did not seem to care.

The two other youngsters, whatever their feelings may have been, had other business on hand just now, the getting of their breakfast. Frank took the two pots and fetched the curious coffee, waiting a moment when he had received it for some sign that there was something else forthcoming. The cook, however, said sharply, "Dat's all. Doan fink you gets scouse any more, do yer?"

Frank retreated without a word, and on reaching the house found that Johnson had been aft and procured about two ounces of butter from the steward wherewith to lubricate their biscuits, and with this and the coffee they made what breakfast they could.

Having appeased their hunger somewhat, they made an attempt to help the sick boy for their own sakes. They dragged him out of his bunk and wiped him down roughly, although he implored them to let him alone; then they did their best to straighten up the extraordinary confusion of his bunk, unrolled his bedding and laid him on it. It was all they knew how to do, and anyhow their time was precious. Frank made a clearance of his bunk too, and some sort of a bed for himself with a curious angry feeling that he ought not to have been allowed to be so ignorant of the commonest duties of life, and that anyhow some one ought to show him how here.

What to do with his many belongings he did not know, there were no lockers, no shelves, just a few nails driven into the bulkheads, and his chest, from having been tousled over in a wild hurried search for things, was so full that it wouldn't shut. At last he said despairingly to Johnson, "I wish I only knew where to put my things, there's no drawers, no cupboards, and I never put anything away at home anyhow."

"Oh, shove 'em anywhere," said Johnson testily, "don't bother me. I've got trouble enough with my own dunnage. Go and get a broom and sweep the wreck up into a corner, I'm going to turn in, I'm as tired as a dog." And suiting the action to the word he flung himself into his bunk just as he was, without even troubling to take off his boots or change his damp clothes.

Frank found a broom and drew together the accumulated rubbish and dirt on the deck, and then feeling ashamed to leave it there in spite of what Johnson had said, scooped up a double handful of it, went outside and flung it over the nearest rail, which happened to be to windward, with the result that it all blew back on top of him, into his eyes and over the clean deck. A yell of execration went up from two of the men who were passing as the dirt blew over them, but beyond cursing him roundly, and suggesting that he had never yet been round Cape Horn, they did nothing to explain the why of his mistake.

He hastily retreated within his den, finding his watchmate already asleep. He felt the call of rest very strongly, but his cleanly instincts rebelled against the fact that for two days he had not had his clothes off, or even an apology for a wash. Still he knew not where to get any water except salt, and that was a task he felt beyond his powers, there were no conveniences of any kind for washing, and he—well, like most boys who go unprepared to sea for the first time, he just did the easiest thing, got into his bunk, and in less than a minute was fast asleep.

CHAPTER III
HIS FIRST GALE

A loud voice shouting in his ear, it seemed, "Seven bells; turn out here, you sleepers," aroused Frank to a consciousness of his surroundings again, to his utmost astonishment, for he felt sure he had only been asleep five minutes.

As he awoke he heard Johnson muttering, "Blowin' a gale o' wind now, I should think, by the way she's kicking about, the old beast. Here, Frank, go an' get the dinner an' hurry up, it'll be all hands directly, I can see."

Frank scrambled out of his bunk, dragged his cap on, and staggered out on deck, to be met as he did so by a heavy spray which drenched him and nearly knocked him down. He gasped and clutched at the side of the house, but did not go back, although he felt a little bit alarmed. He held on his way to the galley, however, and the cook handed him two tin dishes, one with a piece of fat boiled pork in it that made his gorge rise as he looked at it, and the other with some plain pea-soup.

Now he ought to have known better than to have attempted to carry both dishes, having no hand left to hold on with. But he started and got half-way towards his house, when the ship gave a combined roll and pitch that shot him off his legs, and hurled him along the deck as helpless as a dead thing. He landed in the scuppers at the lee side of the vessel, which were a foaming torrent of water, and when he had scrambled to his feet again his dishes and their contents were several feet away.

Pursuing them was out of the question in his then condition, so he grasped his way to the house and told Johnson of his mishap, who bad-worded him severely, winding up by saying, "I suppose I shall have to go an' get it. I never saw such a fool in my life." A common enough expression, but one very rarely justified.

Away went Johnson, presently returning with the food, but grumbling horribly. He made haste to eat some of the pork and pea-soup, but Frank, although savagely hungry, was fain to stay his appetite with a biscuit; that pork was too much for his sight, to say nothing of his stomach.

As soon as Johnson had finished he pitched his plate into a corner, and his knife and spoon (he had used no fork) into his bunk, and lighting his pipe began to put on his oilskins and sea-boots, grimly warning Frank that he had better do the same. Frank obeyed, not without a sense of its uselessness, as he was already fairly drenched, but in the topsy-turvy world into which he had been plunged he did not feel at all sure that it was not the right thing to put waterproof clothes over wet ones. He had hardly dressed himself thus and begun to realise how utterly helpless and clumsy he felt, much worse than he had before, when he heard a shout, "Eight bells! all hands shorten sail."

He tumbled out on deck and looked helplessly around. But Johnson, brushing past him, said, "Come along, you can haul aft the slack anyhow."

To a novice the scene was appalling. As the ship rolled, the seas rising high above her threatened to overwhelm her; the wind roared and howled as if full of rage and desire to destroy, great sails being clewed up, slatted, and banged and crashed, making the vessel quiver as if in pain, and the weird wailing cries of the sailors hauling on the ropes added to the truly infernal din. Without the least idea of what he was doing, or why he was doing it, Frank staggered hither and thither, pulling at ropes and getting pushed about, trodden on and sworn at, until at last there was a general rush of the men aloft, and he, left alone, began mechanically to do the only thing he understood, coil up the straggling ropes upon the belaying-pins.

He was suddenly startled by a yell from the skipper, who from the break of the poop demanded to know why the something or other he wasn't "up lending a hand with that main tawpsle." He might just as well have asked him why he wasn't leading the House of Commons. Frank gasped at him uncomprehendingly, as the mate approaching the skipper made some remark, at which the skipper gave a sarcastic laugh and turned away.

The mate suggested that it was not wise to send so obviously helpless a lad up where he could not possibly do any good, and whence it was more than likely that he might fall and be killed; which proves that the mate's bark was worse than his bite, for I have personally known brutes who would have insisted upon a lad like that going aloft under similar conditions to almost certain death.

Now Frank's plight was bad enough, but his native pluck began to get the better of his physical misery and his mental confusion, and he actually began to think of what a fine story of adventure he would have to tell when he got home again. He had of course not the slightest idea what an ordinary everyday sea-experience he was sharing. He could, however, and did, feel some admiration and envy for the sailors, who, clinging like bats to the yards high above him, were struggling to secure the great thrashing sails, even wished that he could do what they were doing, for he dimly felt that their deeds were heroic, more so than all his reading had prepared him for.

The gale increased in violence very fast, and it was well on to four bells before she was snugged down—that is, reduced to such sail as she could carry with safety—and the wearied men who had been on watch since eight in the morning were able to crawl below and get something to eat. The watch on deck had plenty to do securing spars and other movables about the decks, and Frank watching them wondered why they did not take more notice of the threatening waves and of the great masses of water that were continually tumbling upon the deck of the deeply laden ship. But by this time he had begun to learn the sailor's first lesson, to endure and keep doing what there is to be done with an utter disregard of the body's claims to attention, and had he known it, he had made a long stride in his knowledge.

Bad weather having thus set in, lasted without intermission for several days and nights, during the whole of which our hero never changed his clothes, never washed, and grew not to care a bit about it, although, had he looked at himself in a glass, which he never did, he would have been horrified to find how begrimed and unwholesome-looking he had become. Of course he had the example of the elder boys, who seemed quite lost to all sense of decency both in behaviour and conversation, from lack of any kind of supervision.

The poor little wretch Harry, from want of food and from bad air as well as sea-sickness, was just a shadow, becoming at last so bad that the second mate, who alone of the afterguard seemed to think at all of the boy's plight, taking pity on him, induced the steward to give him a little attention, and a cup or two of beef tea and some cabin biscuits, which revived him and probably saved his life.

It was the second mate too, who, as soon as the weather changed, so far interested himself in the boys as to make them wash and change their clothes and scrub their house out. But if he had been like the mate and captain, goodness knows how they would have fared. It needs no argument, I think, to convince most people that boys at sea should never be left to themselves, even when they have had some previous training, unless there are ample facilities for cleanliness and room to stow their belongings away.

With the setting in of fine weather and a steady easterly wind, there was a great change for the better in the boys' condition. The second mate's admonitions had so good an effect that some sort of order began to be observed in the little house, and the eldest apprentice, Williams, took upon himself to make the two new-comers keep the place clean after a fashion. At the best, however, it was a miserable hole, from which comfort was entirely absent, all the minor decencies of life being also wanting.

But on deck Frank and Harry, who picked up wonderfully quick when once they had got over their sea-sickness, were beginning to be of some use, could handle a broom with a certain amount of ability, and get about without tumbling. They began to remember the names of things, and of the various ropes and sails, also to take an intelligent interest in the work of the ship, although of regular teaching there was none except what the second mate gave Harry, who was in his watch, and followed him about like a dog.

And now, in spite of the many drawbacks and the departure of his illusions about a sea-life, Frank really began to enjoy himself. Being perfectly healthy and robust, the change of food from the best to the worst, and the sordid details of his surroundings below, had no power to make him miserable.

Had the mate and skipper realised any responsibility towards the lads under their charge, he would now have begun to learn at a very rapid rate, for he was full of inquiries upon every subject connected with the work of the ship and the wonders of the sea. But all his inquiries, except those directly connected with the work given him to do, were snubbed by the only persons he was on conversational terms with, the two elder boys; indeed their knowledge of things he wanted to know about, was not much greater than his own. Nevertheless he did learn perforce to do such quite menial work as is required of seamen in steamships, connected almost entirely with keeping the ship clean, finding that any dirty or tiresome piece of work was given to him to save a growl from the men.

To his great delight, however, he speedily learned to go aloft, having strong nerves and not being giddy. At first he felt terribly alarmed when, having climbed as high as the main-yard, he looked down at the narrow space of deck beneath and the wide blue sea around. But before his fellow-apprentice, Harry, had begun to climb at all he had learned how to loose a sail, make up a gasket, and furl a staysail, and had even accomplished the much more difficult task of greasing down, a task that everybody on board tries to get out of if possible, because of its dirt and its danger. For the grease must be plastered on the after side of the upper masts with the bare hands, and consequently the job of holding with greasy hands is a very difficult one, while the manipulation of the grease-pot is a business that worries even the smartest man.

Finding him willing and able, the mate put more and more of such tasks upon him, until, besides being quite the equal of Johnson in ability, he was in a fair way of becoming as useful as the average seaman, except that he could not as yet perform a single piece of "sailorising," as it is called, meaning the various manipulations of rope, such as splicing, knotting, serving, &c., neither could he steer. And all this, because he was "gleg at the uptak," as the Scotch say, before the vessel had got down to the line. This, had he known it, proved the wisdom of Captain Burns in selecting a small ship for him, for in them a boy is bound to learn, there being so many things that a boy can do if he will, and so few men to spare. It also proves the untruth of what is so frequently alleged as to the expense of carrying boys at sea. I have been in a great many ships, but I have never yet been in one where the boys did not earn their pay and keep quite as fully as any man, generally much more so, and where premium apprentices were carried, I have often seen them in their third year doing more and better work than any foremast hand in the ship.

There was one thing, however, that began to worry Frank more than a little. As soon as he became used to his surroundings, and learned to wash himself once a week in his share of half a pail of water, he also began to change his clothes. But what to do with the dirty ones (and they were *exceedingly* dirty) he didn't know. He timidly inquired of Johnson, who said, "When it rains you can wash 'em if you like!" That closed the inquiry, for he was ashamed to say that he had no more idea of how to wash a shirt than of how to make a watch, so he stuffed the foul clothes into his bunk as well as he could and lay amongst and on top of them.

By-and-by they entered "The Doldrums"—that strip of ocean between the Trade Winds, where it seems as if all the rain-making in the world is carried on. The beautiful steady weather they had enjoyed was broken up, and with it went the "caulks" or sleeps during the watch on deck. Now it was pully hauly all night long, amid ever-recurring deluges of rain, and even Frank could see that the ship was making very little progress. Every one seemed to get a rough edge on their tempers, the captain especially, whose language, never very choice, became appalling, and his purple face took on a deeper hue and his eyes were more bloodshot. The men cursed and swore as they hauled the big yards first on one tack and then on the other, and there was never a laugh heard; while ever and anon the rain came down in almost solid sheets of water.

The men forrard found time and opportunity to wash out their miserable bits of duds, and with the cunning of seamen managed to dry them too in the bursts of blazing sunshine, but never a bit of washing was done by any of the boys, while clothes that were hardly soiled but had got thoroughly wet, hung in the house on all the nails, adding another flavour to the many odours. At last Frank, in despair of knowing what to do with all his wet and filthy clothing, took a short way with them: he flung a couple of armfuls overboard at night while nobody was looking. Quite unknown to him, Harry Carter had been doing the same, and for the same reason, because there was no one whose business it was to tell them or show them different.

Frank had now been a month on board, for the ship was a very slow one, and so, although she had enjoyed fair weather, it had taken her all that time to get down to the line. And had he been able to indulge in retrospect he would have seen what an immense change had taken place in himself, and how very far removed he was from the boy who came on board the *Sealark* in Liverpool. To say that he was enjoying the life would not be quite true, yet he was by no means miserable, having that happy temperament which makes the best of things, and besides, he was rather proud of his accomplishments. He was fairly chummy with Johnson his watch mate, who had really never imposed upon him, and the two had many a yarn together about their previous lives and ambitions. They were much happier than the other two boys, for Williams was a cad, and Harry, poor chap, had no backbone, so he just degenerated into a little loafer who skulked out of everything he could, and made the only man who tried to befriend him, the second mate, so disgusted with him that he gave up trying to teach him. Frank, on the contrary, was one of the willing ones, naturally energetic and industrious, and besides, being quite a shrewd lad, he soon noticed that everything came easier when he went at it with a will.

But there was one thing that he secretly craved after, the ability to steer. He felt quite a fierce envy of the men who stood nonchalantly at the wheel for two hours at a time, keeping the ship on her course by just twiddling at the spokes as he thought. At last this longing grew so great that one Sunday afternoon when there was nothing else doing, and the ship was gliding steadily along with all her sails just full over an almost smooth sea, he took his courage in both hands and going up to the mate said, blushing furiously as he did so, "Please, Mr. Jenkins, may I learn to steer?"

The mate looked at him steadily for a moment, and then grumpily replied, "Yes, I s'pose so. Hansen!" (to the man at the wheel), "show this boy how to steer."

Now Hansen was a young Dane, a smart seaman and a kindly fellow, and the duty now fallen upon him was quite to his taste. Indeed most foremast hands are willing enough to teach a boy anything they know themselves in the way of work, if only the boy be smart.

So the lesson commenced, Frank standing on the lee side of the wheel, and Hansen pointing out to him the little black mark on the compass bowl in which swung the card, and explaining how his duty was to keep a certain point on the card in line with it, said, "Ven de lubber point moof away from de point you steering by, you pushes de veel as if it vas fast to de lubber point, see," suiting the word to the action. "But you ton't push de veel too much, 'cause if you do, de lubber point sving too far de oder vay, unt den you got to pull it more to get it back, unt so de ship don't steer steady, see."

After a few minutes he allowed Frank to take the wheel, himself going to the other side and explaining, helping too, so that the old man dozing in his state-room below should not note, by the tell-tale compass hanging there, that the ship was too much off her course.

In half-an-hour Frank could keep her fairly straight, and had learned not only to watch the compass, but the ship's head against the sky, which, he was bidden to notice, gave him warning of the movement of the vessel and of the way she wanted her helm before the compass did.

Frank was so interested that the time flew, and he felt quite sorry when eight bells sounded. Mr. Jenkins came aft and looked at him steering, and when he saw that the ship was going fairly steady on her course, said, "Well, quartermaster, how d'ye get on, hey?"

Frank answered diffidently, "I think I know how to do it now, sir."

"Oh, ye do, eh! Very well, we'll see you get yer trick reg'lar, then."

And that was all from the mate, but Hansen whispered as he was relieved, "If you likes I shows you how to box de compass ven ve goes forrut."

Frank, entirely glad, followed Hansen down to the lee ladder and there began an acquaintance which was of the highest possible service to our young friend. For Hansen was, like most of his countrymen going to sea, a well-educated man, and besides he held a Danish certificate entitling him to take a position as chief mate as soon as he should have served the necessary time at sea. And he was delighted to have some one to whom he could impart his knowledge, some one like Frank, who was not only willing but eager to learn.

From that day forward Hansen and Frank were inseparables whenever it was possible for them to be together by night or by day, and Frank learned with great rapidity. For he was in the proper educational position, keen to learn and blessed with a teacher full of theoretical and practical knowledge. Not only did Hansen teach him the theory of navigation as far as he could absorb it, but he also taught him practical seamanship as far as the manipulation of knots and splices in rope and wire were concerned, and, whenever possible, gave him a lesson in the handling of sails aloft.

Nor was this all, for Hansen found out how very much troubled the boy was about the condition of his clothes, and he gave him practical instruction in washing and mending, which was of the highest possible value to him. But I want to make it quite plain that this blessing for Frank came about quite accidentally or providentially, and that as far as his rightful teachers were concerned he might have remained in the position of a mere unskilled deckhand, as the other boys undoubtedly were still. Of course much credit was also due to Frank for his willingness to learn, without which this splendid opportunity of instruction would have been wasted. As it was, he much begrudged the time he was compelled to keep watch on the poop at night where Hansen could not be with him, and when it happened that he had one wheel or look-out and Hansen the next, a whole watch on deck at night might be wasted, except for such mental exercises as he could perform by himself.

He could not help sometimes comparing his present educational processes with what he remembered of his school days, where all the conditions were of the most favourable kind, every appliance and comfort were at his command, but the true spirit of learning, as well as of teaching, was entirely absent. Now he had nowhere to write or cipher even, except in his bunk; and unless willing to strain his eyes in the glare of the tropical moonlight on the main-hatch, there was absolutely no place where he could work in comfort.

There was another matter which gave him some trouble, the undisguised hatred and jealousy of his housemates, who lost no opportunity of annoying him and putting hindrances in his way, while their sneers and jeers were incessant. Fortunately he he was one of those fine lads to whom hindrances only act as incentives, who may be spoiled by ease, but are stimulated by obstacles, and so he went on his way learning in spite of all.

At last, however, he felt he must put his foot down, and the occasion for doing so quickly arrived. Johnson, his watchmate, had, among other petty annoyances, developed a very tyrannical spirit towards him, aided by the other senior apprentice, Williams, and was always hindering him in his learning in his watch below by putting all sorts of unnecessary duties upon him, fagging him in fact.

One day Frank having made up his mind that he would have no more of this, as soon as breakfast was over got into his bunk with his books and began to work out some problem that Hansen had given him the night before. He had hardly settled down before Johnson said, "Look here, Brown, you've got to clean the house out this morning, you're getting thundering lazy, and I won't have it."

Frank looked up, and quietly said, "I did the house out last time, it's your turn now. I'll do my share, but I won't do yours. I've got something else to do."

At this Johnson burst into a storm of abuse, and wound up by snatching Frank by the legs and dragging him out of his bunk. For the next few minutes there was a fierce fight, go-as-you-please, no room for science and boxing. Just like a pair of wild cats they struggled and tore at each other until the second mate, passing by and hearing the uproar, burst in and separated them. Then as they stood before him all torn and bleeding and panting from their exertions, he sternly demanded the reason of this behaviour. Johnson having first say, complained that Frank wouldn't do his share of the housework. Then Frank gave his version, and in the upshot they were both hurried before the skipper.

Now I have hitherto left this worthy severely alone, for, indeed, as far as the management or handling of the ship was concerned he might as well not have been on board. He was one of a type that now, thank Heaven, has almost disappeared from the sea, a drunken, worthless man who by sheer lying and hypocritical professions had imposed upon the owners and obtained a command for which he was entirely unfitted. He was always more or less under the influence of liquor, and, having a certain amount of cunning, left everything to the mate, who ran the ship with a fair amount of success, although naturally she did not get along very fast.

Now when the two lads were brought before him he sat endeavouring to assume a judicial air, and heard the story from the second mate; but his muddled brain could not sort the items out, and so he said in a thick voice, "Now look here, if I have any more of this I'll clap ye both in irons. I'm the only fighting man ther' is aboard this ship, an' if ye want t' fight I'll fight ye an' beat ye too. Stoord! stop these boys' allowance o' marmalade for a month. Go forrard and behave yerselves, an' don't you let me hear of ye misbehaving yerselves again."

It may be here explained that in this ship twelve ounces of butter were allowed to each man one week, and a pound of marmalade the next week, and so on alternately. It was not much, but the deprivation of it left a great gap, and did not tend to make the boys feel very benevolent towards each other or the skipper.

There was another serious annoyance threatening Frank's advance in learning, a peculiarity of the sailor mind, which is prone to jealousy. The constant association of Hansen with Frank led to all sorts of scurrilous remarks from his watchmates in the forecastle, who felt in some dim indefinite way that he was worming himself into the confidence of the people aft, their natural enemies. But Hansen was a sturdy soul who was apt to go his own way without bothering his head much about other people, and so, except for two or three rows which did not get as far as a fight, the bad feeling made no difference to Frank. Indeed I only mention this rather sordid detail to show how curiously difficult it is for a keen apprentice to learn his profession at sea, how he is beset by all sorts of hindrances undreamt of by his friends ashore, and how easy it is for him to take the line of least resistance, and let things slide, except where he has the good fortune to be under the command of a conscientious captain who feels it his duty to teach the apprentices committed to his charge their business.

And now I come to Frank's first adventure. Hitherto, interesting as his life had been to himself, the recital of his progress must appear rather humdrum, especially as so much of the vessel's progress must be left to the imagination, since we have been largely dealing with an individual.

Owing to his advance in the art of steering he had been made a regular helmsman, taking his "trick" at the wheel in regular rotation, and giving perfect satisfaction to the taciturn mate. The ship had reached the heart of the south-east Trade Winds, and was carrying all sail to a strong breeze, when Frank came to the wheel at two o'clock one morning. He had been at his post about half-an-hour, and was thoroughly enjoying the work of keeping the noble craft on her course, when he saw a figure emerge from the companion. He knew it was not the mate, for that officer had gone forrard some time before and had not returned, and besides he never came up the companion unless he had previously gone down that way. The figure stood for a moment or two at the top of the steps as if irresolute, and then coming aft to Frank peered in his face. It was the skipper, and his breath seemed to be almost scorching, while his eyes glared unnaturally. Frank felt uneasy, but steered on until the skipper said hoarsely, "Put your helm down, don't ye see you'll be into her in a minute?"

Mechanically Frank obeyed, for he had already learned the seaman's duty of unquestioning obedience, spun the wheel hard down, and the vessel, which was close-hauled on the starboard tack, flew up into the wind, bringing all the sails aback and causing naturally a tremendous commotion. The mate's great voice was heard above the flapping of the sails and the snapping of the gear shouting, "What the — — so and so is the matter?"

The skipper burst into a series of unearthly yells, almost paralysing Frank with fright; but the latter held on to the wheel according to his orders. The mate came rushing aft, and met the skipper in full career, who flew at him like a tiger, and the two were immediately locked in what appeared to be a struggle for life. The watch came rushing aft in utter bewilderment, and flung themselves upon the combatants, succeeding at last in separating them. There was an extraordinary mêlée before they were both secured, no one knowing in the least what was the matter, until the mate, finding his voice again, shouted, "Secure the skipper, men, he's gone mad." It was even so. His long debauch had culminated in a terrible attack of delirium tremens, rendering him for the time being an appalling danger to the ship and all hands.

He was quickly secured and carried below, the steward being called and given charge of him, while the mate and all hands, who had rushed on deck thinking that some terrible catastrophe had taken place, were busy for the next half-hour in restoring the ship to her normal condition and getting her on her course again. Fortunately for them all the breeze was not strong enough for any actual damage to be done, but it was a terrifying experience, and there was no more sleep that night for anybody. Below in the cabin the wretched man who was the cause of it all was apparently suffering intolerable torments, writhing in his lashings so severely that the lines literally cut into his flesh, yet it was impossible to release him. It was a very serious situation for the mate, who, however, rose to the occasion, and made it his first duty in the morning to rummage every corner of the skipper's state-room and the lazaret—where the small stores are kept—and every drop of intoxicating liquor that he found was at once hove overboard.

Frank was mightily impressed, but quite satisfied, after having been questioned most severely by the mate, that he was in no way to blame, for even had he known enough to disobey the insane order given him, he would no doubt have been attacked by the madman. But he, like every one else on board, felt that he had narrowly escaped a very great danger.

And now as the skipper lay slowly creeping towards convalescence, the *Sealark* began to draw downwards towards the stormy latitudes, and the mate was in a state of perplexity as to which course he should take, not knowing the skipper's intentions. The first port of call was Levuka, Fiji, and it was possible to go either east or west, the former being the most natural and easy way. But still he hoped that the skipper would get well and take the responsibility again, his position being an extremely awkward one.

And in the meantime the mixed crew forward were getting very unruly, as such crews will when there is anything wrong in the after part of the ship. However, the skipper was very slow in his progress towards convalescence, and so Mr. Jenkins made up his mind to run east, a decision immediately noted and approved of by the crew, who dreaded the passage west around Cape Horn. And gradually things settled down again into a sort of armed neutrality, the crew grumbling and growling at every order given, and doing as little as they possibly could.

But out of this unsatisfactory state of affairs grew one blessing; the boys, with the exception of the weakling Harry, rose to the occasion, sinking their differences and rallying to the aid of the two officers, who noted the change, and signified their approval by giving the youngsters better food and treatment, besides encouraging them to take a more active part in the handling of the ship. Now Frank's assiduous study during the fine weather placed him on a footing of perfect equality with Williams and Johnson, indeed he was their superior in many things, if comparison had been made. They began to recognise a community of interest, to look upon the crew as possible enemies, and upon the officers as their natural and proper friends. Frank thought wistfully of Hansen, who in the present state of affairs was entirely debarred from communication with him, and was very sorry.

In this unsatisfactory condition, but with the machinery of the crew still working almost automatically, they began to run the easting down, to rush along that enormous stretch of ocean which embraces the southern hemisphere of our globe. The wind increased steadily day by day, the sky took on a permanent grimness of aspect that shut out the blessed sun as if with an impenetrable pall of rushing cloud, and the sea rose into mighty rolling waves that extended from one side of the cheerless horizon to the other.

The *Sealark* did not behave well, not that she was overloaded but badly loaded, her general cargo being largely composed of iron, which lay heavily in her bottom and made her dull and uneasy in a seaway. She rolled tremendously and shipped on either side enormous quantities of water, keeping the decks awash from end to end. Yet it was essential to her safety that she should carry plenty of sail so as to keep well before the ravening sea, which threatened to overwhelm her, although it was exceedingly doubtful whether the crew were sufficiently strong, even had they been most willing and full of ability, to handle the sails promptly in an emergency.

It was a trying time for all, but especially for the mate, for the skipper seemed to have lost all his manhood, and although he was fully capable of resuming command he showed no desire to do so; he just lay in his bunk and smoked and dozed, apparently quite oblivious of his responsibilities.

But strangely enough he seemed to have been nursing a sense of grievance against the mate, who had acted like a good man and a thorough seaman, and really saved his life by depriving him of liquor. This curious twist of the skipper's mind, however, did not become fully evident until he had resumed command, which he did one night in the middle watch as suddenly as he had interfered before.

The ship was running dead before the wind with the maintopgallant sail set, which was just as much as she could bear. The darkness was profound, except for the unnatural glare of the foam rising high on either side as if about to overwhelm the flying ship, while every few minutes a furious squall came hissing along, laden with stinging snow-particles and making sight impossible.

During these squalls the force of the gale seemed to be doubled, yet nothing could be done but hold on and hope the gear would stand the tremendous strain, while the helmsman needed all his ability and strength to keep her going straight, knowing that a very small deviation from her course at such a time would mean her "broaching to," or flying round suddenly into the trough of the sea and most probably foundering at once with all hands. The mate stood near the wheel in readiness to help the helmsman in case of any sudden jerk of the wheel being so heavy as to overpower him; while both watched the compass with straining eyes, at the same time keeping a knowledge of the way the wind was coming by the sense of touch.

To them came suddenly the captain with a swagger, who blusteringly demanded of the mate why he was not carrying more sail. The mate was for the moment too much astonished to reply, but stood gazing at the apparition before him, while the helmsman's attention being diverted from his business, allowed the ship to take a sheer which was nearly her last.

CHAPTER IV
A GREAT FIGHT

That was a dramatic moment for at least four people, Frank being within close distance. The ship, feeling the enormous pressure of a mighty sea against one side of her rudder, swung up to meet the wind, and the strain upon the wheel was so great that the man steering could not move it. The two men who should have been most fully alive to the danger stood glaring at one another, while the lives of all on board trembled in the balance. But by some impulse which he did not understand, Frank flew to the helmsman's aid, flung all his weight upon the lee side of the wheel, and between them they got the helm up, only just in time to save the ship from broaching to. She gave one mighty swerve as if suspended in some huge sling, with such rapidity that for all their seasoned sea-legs the two officers were flung off their feet and rolled helplessly on deck. At the same moment a massy hill of water, the glare of whose foaming crest lit up the whole stormy scene, burst over the whole length of the starboard side, filling the decks fore and aft, and smashing everything in its way which was not of the most permanent character.

Both the skipper and the mate, apparently forgetting their quarrel in the face of this terrible common danger, as soon as they regained their feet rushed forward and took their part in the work of saving as much as possible of the floating wreckage of the deck from destruction. Frank and Hansen, for it was he who was helmsman, strove manfully to keep the maddened vessel on her course, feeling sure that it was their only hope of life, and yet unable to realise that they would be able to do so. It was then that Frank knew the dignity of the sailor's calling, as never afterwards. It was great to feel the power of command over the great fabric beneath him, to know her obedience to the helm, and to understand the movements of the wind and sea which were being compelled to serve him.

On the main deck there was a scene of ruin. A large portion of the bulwarks was gone, the spare spars on either side were loose in their lashings and threatening to break adrift altogether, while various portions of wreckage were floating and dashing from side to side of the flooded decks. The cabin was gutted, the deck-house had one side smashed in, and all hands were in doubt as to what extent the ship had been damaged.

Moreover the ends of the gear had been washed into all sorts of entanglements, so that shortening sail for the time was impossible, at least until halyards, sheets, clewlines, and downhauls had been cleared. And to add to the difficulty, there was the all-embracing blackness and the surging of the waves over the ship.

At such times as these sailors live only by permission or sufferance of the elements, for in her then helpless condition the slightest addition to the weight of the sea crashing aboard, or the force of the wind, would most probably have rendered all seamanship or courage of no avail. But mercifully the good sails held, the staunch masts, rigging, and running gear bore the tremendous strain, and the two brave fellows at the wheel kept her directly before the wind and sea. It was piercingly cold, and their long spell was so arduous that they felt as if they would have given anything for a few minutes' rest, while, in addition, there was the appalling uncertainty as to what damage had really been done by that mighty sea.

But they endured as sailors do, until, just as the grey, cheerless dawn began to break, they saw a figure come creeping aft, water streaming from him as if he had just been overboard. It was the second mate, who said as he reached the binnacle, "Well, boys, I suppose you're most done up, but you've had the best of it up here after all. Its nearly four bells in my watch, but you'll have to hang on a bit longer till Jem gets a drop of coffee and comes to relieve you. 'She steerin' any easier?"

Hansen replied, "She ain't safe mit von hant, sir. She gripes efery now and den like de deffil. I nefer ben able to steer her at all if it ain't ben for Frank here, goot boy."

"All right," rejoined Mr. Cope, "I'll see that there's a stand-by at the relief, and, say, Frank, you'll have to go into my bunk, your place is just washed out."

All Frank could say was "Thanks, sir," for he had almost arrived at that point when nothing makes any difference, the mercy point I call it. Only the higher the intelligence and sense of responsibility, the longer it takes to reach the point when nothing matters. It is this which softens the terrors of most of the awful situations in which men are placed, when the fear of death, natural to all of us, has taken its proper place, and there only remains a sort of dim compulsion to go on doing our duty.

When Frank was relieved and made his way forrard, he found, to his amazement, that he hardly knew the ship, the damage done was so great.

But his own particular corner was not so bad as the second mate had led him to believe. True, the side of the house was smashed in, and the sea had evidently made a clean breach through, but it had not washed his bunk out, nor torn his chest from its lashings. And so after a pannikin of steaming coffee and a couple of handfuls of broken biscuits he turned in just as he was, and in a few minutes was fast asleep and perfectly happy.

He was aroused next minute, as it seemed, by Williams, who assailed him with bad words for being so hard to wake. Realising that it was seven bells and breakfast-time, he sat up, wrenching himself from sleep with all the reluctance of healthy youth that has been over-tired and has not had nearly sufficient time for rest. But as he awoke fully to the fact of Williams's abuse, he felt an accession of sudden rage, all the man awoke in him, and springing out of his bunk he seized the fellow by the head and throat, and with one tremendous effort dashed him out of the wide-open door on to the flooded deck.

Then in a voice that almost startled himself he shouted, "No more of that from you or anybody else in this ship. I can do my work, and I won't be bullied. I'll die first." Then turning away from the thoroughly discomfited Williams, who, dripping with his ducking, dragged himself to his feet and slunk away, he seized Johnson by the shoulder and said roughly, "Here, Johnson, seven bells. Go and get breakfast, and look sharp about it. You know it's your turn, so no skulking."

Johnson hoisted himself out growling under his breath, but he did not refuse, for even he recognised a new note in Frank's voice, and knew that the boy had found his manhood.

Now I do not wish to give the idea that either Williams or Johnson were no good, because they were very fair specimens of stalwart boys in their second year at sea, and could do their work fairly well, but they had no ideals, they had lost them early, while Frank seemed as if he were not only going to keep his, but was increasing their number by adding thereto real knowledge of the facts of a sea-life. This, coupled with his fine bodily strength, made him already as useful as either of them, and more reliable than either.

Poor little Harry, on the other hand, had only developed the cunning of the weakling, and gave the second mate no end of trouble hunting him out of holes and corners where he would hide himself at night. And so he had been let pretty much alone, as it was more trouble than it was worth to get him to work at all. At the present severe time he was suffering very much, he was just a picture of abject misery without a dry rag to his back or a warm corner to snuggle into, and bitterly indeed did he repent his folly in wanting to go to sea.

Meanwhile matters on deck were very bad. Apart from the damage done by the sea, there was constant friction between the mate and the skipper, quarrels in front of the men, and every hindrance possible put in the mate's way, while worst of all he was prevented by the skipper from working the ship's position, and in consequence knew no more where she was than did any of the sailors. These latter, too, were as usual quick to seize the advantage they had in the disagreement of the officers, and so did nothing without a great amount of grumbling and swearing; in fact discipline was almost at an end, although there was no actual outbreak as yet. Which of course made things all the worse for the boys, who were kept at work of the hardest, doing those duties which in a properly regulated ship would have been performed by the men.

Fortunately the wind held steady if strong, and none of the sails blew away. So that beyond occasionally repairing the bending of a sail or securing some of the "Irish pendants" (flying ends) aloft, there was little to do of necessity, and what there was done fell to the boys, even to scrubbing off from the decks, incessantly washed by the sea, the slimy sea-grass that grew thereon.

At last matters grew so bad that one of the men, a huge German named Müller, who was in the mate's watch, upon being ordered by the mate to go aloft and secure a chafing-mat upon the main-topmast back-stay, refused most insolently, saying that he didn't intend to do anything more while he was aboard than steer and take his look-out. "Let de boys do it," he said, "or ellas do it yorselluf."

The mate flushed and clenched his fist, but he would probably have swallowed the insult if it had not been for the skipper's mocking laugh just behind him, one of those devilish inspirations that have been the cause of so many murders. It decided the mate, who sprang at Müller's throat, and the pair came heavily to the deck. Almost as if by preconcerted signal the watch below rushed out, it being nine in the morning, and flung themselves at the pair, evidently intent on murdering the mate. But the three boys with one impulse hurled themselves into the fray, fighting like wild cats, not that they loved the mate, but because their instincts were on the side of law and order.

There was a very pretty scrum for a few minutes, the old man looking on from the poop with an amused air as if he were enjoying himself, until the second mate, who had been busy in his cabin, rushed to the rescue, armed with an iron belaying-pin, and almost immediately settled the business by giving the foreigners some reminders of authority that they did not forget in a long while.

Helping the mate to rise, and finding that although considerably pumped, he was not hurt, the big German having only clawed at him like an old woman, the second mate roared, "Get forrard, you curs, or I'll shoot some of you," producing at the same moment a revolver from his jacket pocket.

He did not have to speak twice, the motley crowd recognised their master, and hustled forrard out of his way on the instant.

Then turning to the mate he said, "Hope you're all right, Mr. Jenkins, those brutes didn't seem to do much but fumble."

"Yes, thanks, Cope," growled the mate, "I'm all right enough; but I've got a score to settle with one man that won't wait any longer, and if it costs me my life I'm going to put it through now."

And at the word he rushed up the poop-ladder and straight at the grinning skipper, who, unable to get away, put up both arms to guard his head and cowered before the mate's mad rush at him. With a blow like a blacksmith's the mate's fist smashed through his feeble guard and brought him to his knees, then another crashing punch flattened his purple nose, from which a stream of dark blood spirted over his straggly beard. Again that vengeful fist was raised, but it did not fall, for the second mate and the three boys had by this time reached the furious mate, and clinging to him, implored him to desist. While they held him the crestfallen skipper crawled away below, and gradually Mr. Jenkins calmed down, only expressing the fervent hope that he had put a mark on his commanding officer that he would carry to his dishonoured grave.

"I'm all right now, Cope," he said in almost jubilant tones, "and from this out I'll run this ship on different lines, I'll swear. Just a minute," he continued, and he dived below, returning with a revolver in his hand and brandishing a fistful of cartridges.

"Now," he said, as he loaded the weapon, "we'll have a change. Go below, Mr. Cope, and thank you for your help. I think I can manage now. Lay aft the watch!"

The last words, uttered in a tremendous voice, brought the four members of his watch along in a hurry, the first one being Müller. As they came up to the break of the poop, the mate looking down upon them with the utmost scorn, said, "Get the slush-pots and lay aloft an' grease down, you dirty scum. I'll show you who's boss of this packet. You'll do what you like, will you? Think the skipper'll back y' up, do ye? I'll look out for all of ye and get plenty of sleep, and if one of you so much as whimpers, d'ye see this?" brandishing the revolver, "I'll shoot ye as soon as wink."

A tremendous change had come over the man once he had freed himself from the fear of losing his certificate, which so often makes cowards of the best of seamen under a worthless master. He was now a savage bully, and woe betide the man who crossed him.

Within ten minutes the thoroughly cowed men were strung aloft busily slushing down the masts, while Frank and Johnson were finding something to do, and chuckling to themselves at the turn which affairs had taken, for they had long been disgusted at the way in which all the dirty work had been put on them while the men were just loafing about.

But Mr. Jenkins had not quite finished his little programme yet. Having seen the men slung aloft, he strode into the cabin and up to the captain's state-room door, at which he knocked with a determined fist.

"Who's there?" quavered the skipper.

"It's me," answered the mate, "an' I want a word or two with you, Captain Swainson, before we go any further."

"Go away, Mr. Jenkins," replied the skipper in a tremulous voice, "I'm too ill to talk to you now."

The mate's answer was to fling the door wide open.

Then confronting the cowed man he said, "Now, Captain Swainson, understand from this out that I am the mate of this ship, fit and able to do my work, and determined to have the respect due to me from every man on board, beginning with you. I have put up with all the slights and insults from you that I intend putting up with, and now if you don't treat me as I deserve I'll take the command from you and keep you under arrest until we reach Levuka. I'm going to work the ship's position every day and know as much about her as you do, if not more. I've let you have your fling until you raised mutiny, which, thanks to the second mate and the boys, has been stopped. Now understand there's to be no more fooling. Treat me properly and I'll behave as your mate, try any more of your miserable games on and I'll do just what I've said. That's all."

And with the air of a conqueror Mr. Jenkins strode away, leaving the skipper in about as abject a condition as a man could well be. And so the ship was saved for the time, but only, as you see, because a law-abiding man had been driven to desperation and compelled to cast all fear of his future away and take the place he never ought to have relinquished.

Frank was astounded at the change in everything on board which almost immediately took place, and it made an impression upon his mind which never left it, of the value of discipline and of having some strong man to command. More than that, the part which he and his two seniors had played in rallying to the support of their officers in the face of a common danger gave them a sense of their own importance in the scheme of things which did them much good, and knit them together for the first time. They squabbled among themselves no longer, and instead of the aimless tattle, sometimes evil and always useless, which had characterised the yarns of Williams and Johnson with each other, discussions about the way to do things and the prospect of promotion were held.

But they were unanimous on one point especially, which was that since Master Harry had chosen to develop into a loafer as far as his work on deck was concerned, they would take care that he did all the menial work when he was below, and so with a great deal of protestation on his part and rather severe coercion on theirs, he was made to wait on them and keep the house clean—himself too. And it was astonishing how particular they became when they had some one whom they could make do things for them instead of having to do them for themselves.

On deck they learned rapidly now, for although neither the mate nor the second mate gave them any definite teaching, they were treated exactly like the men, and found that as they learned their work they were allowed to do things that in the ordinary way they would never have got a chance at. But it was very curious how in the new order of things the skipper was ignored. The mate was really in command of the ship, for Captain Swainson never interfered in any way; he was more like a passenger than one concerned in the ship's business. He was treated with studied courtesy by everybody, for somehow, without any definite orders having been given on the subject, all felt that the mate would speedily have punished any attempt at insolence to the captain. Mr. Jenkins was far too good an officer to allow any such insubordination as that, now he had regained his rightful position on board.

Still the skipper's position was painful and lonely in the extreme. Deprived of his beloved stimulant, which had always made him feel dignified and important, and conscious of the feelings of all hands towards him, he felt a deep craving for society, and, like the weakling that he was, fell back on the steward, with whom he came in more frequent contact than with anybody else. And when a skipper does that he is very far gone indeed. He is like a housewife who has forfeited all the love and respect of her husband and children by evil behaviour, and has fallen back upon her servants for company.

And still the ship sped on her long journey. For a ship is somewhat like time, whatever be the conditions on board short of disaster, slowly or swiftly she goes on towards her appointed goal. Wheel and look-out are relieved, sails are trimmed, watches succeed one another, and however long the way may seem, the miles are eaten into one by one, until looking back it seems wonderful how she has come so far in so short a time.

The *Sealark* was no clipper, as I have said before, and met with only the usual weather prevalent on that passage, and so at the end of four months she had passed the great Australian continent, and heading northward, soon changed the fierce stress of the westerly gales for mild and gentle breezes, the cold grey skies of the Southern Ocean for the deep blue vault of the Pacific heavens with their myriad burning brightnesses, and the mighty rollers of the Antarctic for the gentle waves, milk warm and coruscating in the sunshine by day, blue-black and shot with lambent flame by night, of the vast peaceful sea.

And now Frank really began to enjoy life. He could not have stated it in so many words, but he felt as if all the stern experiences which he had endured at the outset of this voyage, dreadful as they had seemed to him at the time, were a small payment for the present sense of reward. He drank in the beauty of his surroundings with the keenest physical delight, felt himself strong, and worthy, and proud, and, if he had not been too much of a man now, would have liked to dance and sing for sheer delight of living. But he felt a deep and certain satisfaction in the knowledge that he had chosen his vocation in life aright, and went about his work springingly.

I hope it will not be thought that I am painting my hero in too favourable colours, because I can assure my readers that he is not at all an uncommon type of boy, but one that I have often had the pleasure of meeting and being associated with, both afloat and ashore. And for one good thing there was no nonsense about him. He might, it is true, have given more thought than he did to those dear ones he had left at home, but he found out experimentally that when he did he was apt to get discontented with his surroundings, and a bit homesick too, so he deliberately tried not to think too much about dear grimy Dewsbury and those who dwelt there, except in picturing his triumphant return.

Now, as the weather grew so fine and the nights were so delightful, he courted Hansen's company again, and with more ease, because Mr. Jenkins had, ever since the great change, dispensed with the boys' keeping watch on the poop at night on their promise to keep within hail. And now he was joined by Johnson, who, being a good fellow at bottom, and only a bit lazy, felt that if he didn't mind Frank would get away ahead of him; and so they both sat and talked sea-lore all through the night watches on deck when they had neither wheel nor look-out, and accumulated knowledge apace.

Then came the great event of the voyage so far for Frank. He was on the main-royal yard one morning at daybreak busy at some small task, and when he had completed it, instead of coming down at once, he sat still a minute or two gazing around him at the gorgeous beauty of sea and sky, feeling tremendously impressed, in spite of his matter-of-fact nature, with his marvellous surroundings.

And then as the sun emerged majestically from the sea upon his right, and flooded ocean and heaven with a golden glow, he saw right ahead what even he could not help knowing was land. It was a solid black irregular lump clearly defined against the brilliant sky, such as he felt sure no cloud could ever look like. Strange as it may appear, the vessel had not sighted land since leaving Britain, which accounts for his excitement. He trembled so that he could hardly hold on, and stared at this new sight as if his eyes would pop out of their sockets. Then recovering himself he slid down the backstays, and running aft to the mate, reported what he had seen.

To his great surprise the mate received the news very quietly, saying only, "Yes, I expected to sight it this morning; it's Norfolk Island."

But Frank was full of the wonder at having come straight to this little spot upon the ocean's surface after nearly four months' journeying over the trackless ocean, and just bubbled over with enthusiasm about it, which Johnson did his best to damp, saying, "I don't know what you're making all the fuss about; it's nothing. Didn't expect we should lose our way, did you?"

By noon they had drawn close up to the beautiful island, so near indeed that the forests which had looked at a distance as if the hills were covered with dark-green grass, now showed up in all their magnificent beauty of great trees, with towering cliffs and deep ravines into which the sea rushed sullenly, and recoiled in a smother of snowy foam.

Nearer and nearer still they drew, until to Frank's delight they saw several canoes making towards them. As these came alongside, Frank, who was eagerly looking forward to seeing some picturesque savages, was somewhat disappointed to see that the dark-skinned boatmen were all clothed in shirts and trousers, and was still more astonished to hear the vessel hailed in good English, "Ship ahoy, where are you bound to? may we come aboard?"

Permission being given and a rope thrown to them, several fine sturdy fellows soon flung themselves inboard and greeted every one whom they met effusively, as if they were old friends.

They had brought a plentiful supply of fruit, vegetables, fowls, and eggs, and very quickly hoisted their wares on deck. Until then Frank had scarcely realised the privation of the voyage in respect of food, the weary sameness of salt beef and pork, pea-soup and duff, with one mess a week of tinned mutton and preserved potatoes, which he loathed, yet had to eat because there was nothing else. He found himself dribbling at the mouth with eagerness to taste those beautiful oranges and bananas, to say nothing of the fowls, eggs, and vegetables.

He rushed to his chest and got out his money, his father having given him three pounds for pocket-money when he left home, a fact which he had quite forgotten until now. But when he came rushing back with his coins in his hands and inquired the price of the fruit, he was amazed to find that these civilised islanders wanted clothes in barter, not money at all, and that moreover the commodities they had brought were rapidly disappearing, the steward buying largely for the cabin, and the men were eagerly offering shirts and trousers for quantities of food which were far below their value.

Poor Frank was almost desperate, and quite unaware of how he was delivering himself into the hands of these astute islanders, who were adepts at dealing with sailors ravenous for fresh food after a long passage at sea. In the end he became possessed of about a dozen oranges, a small bunch of bananas, about thirty, and two eggs, for two shirts which were nearly new, and had cost four and sixpence each in Liverpool. The total value of what he had received in exchange being about one shilling.

He was not to be blamed, for his experience was quite a common one. I myself have given two shirts worth at least six shillings for a dozen baskets of sweet potatoes, whose total weight was certainly not more than twelve pounds. This was in the Straits of Sunda, and the astute Javanese had packed the bottoms of the baskets with leaves, putting just three or four potatoes on the top, and not allowing examination until the bargain was made and the garments handed over. They knew the simplicity and gullibility of the sailor as well as any longshore man at home, and took full advantage of him. As everybody does in all parts of the world, except those who seek him for his good.

Having sold out their wares, the islanders scrambled into their boats, and pushing off in high glee made for the shore with their spoil, while the ship, struck by a heavy squall, such as will always be met with under high land, sped rapidly past the island, and was soon well on her way with a new departure for Fiji.

But no one could calculate the value of that little episode in the passage to these long-suffering ones, or the benefit that the fresh food was to their salt-saturated blood. Frank thought that never in his life had he tasted anything so delicious as that fruit, and as for the eggs, well, Williams and Johnson had succeeded in obtaining two dozen, and as they had got no fruit there was a grand exchange, and at supper-time a feast of hard-boiled eggs, when the whole twenty-six were wolfed by the four boys without any feeling that they were playing the glutton.

Thenceforward the ship seemed to have entered a new world. The sea was full of wonders. Strange birds and multitudes of fish, with occasional troops of whales of various kinds, queer floating things, and sounds at night also made Frank feel that all his early dreams of the delights of a sea-life were more than realised; and he confided to his friend Hansen his perfect satisfaction in his choice, saying again and again that he felt sure he was right when he chose the sea as a profession, and now he knew that it was the only life he could ever have lived.

Hansen looked upon him pityingly, benevolently, but said nothing, feeling, perhaps, the uselessness of doing so, but at the same time he felt that Frank's enthusiasm, beautiful as it was, would soon fade in the face of the stern realities of a sea-life when once he had reached man's estate. And yet, there was Harry Carter, of Frank's own age and with all of Frank's opportunities, who had degenerated into a wastrel, who bent all his faculties to the hard task of shirking work, who wouldn't learn and who would loaf, devoting as much brain power to getting out of the performance of his legitimate duties as would have made a man of him had he used them in the proper way.

One hundred and thirty-one days from home, and the joyful cry came ringing down from the mast-head of "Land-ho!" It was the voice of Hansen, who had been sent aloft by the mate to see if he could see anything, and from the fore-topsail-yard had sighted the beautiful outlines of Kandavu, an island of the Fiji group just south of Viti Levu, where the mail steamers from San Francisco used to call on their way to Sydney. The south-east Trades blew fresh, and the ship seemed to feel the call of the land, so that by sunset, amid wonders of nature that Frank felt could not be surpassed on earth, the *Sealark* anchored in the pretty bay of Levuka.

"The Sealark" enters the bay.

Who could hope to describe the tumult of mind experienced by Frank that evening, as he witnessed the fish-like gambols of the Fijians who came off in their canoes, or disported themselves around the ship like so many seals? How he listened to the strange mellifluous language they spoke, and the extraordinary attempts at English they made; how he feasted upon eggs and fruit, and vegetables and fish, until he felt a very glutton, then sat on the rail under the broad glare of the blazing moon and listened to the strange sounds, sniffed the curious sweet fragrance of the land, and dimly tried to recall the tales he had read of the far-off cannibal islands in his childhood.

Then tried to realise that he was really here—and right on the other side of the round world was that little family group whom he knew were always thinking of him. A sudden sense of the vast distance he had traversed came over him, a feeling of utter loneliness and longing to see the faces of those dear ones seized upon him, and to his own utter surprise a few hot drops came stealing down his cheeks, reminding him that for all his manly experiences he was but a boy after all.

That made him angry with himself, and roughly brushing away the tell-tale moisture he strode into the house and lit his pipe (I hadn't mentioned this acquisition of his) and began to laugh and banter Harry, the butt of the house, who was as usual in trouble for forgetting to wash up the supper traps. But at the earliest moment he sought his bunk, for he wanted to forget his sudden homesickness, and in that dark corner was almost immediately lost to all his external surroundings.

CHAPTER V
AMONG THE ISLANDS

Many masters of our beautiful language have endeavoured to depict the glories of a morning among the South Sea Islands, and I am in no mood to emulate their achievements. I can only say that when Frank, after a long night's sleep, the first really satisfying sleep he had enjoyed for five months, arose at the call of "Coffee" at 5 A.M., he emerged into a sense of loveliness that, boy as he was, sank into his very soul. The atmosphere was so sweet and pure, the odour of the land so entrancing, the beauty of the islands and limpid seas so far beyond anything he had ever dreamed of, that he found himself wonderingly comparing his surroundings with what he remembered of his childish dreams of heaven.

But he was rudely awakened from these unwonted visions by the hoarse voice of the mate shouting "Turn to."

He hastily gulped down his coffee, regretted his loss of a smoke, and strode out on deck ready for work. The men forrard made no sign of their existence, and after waiting about two minutes Mr. Jenkins turned to the second mate and said, "Go forrard, Mr. Cope, and give those fellows a rouse. I s'pose they've overslept."

The second mate marched to the forecastle door and reiterated the mate's order to "Turn to," but was met with a volley of oaths and evil advice as to his future.

He made no reply, but returned and reported to the mate, who immediately seized an iron belaying-pin and was about to rush forward when he was stopped by the second mate, who seized his arm, and pointed to the space between the ship and the beach, where only a very short distance away a whaleboat was coming at a great rate directly towards them.

"It's the old man," said the second mate in a low tone, "and he seems to have a pretty gang with him. I shouldn't wonder if he means mischief; at this time in the morning, too."

The mate looked thoughtfully at the boat for a moment, and then turning to the second mate said quietly, "I believe you're right; at any rate I'll get ready for emergencies before they arrive, and you'd better do the same."

So they both hurried into the saloon, and seeking their berths, charged their revolvers and pocketed them; then coming on deck, the mate awaited calmly the arrival of the boat alongside with the skipper, who had gone ashore overnight in the first boat that was available. He had not long to wait, for the boat, propelled by four stalwart natives, dashed alongside in great style, and the mate standing on the gangway saw to his disgust that the superior officer was drunk, and that he was accompanied by three men who had "beach-comber," or unattached loafer, writ large upon them. However he waited quietly until the skipper swayingly mounted the rail, then said calmly, "Good morning, Captain Swainson."

I cannot put the skipper's reply down, because it was not only abusive but couched in very foul language. It raised the mate's wrath, and he was about to make a hot reply when he became aware of the presence of one of the beach-combers, a huge brutal man who looked ripe for anything from pitch-and-toss to manslaughter. This visitor laid his hand on Mr. Jenkins' shoulder, saying, "Now, Mister Chief Mate, mind yer stops. I'm a friend of the cap's, and I've come off to have a little sociable conversation with you about your mutinous behaviour on the passage out."

"And I'm another friend of his," said the second visitor, pushing in.

"Count me in," shouted the third, who had now gained the deck, and there the mate stood, confronted by as nasty a situation as could well be imagined.

The skipper, looking as malignant as a monkey, rubbed his hands and emitted an exultant chuckle, then said, "Aha, me hero, boot's on t'other leg now. I'll make ye sing small enough before I've done with ye. Will you kindly inform me" (with profound sarcasm) "why the hands haven't been turned to yet? I want you to understand that I'll have discipline aboard this ship or I'll know the reason why."

The mate only turned on his heel and replied, "I'll talk to you when you're sober. As for you," turning fiercely to the loafers, "if you interfere with me in any way, look out for yourselves. I'm heeled and don't fear a whole regiment of beach-combers. Come on, Mr. Cope, let's leave these gentlemen to their pleasures and get the hands to work."

So saying he strode forward, gripping a belaying-pin from the rail as he went, and on arriving at the forecastle door he shouted, "Now then, are you fellows all dead in there? Turn to."

There was an almost inarticulate rumble of oaths in reply, but the mate had heard enough to put the draught upon his smouldering rage, and leaping into the forecastle he seized the foremost man, the big German, by the throat, and flinging himself backwards, they both fell in a kicking heap on deck. The second mate sprang forward, and dragging the sailor off the mate flung him sideways into the scuppers, the mate just springing to his feet in time to meet the rush of the other men. Unfortunately he had dropped his weapon in the struggle with the first man, and had not time to get his pistol out.

The second mate was in the same case, and for a moment it looked as if they would be overpowered. But as usual the unexpected happened, there was a scuffling rush from aft, and into the fight broke the three visitors like a whirlwind, striking and kicking with such hearty goodwill at the mutineers that in the short space of a minute the struggle was over, and the victory of law and order was complete. The mate and second mate, panting and bleeding, stood astonished and glared at their helpers, the foremost of whom said, "It's all right, Mister Mate, I come aboard with the idea of puttin' you through, but I ben skipper myself too long an' ben in too many tight places to have any sympathy with mutineers, and I'm glad to have ben of any service to ye. My name is Haynes, an' I'm willing to be chummy if you are. Shake," and he held out a hairy fist.

The mate gripped his hand gratefully, and said, "Thank'ee, Cap'n Haynes, but now if you'll excuse me I've got to get these blighters goin'; duty first, y'know." And turning to the discomfited crowd he shouted, "Now get along an' wash decks, an' the first man I see skulking I'll clap the irons on him."

There was an immediate move to the work, and in five minutes the usual everyday business of cleaning the ship was going forward as if nothing had happened.

This time Frank and his chums had taken no part in the proceedings, but they had not failed to notice all that went on, and as they handed along water or worked at the pump they meditated upon the advantages of a plucky front shown to opposing forces. And when breakfast-time came they eagerly compared notes upon the upshot of the morning's work, much to the advantage of the mate and the disadvantage of the skipper.

But they soon forgot all about it in their admiration of the natives, who as the day set in had come off laden with fruit and sundries for sale. They were a splendid set of fellows, looking fierce enough for a regular cannibal raid, with their enormous bushy heads of hair frizzed out like a huge halo all around, and their necklaces of sharks' teeth gleaming upon their shiny, tawny bodies. But they were peaceable enough now and only bent on trade, on getting rid of the loads of fruit they had brought in exchange for money, Frank being astounded at the quantity he obtained for a shilling.

He however could not think of much else because of his admiration of the antics of those islanders in the water. They seemed to be even more at home there than in their canoes, and as a good swimmer himself he felt what a difference there was between what we know as swimming and the fish-like antics of men who were almost brought up in the water. What with the noise and excitement consequent upon the constant arrival of more and more natives Frank got no breakfast, only a little fruit, so that when turn-to time came he was angry with himself, and loath to turn away from this most interesting experience.

But there was much work to be done, and the mate was obviously bent upon getting a full day out of his men, although in doing so he gave himself no rest, and of course the boys had their full share. So busy were they that they did not notice the absence of the skipper and his body-guard of beach-combers, who, finding no liquor on board, had not tarried to breakfast, but had gone early, taking a ceremonious leave of the mate, and assuring him of their readiness to come and help if he had any more trouble with his crew. He did not answer, but smiled grimly, thinking that any trouble that he was likely to have would probably come from quite a different direction, that is, from the skipper.

Now began for the boys, who had indeed well deserved it, a really first-class time. The mate and second mate having obtained the upper hand of the crew, kept it by making them work, getting the ship in apple-pie order after her long passage, and the boys were put upon all the best jobs, working at whatever they could do that would teach them to have confidence in themselves; while the usual scheme of things in such ships was reversed, that is, all the dirty, and what is generally known as menial work, instead of being put upon the boys, was done by the men.

If this should seem unfair to any reader, I would beg to remind him that these lads, having paid liberally for the privilege of being taught their profession, had no business to be placed in the position of lackeys to the men, who are always ready to shift all unpleasant work upon boys' shoulders, whether they are premium apprentices or not. But their present position was entirely due to their own efforts, and the extraordinary condition of affairs on board. Moreover, although neither of the officers dared go ashore, knowing the simmering state of revolt among the men, they gave the boys every chance to do so, and thus the lads got a knowledge of boat-handling which is so very useful to a sailor.

But this I am sorry to say had its evil side, for the two seniors having had experience of shore-going pastimes on the previous voyage, when they were under no sort of supervision, took advantage of their liberty to introduce Frank to the dubious delights of Scotch whisky, for which he was proud to pay as being the only possessor of cash in the house. And it was curious to see how the shirker Harry, who, as we have seen, was almost useless on board, became when on shore quite a swaggering tar, and put on so many frills that it became necessary to take him down a few pegs and threaten to stop him from coming ashore at all by reporting his behaviour to the mate. This he resented exceedingly, and sulked a good deal, but little was thought of that until, one evening when the boys had been allowed to run ashore as usual, Harry was missing.

Now they had all four mixed freely with the natives; had visited their houses, and taken part in some very curious and unconventional proceedings which need not be particularised, except by the general statement that these boys were growing into men very fast. Yet as far as was known by Frank and the two seniors, Harry had never dreamed of desertion; in fact the idea, when first mooted by Williams, was scouted by the other two as absurd. However, after scouring the town and visiting all their accustomed haunts until they were ready to drop from fatigue, they were compelled to return to the ship without him.

They met the mate at the gangway, and the first thing he said was, "This is the last time you go ashore here with my leave, you ungrateful young swine. It's always the way. Be easy, and you get imposed on. But where's Harry?"

There was a dead silence for a few moments, the lads feeling as if they could hear their hearts beat.

"D'ye hear me?" roared the mate, now thoroughly alarmed.

Frank faltered out, "We don't know, sir, we couldn't find him. We've hunted everywhere we could think of, and that's what made us so late."

As soon as the dread truth soaked into the mate's brain, his fury was terrible to witness. He was almost insane at the thought that after all his care in dealing with his worthless skipper, and his mastery over the very difficult circumstances of his position, this calamity should fall upon him, Harry being the son of a particular friend of the owners', who had especially commended him to the mate's care. Matters were all the more complicated, in that the skipper had not been near the ship since he had gone ashore the morning after her arrival, and although this was nothing less than criminal on his part, it would not in any way absolve the mate for losing the boy.

In vain did the second mate try and comfort him, pointing out how absolutely free from blame he was except in the one detail of letting the boys run ashore for an hour. But the poor fellow could not pardon himself, and sleep being an impossibility, he sat and suffered through the night.

About 3 A.M., when he had arrived at that stage of sleeplessness when the idea of ever having slept seems ridiculous, and had turned over in his mind a thousand schemes for recovering his lost apprentice and had rejected them all as useless, he thought he heard a sound on deck.

Now there is no place so quiet as a ship at anchor in a snug harbour on a calm night, and there is no place where an unwonted sound is so easily heard. Consequently the mate fairly bristled with apprehension, and as he lay in his bunk he was like a cat ready to pounce. Then he saw a gleam of light flash across the cabin, and in a moment he was out of his bunk, his trusty revolver clutched in his right hand, and peering out of the pitchy dark of his cabin he saw the forms of three men in the pale glimmer of the young moonlight stealing across the saloon deck. Without a moment's hesitation he raised his revolver and fired three shots in quick succession, the noise and stench of the exploding powder filling the narrow space almost to suffocation.

There were many confused noises of pain, of rage, and of fear; but Mr. Jenkins calmly retreated to his room, and lit the dark lantern which all ship's officers possess, and emerging once more from his cabin met the second mate, also with his lantern and weapon in hand. Their greetings were curt, and their investigations resulted in finding two badly wounded men of the crew, the big German before mentioned, and an Irish-American of whom I have hitherto said nothing.

These culprits were too frightened and weak from loss of blood to say anything in reply to questions, so leaving them for a while the two officers hurried on deck, finding no one there; but the second mate rushed to the stern, remembering that the boat had been passed there instead of being hoisted, and flashing his lantern down at her, saw two cowering figures in her stern-sheets completely demoralised with fright. He sternly bade them come up, emphasising his readiness and willingness to shoot if they did not.

Tremblingly they answered, "Ay, ay, sir, we'll come up; don't shoot, for God's sake," and began to haul the boat alongside. They mounted the ladder and began to scurry forward, when the second mate stopped them and bade them carry their shipmates with them, the mate having in the meantime roughly improvised a couple of tourniquets for their wounds, and stopped the bleeding therefrom.

They did so very humbly and carefully, and when they had gone the mate said solemnly, "Looky here, Cope, I believe if it hadn't been for those blessed boys you and I would have had our throats cut to-night. I've heard say that it's an ill wind that blows nobody any good, but I feel sure that we owe our lives to the misfortune of that infernal young scalawag Carter having chosen to-night to run away. I don't care now. I feel regularly happy. And if I only had a drop of something stronger than this pump grog I would celebrate."

"Yes, an' it would go to your head like fire," said the second mate. "Be thankful, man, that they can't say that about us. I like my tot as well as the next man, but I'm bound to say that when there's trouble about I want to be able to say there wasn't any grog in it, anyhow. Now go and turn in, and I'll keep watch until daylight. I've had a good sleep, while you must be regularly fagged out."

"Thankee, Cope, I will," replied the mate, "but keep your eyes skinned for those devils in case they are up to mischief again."

"All right, sir," rejoined the second mate, "I'll keep my lamps trimmed for them. But you try and get some sleep."

So the mate went to his bunk and fell instantly into a sound sleep, while Mr. Cope paced the deck and watched the gentle night fade away and take on the glory of the dawn, but never for a moment did he relax his vigilant watch on the fore end of the ship. And as he pondered over the events of the voyage so far, he felt sad to think how the mate, who was one of the kindest and best-natured fellows alive, should have been driven by untoward circumstances to become in the eyes of some of his fellow-men a veritable tyrant, enforcing his will by the use of deadly weapons.

But he was a healthy-minded young man, and soon shook off any morbid feelings that the hour and the reaction pressed upon him, and so fully did he occupy the time with these various mental exercises, that it gave him quite a start to hear the cook call out "Coffee." He slipped below and warned the steward not to awaken the mate. Then having swallowed his refreshing draught, he went forward and had a quiet chat with the boys as to the possibilities of Harry being found, but without much hope of anything being done.

Then a man from forward approached and diffidently said that the two wounded men were in a high fever, and evidently very ill. This immediately reminded Cope of his first duty, and he went and hoisted an urgent signal for a doctor and the police, feeling sure that it would be just what Mr. Jenkins would have done.

Then, having started such of the hands as were capable of working to wash decks, he went and called his superior and informed him of what he had done, being delighted to hear in return that in Mr. Jenkins' opinion he had done just right. In half-an-hour a police-boat was seen coming off with the doctor on board. She was soon alongside and the officer in charge put in possession of the facts. The doctor and the second mate went forward to the forecastle, and for the next hour that gloomy chamber bore no bad resemblance to a dirty hospital ward, while the groans of the sufferers were pitiable to hear.

At the same time the police-officer was in nowise astonished to hear that the mate had not seen his commander since the day after their arrival, and told Mr. Jenkins that the consignee of the cargo had seriously debated the question of putting him on board his ship by force, and daring him to come ashore again. The officer said, moreover, that from the capers the skipper had been cutting, it was certain that he must have spent a good deal of money or accumulated a heavy debt, which would certainly have to be liquidated before the vessel's departure. He, moreover, promised to leave no stone unturned to secure the restoration of the runaway apprentice, but owned that in a port like Levuka, where there were so many schooners popping in and out, it would be difficult indeed to catch him if he had chosen to go to sea. Ashore, he could almost guarantee his being caught. And with this scant comfort Mr. Jenkins had to be content.

Presently the doctor reappeared, looking as became a man who had done a good day's work. He said, "Well, Mr. Mate, you've given those fellows something to remember you by, and they won't forget me in a hurry either. My word, but they did squimmidge. Never mind, it's all over now, and they are doin' as well as can be expected. Here are the pills," and he held out two small bullets. "And now, Mr. Mate, just a toothful of whisky or squareface or anything of that nature, and I'll absence myself chop chop. I've got a lot of grousing beggars ashore waiting for me who'll swear I've been neglectin' them on purpose."

"So sorry, doctor," replied the mate, "but there isn't so much as a smell of firewater aboard this ship. I had to give it all a passage coming out, or I'm blessed if I think we should have got here at all."

"Oho," the doctor laughed, "that's the explanation, is it? Well, Mr. Mate, you have my sympathy. But I'm not surprised, judgin' from the way your jovial skipper's been making Rome howl since he came ashore. He's one of my patients now, you may like to know. I'm doin' my best to save him from a fit of the rats, but I don't know how it will turn out, I'm sure. He's very shaky. Come on, inspector."

"I think not, Doc," answered the police-officer. "I'd better stay aboard here and let Mr. Jenkins go ashore and see his skipper. He's got a report to make that won't keep, and from what I can see of things, the ship won't suffer from my presence here until he comes back."

And then, while the mate bent his shore-going rig, the police-officer held an earnest colloquy with his chief boatman as to the disappearance of Harry, making arrangements for a thorough scouring of the countryside for the foolish lad.

Five minutes afterwards the mate was hurrying shoreward, while, to a casual observer, nothing unusual was taking place on board the barque. The available men and the lads were busy about their usual duties getting the vessel ready for sea, her Fiji cargo having been discharged, and nothing remaining to be done but prepare for the resumption of the voyage.

Frank and his two chums went about their work with a penitential air, the sense of disaster impending, although they repeatedly assured themselves that they were in no way to blame for the loss of their berthmate. In addition, they were puzzled beyond measure at the extraordinary events which had taken place during the night, entirely outside their knowledge. They had slept so soundly that no item of the fray had reached them, although if it had they would have been scarcely surprised, for by this time all three of them, Frank especially, had grown to regard such events as quite within the range of any day's happenings, so speedily do we all become accustomed to our surroundings.

It was nearly noon before the mate returned, looking triumphant, like a man who had overcome all his difficulties. It appeared he had met the skipper in the presence of the ship's agent, and had completely justified himself in the latter gentleman's eyes, and also in the opinion of the authorities, who, with a common sense which may be looked for in vain in older countries, considered that he had acted extremely well, and told him so.

The episode of the boy Harry's loss had been lightly glossed over as a thing that boys were prone to, and the mate completely exonerated. No wonder he was exultant, and if occasionally he wondered how he should meet the father of the lad upon his return home, he consoled himself by remembering that the skipper would have to answer for it first.

So things resumed their normal course on board, except for the two wounded men in the forecastle, who were indeed in evil case, full of pain and the consciousness of frustrated designs. Otherwise everything went on just as usual. It does, you know, on board ship as well as on shore. There must indeed be an utter break-up, an entire disintegration of all things when the ordinary work of getting meals goes wrong. Whoever mutinies or fights or gets killed, the cook and steward keep busy with their pots and kettles, and the grub comes up to time whether there is anybody to partake of it or not. It is the necessities of life which bind our doings up, not the great heroic deeds. I have seen a cook rise calmly and go to his galley at 5 A.M. to prepare coffee when everybody else in the ship except the steward felt certain that she would not live through another watch. And we were all so glad of that coffee, although we did not praise the cook.

The next morning brought the skipper on board in charge of an official who said that if the ship was ready for sea it would be well if she went at once. To which the mate was most agreeable, only making slight demur on the ground that he was two hands short. That, said the official, he had considered and had brought with him four Hawaiian Kanakas, well-drilled seamen who would work their passage to Honolulu with great pleasure.

In respect of the missing boy, the official gravely said he was very sorry, but not a trace of him could be found, and the ship could not be delayed while a fruitless search was being made for a youngster who, by all accounts, was a wastrel who would never be any good. With this the mate was fain to be content, and, having seen the skipper comfortably bestowed in his bunk, with the prospect of an acute attack of delirium tremens before him, Mr. Jenkins returned on deck and gave orders to man the windlass, the wind being very kindly for departure.

The anchor came up easily, the four Kanakas being stalwart, cheery fellows, who gave all the strength they had to the work, and paid no heed to the lowering looks of the white men who unwillingly toiled with them. And in an hour the *Sealark* had her white wings spread again for the long sea-road to the Sandwich Islands, where she was to discharge the remainder of her cargo.

It happened to be Frank's trick at the wheel as the ship sped away from the land, and do what he would he felt unable to help being sorry to put to sea again. Having cultivated the ability common among sailors of detaching his mind entirely from the business of steering, which he did all the more perfectly because mechanically, he dwelt mentally upon all the strange scenes he had witnessed in the semi-savage town they were just leaving. Then he thought of Harry, the misguided youngster who had taken a step which would probably break a fond parent's heart, who had thus flung away as a dirty rag all his prospects, and proved his utter inability to understand the meaning of life.

This led him to think of his own dear folks at home, and to remember with a start that it was now six months since he had heard anything of them. Whether it was the soft influence of parting from the first port he had ever visited, with all its varied and pleasant associations, he did not know, but as he thought of home he felt curiously choky and unhappy, while his eyes grew dim with tears.

He was quite lost to all his surroundings on the narrow quarter-deck, the white sails above him, and the resplendent sea and sky, when, with a sudden tightening sensation at his waist and a cold chill over his scalp, he became aware of the skipper standing before him with an awful face. The glaring eyes protruded from between swollen, reddened lids, the cheeks looked like slabs of diseased meat where they were not overgrown with weedy hair, and from between the thick purple lips came a breath so foul that quite involuntarily Frank turned his head away.

A voice as harsh and unnatural as a dead man's might be imagined to sound said, "Boy, what are all these devils doin' aft here? You're a devil too, ain't you? I'd kill you if I could, but I can't kill the devil, I can't kill the devil. Ah, spare me, spare me," and the miserable man sank down on his knees muttering terrible things which, fortunately, Frank did not understand.

Of course Frank was frightened, but I like to remember that he kept on steering even though his heart was bumping against his ribs as if it would break through. Then he lifted his voice and yelled at its utmost pitch, "Mr. Jenkins, Mr. Cope, come aft, the captain's mad!"

Immediately the poor demented creature sprang to his feet and flew at Frank, who, agile as a monkey, vaulted over the wheel-box and seized the wheel on the other side, still shouting lustily and keeping a keen eye on the maniac, who now, by some sudden twist in his poor brain, dived under the grating, and with a horrid chuckling laugh began playing with the gear by which the rudder was moved.

Fortunately by this time Frank's cries had been heard, and the two officers, hurrying aft with eager inquiry, flung themselves upon the skipper and dragged him below. There they secured him so safely that, strive as he would, he could not get loose again. Then, with the versatility of sailors, they returned to their work of getting the anchors and cables secured and the ship prepared for open sea. All the attention they had paid to Frank was comprised in the simple question Mr. Cope put to him, "Did he do anything to you?" And when Frank answered "No, sir," he expressed his satisfaction by a curt nod.

But Frank had received a shock that left him shivering as if from cold. It was far too heavy a strain to put upon a lad of his age. And it is all the more satisfactory to be able to record that he stood it successfully and still steered the ship as straightly as before. Yet he did not at all realise what was the matter with the skipper, until being relieved he went forward to his berth, and in answer to the eager questioning of Johnson, told him of all that had happened, with as much of the skipper's conversation as he was able to recall.

"Ah," said Johnson, wagging his head wisely, "the old swine is paying for his fling in Levuka. He's got what the Yanks call snakes in his boots, and serve him jolly well right too."

"Snakes in his boots!" replied Frank in a horrified tone; "whatever do you mean?"

"Why, what the doctors call delirium tremens," said Johnson sententiously. "When a man has been drinkin' heavy for a long time he gets a fit of madness, sees things that ain't there, mostly snakes, and spiders, and rats crawling all about where he is, and carries on something shockin'."

"Oh dear, oh dear!" shudderingly rejoined Frank. "I wonder you can talk about it like that. What a frightful thing. I feel half mad thinking of it. And if you could have seen his face! It frightened me almost to death. If that's the fruits of drunkenness, I'll never touch another drop of the beastly stuff as long as ever I live."

"Good boy," sneered Williams, who had just come in, "that's what they call in the books, the effect of a horrible example. But who's going to be such a juggins as to get like that? Not me, anyhow. I'm going to have my grog and enjoy myself."

Frank didn't see his way to any reply, so he remained silent with the skipper's awful face in his mind's eye.

These unpleasantnesses, however, did not long affect the lads, who had far too many objects of interest around them to allow them to dwell upon the troubles of other people. They were now sailing through perhaps the most romantic and beautiful sea in the world, their route being studded with lovely islands, the sea swarming with fish, the air joyful with birds. They had, moreover, frequent visits from passing canoes, for the natives of those islands, confident in the quietude of their environing seas, think nothing of journeying a couple of hundred miles or so in craft that civilised men would hardly care to cross a narrow river in.

It was great fun to see the four jovial Hawaiians exchanging salutations with these wanderers, and greater fun still to learn from the dusky mariners how to snare the many fish that gambolled about them by day and by night. They, of course, thought nothing of the tremendous strain upon the mate of having to navigate the ship amidst that maze of islands, having the entire responsibility thrown upon him without any recompense or compensating circumstances. And all the while the man who was receiving pay for this onerous work was lying helpless below, having gotten over the worst of his madness, and was now slowly working his way back again to complete health under the careful attention of the man to whom he had behaved in so shameful a manner.

But taking it all round there was a peaceful, happy time for everybody. The men forrard, having lost the two malcontents, had settled down to their work in good shape, and finding that the Kanakas were rattling good seamen at all such work as handling sails, steering, and keeping look-out (at this last their eyes were like twin telescopes), besides being ever good-natured and willing, they chummed up with them splendidly.

Then the food was good, for Mr. Jenkins had laid in a good supply of vegetables and fruit, having been empowered to do so by the consignee, after that gentleman had found out how helpless to attend to business the skipper was. And to crown all, the weather was persistently fine, even delightful, while the ship, owing to the way in which Mr. Jenkins had kept the hands at work in harbour, was in splendid trim, working easier than she had ever worked before during that passage. So day by day slipped away, Frank feeling more and more satisfied with his lot, putting on strength both of body and mind, and accumulating unconsciously a store of reserve force against the time when it should be needed in other and stormier scenes.

At last, when they had cleared the Phœnix Islands and had a clear long stretch before them up to the Sandwich group, the skipper made his appearance on deck, a mere shadow of a man, looking as if he had still one foot in the grave. He was treated with grave and distant courtesy by the officers, but took no part whatever in the working of the ship. But neither did he make any admission of his wrong-doing or appear at all grateful for the faithful service bestowed upon the ship by those under him, service which had saved her from disaster and everybody on board from innumerable miseries.

As an instance of the depths to which his neglect had dragged him, it was not until they had been out a fortnight from Levuka that the mate came forward one morning to the boys' house and handed to each of them a letter which he said the captain had found among his papers, letters which had been waiting in Levuka for the ship's arrival, and had thus been kept from their rightful owners.

This sounds almost incredible, but I know of a case in a ship upon which I served where the skipper actually destroyed in a drunken fit all the letters for the crew which he had received in Rangoon, and scoffingly said that his action "would save 'em a lot of trouble; what did they want with letters?"

Of course Frank could not help feeling indignant at this shameful treatment, but the joy of thus receiving unexpectedly in open sea a budget of news from his loved ones was so great that he speedily forgot the offence and lay upon the main hatch in the beautiful sunshine (it was Sunday afternoon and nothing was a-doing), soaking his soul in the outpourings of love from that far-away home circle.

How he regretted now the curt letter he had sent home from Levuka, for, smarting under a sense of neglect, he had merely told them that he was well and liked the sea, and that he hoped the voyage would be a long one, thinking that they had forgotten all about him. And now here was the proof of their never-ceasing thought of him. As he realised how great a sin that drunkard aft had committed against him and them, he felt beside himself with rage, the rage of the budding man, and he rushed to his bunk, got out his writing materials, and in his first fury wrote such a letter to his people as he had never dreamed himself capable of putting on paper.

And still the good ship glided on o'er sunny seas 'neath glowing skies, until the glorious panorama of Oahu burst into view at the break of a golden morning, and Frank wondered that the thrill he felt at the sight of Kandavu would not come again. Speedily and in seaman-like fashion the *Sealark* was brought to her moorings, the anchor rattled down, she was safe in port once more, and—the credit of it all went to the creature who had been a positive danger to her instead of any help whatever. This is one of the grim ironies of sea life, but fortunately did not touch Frank's mind; although he knew it, he did not feel it, and it was well.

Now Honolulu is a far more advanced port than Levuka. But there are many opportunities for debauchery, and this doubtless Captain Swainson well knew as he rigged himself out in his best clothes and prepared to leave his ship again.

But Mr. Jenkins was waiting for him as he came on deck with the jovial agent by his side, to whom the skipper had been unreeling a lurid yarn about the difficulties he had overcome of worthless officers and mutinous crew.

"I want a word with you before you go ashore, Captain Swainson," said the mate in grim, dry tones.

"Oh, I can't stop now," hastily replied the skipper. "Can't you see I'm busy? And the agent's waiting too. I'll see you later on in the day. Get the——"

But he got no farther, for the mate, standing squarely in front of him, said—

"If you don't care to listen to what I've got to say quietly, and while you are sober, I shall say it before such listeners as you will tremble to see. I've had enough of your capers, and I'll have no more."

"Now look here, Mr. Mate," interrupted the agent, "this won't do, you know. You mustn't behave like this. You forget yourself."

The mate's blood grew hot. But he restrained himself with a mighty effort, and answered quietly—

"Oh no, I don't, sir. I forget nothing. But that man there was drunk all the time the ship was in Levuka, and mad with the horrors half the way here, and if he's going on the same way in Honolulu, I'm going to stop him, that's all, if there's any use in a British consul."

The skipper looked at the agent in helpless fashion, and the agent, putting on a big official tone, said, "Now, Mr. Mate——"

But Mr. Jenkins stopped him, and said in a tone that carried conviction—

"Now, Mr. Agent, I have nothing to say to you at all. Only if Captain Swainson isn't on board this ship to-morrow attending to his duty, it will be my business to know why, and the telegraph office is as free to me as to anybody else. That's all I've got to say; and now I've my duties to attend to, and I wish you good day."

And he turned on his heel, and left the pair to digest his words.

They got into a boat and went ashore, wondering what the outcome would be, while the mate's orders flew like hail, and the ship was rapidly put in harbour trim, and the discharging gear got ready for transhipment of cargo. In this way the day passed rapidly, and Frank hardly had time to note the beauties of the island harbour wherein they lay until knock-off time, when the gentle native folk with soft caressing words came on board, bringing loads of gifts as they called them, but really gifts that called for a far greater return.

The four Hawaiians were now in their element among their fellows, and full of glee at being home again. They repaid with rich interest the kindly treatment they had received, and introduced the visitors with rapid outpourings of broken English. There was, however, one serious bar to any extended trade—no one had any money. Frank's little store had all been spent in Levuka, and the sailors had not received a penny, although they had now nearly seven months' wages due, and by unwritten ship law were entitled to liberty and a month's wages. This, however, they could not get from the mate, they knew; and so they did not ask, hoping to get at the skipper some time when he was on board.

Now the mate's spirited protest had much impressed the agent, who was a keen tradesman, and without unduly pressing the skipper, he made it clear to him that it would be well to go slow, in case the mate should "behave ugly," as he put it. And so he kept the skipper well in hand, allowing him to have only a gentle fling, and seeing him depart from the beach that night for his ship only partially drunk, and without any means of strengthening the hold the liquor had got upon him. The mate was on deck when he came, and duly noted his condition, but said not a word. And the skipper reeled to his bunk, his head all awhirl with projects for the mate's discomfiture, but saying nothing at all.

CHAPTER VI
INTRODUCES AMERICANS

Whew! but that was a long chapter! And, moreover, I feel that it was far too full of creepy things. I don't want you to think that those boys had no fun, only I get so full of the hard side of things when I remember how little of the soft came my way at sea, that I commit the bad mistake of forgetting the joys of life. Believe me, in spite of the seriousness of the situation on board the *Sealark*, there were times in the evenings when the laughter of those boys and the fellows forrard was simply uproarious, partly because they were well fed and fully employed, but principally because of the four Hawaiian seamen, who were, like most of their race, just bubbling over with happiness, simply because they were alive. It is perhaps a poor sense of humour that makes us laugh at mistakes in language, absurd perversions of speech, but it argues, I think, a beautiful mind, when those whom we laugh at, being full of intelligence, will take no offence, but improve the occasion, in order that more fun may result. Already I am beginning to feel my space run short, but I really must quote one little snatch of conversation which Frank held with Oonee, one of the Hawaiians, giving it as near as possible verbatim.

Frank. "You was once a cannibal, wasn't you?"

Oonee. "No, Falankee, not me. My father, he eatee plenty mans."

Frank. "Now look here, Oonee, d'you mean to tell me that you've never had a steak off a man?"

Oonee. "Yes, Falankee, I tell you taloo (true). But looka. My Baluther, he go livee 'nother islan'. Velly bad man there. I can't forget (remember) what you call 'im. One time mishnally come. Evelly body glad, because no fight longa time so no eata longa pig. Kanaka call man longa pig when him bake. Take the mishnally 'way velly quick, cut 'im neck, put 'im in Kanaka oven all same pig. Bimeby done, all hands come make feast. No knife, no follok, every man pull off bit. Bit hat, bit coat, bit boot, too much plenty velly hard. Bimeby one man he say, 'Mishnally no good ki ki, he makee eatee some nutting, no good belong spoil 'im. Flow 'im 'way.'"

This Oonee was a humorist of the first water, and very proud of his English-speaking abilities. A favourite yarn of his was how once being adrift in Hobart Town when on leave from a whaler, he stopped outside of a shop, and inquired of a strangely-attired gentleman who was standing there the way to his ship. The gentleman, who happened to be a full-length Highlander, used as a tobacconist sign, made no response, and to quote Oonee, "Him no say nutting, no look me, no more. Me touch 'im, feel all same wood, me flightened 'im; lun 'way. I no savvy what thing man that belong."

But I know young people are uneasy with dialect, and so I must discontinue giving Oonee's remarks, only adding that in ability and industry he was as prominent as he was in good-humour and wit. Fortunately for everybody, I think, the Hawaiian seamen were not anxious to terminate their engagement. They had in some mysterious way grown to like the ship and her crew (the old man they knew nothing about, of course, looking upon him much as a schoolboy looks upon x on his first introduction to algebra). All they wanted was to be allowed ashore each night after knock-off time; and this was readily granted them, on their promise to return in time for work in the morning, which promise was always faithfully kept.

But this preferential treatment was deeply resented by the rest of the foremast hands, who indeed had some right to feel aggrieved, not having had any liberty now for the best part of a year. When, however, they came aft and laid their grievances before the mate, he grimly referred them to the skipper, who was as difficult to see as a monarch. Thoroughly frightened by the mate's determined attitude, he had slept on board every night and confined his drinking principally to his own cabin, and although he entertained a good many keen-looking visitors, he was hardly ever seen on deck. Therefore when the steward brought him word one Sunday morning that the men wished to see him, he immediately fell into what is vulgarly known as a blue funk. He could not consult with the mate, who he felt sure sent the men to him, and he felt as if he dared not meet the men, knowing very well what they wanted. At last screwing up his courage to the sticking-point, he ordered the steward to request Mr. Jenkins to step down and see him, and when the mate came to remain handy in case of accidents.

Down came the mate, making an almost involuntary wry face as he passed into the acrid atmosphere of the skipper's state-room from the pure air above. "You sent for me, sir?" he said, and waited.

"Ye-e-s, Mr. Jenkins," stammered the skipper, "I want you to find out what the men want. I—I—I'm not well enough to come on deck just yet."

"What they want, sir, and what I don't see how they can be refused, is some liberty and money. May I remind you that they have been nearly eight months on board and have had no liberty yet?"

"Well," answered the skipper petulantly, "let 'em go, let 'em go, but I've got no money for 'em. What do they mean by coming worrying me for money on the Sabbath? They ought to know better."

The mate stood looking grimly down at the pitiful creature before him in silence for a few moments, and then said, "Do you wish me to convey this to the men then, that they go on leave to-day, but you can give them no money, and it being Sunday you can't get any?"

"Yes, yes, that's it, that's it, do 'em good. If I gave 'em money they'd only spend it in drink like all the rest of the silly sailors. Thank you, Mr. Jenkins, I think I'll get a little rest now," and much relieved he snoodled down under the blankets again. But had he seen and been able to appreciate the bitter scorn and hatred in the mate's face as he turned away, I do not think he would have felt so comfortable.

On deck the mate found the crew awaiting him. Without any preliminary he repeated the skipper's message, looking straight at the men as he did so. And when they began to growl he said quietly, "Now go forrard and do your growling, I've given you the skipper's words. Any complaints you have, make them to him when you meet him. In the meantime I am responsible for the discipline of the ship, and I'm going to maintain it."

They, knowing him, took the hint and slouched forrard, muttering under their breath. But things were not as bad as they had feared, and the Kanaka seamen who manned the boat to take them ashore behaved like the generous kindly souls they all are, and the result was that those ten men (Hansen didn't go, preferring to spend the day with his pupils) had as good a time, nay, better, than they would have enjoyed with their pockets full of money.

But Frank and his chums dared not again ask Mr. Jenkins for leave, for the second mate had informed them privately that so deeply had the desertion of Harry Carter troubled the mate that he had declared that as far as he was personally concerned no permission should again be granted to the boys to go ashore until the ship returned to England, which meant, of course, that they must get leave from the skipper himself, or not at all. So, as they felt unable to approach the skipper, their prospect of seeing anything of the shore except from the ship's decks looked remarkably small.

However, like sensible lads they made the best of their position, and having taken to fishing under the guidance of Oonee, they managed with that and swimming, and skylarking with the jolly natives who came on board, to pass the time very happily. More than that, their studies, which all three of them were now going in for with the greatest interest under the watchful care of Hansen, absorbed a good deal of their time, and had such good results that I doubt if any youngsters of their sea time could have compared with them in their working knowledge of their profession.

Meanwhile the armed neutrality which still existed between the skipper and his officers showed no signs of being improved into cordiality, and although the captain spent all his days ashore, he never again dared to remain on shore at night, being afraid of what the mate would do to carry out his threat. Unfortunately the skipper's drinking had been going on worse than ever, and stray reports occasionally reached the mate as to the way in which the old man had been rioting ashore, reports which he received with a shrug of the shoulders as who should say, "Well, it doesn't concern me."

Whether he would have taken any action on this account I do not know, but one morning when the ship was all but ready for sea, he received a visit from the vice-consul, who, after introducing himself, told Mr. Jenkins that his errand was about the behaviour of the captain, which was causing quite a scandal ashore, in a place where they were not at all thin-skinned either.

The mate listened gravely, and then calling the second mate as a witness, gave the vice-consul a brief account of the happenings since the ship had left home. He wound up by saying that he was now perfectly comfortable and wished only that things might be left to take their course, for he could take care of himself.

"Well, Mr. Jenkins," said the vice-consul, "I happen to know that you are going on from here to 'Frisco, and whether you have ever been to that grand city or not before, I warn you to keep your eyes peeled, for if Captain Swainson wants to do you an ill turn he has only got to put up the price. If I were you I wouldn't go ashore at all there, and I would keep a bright look-out on board too. Of course you'll lose all your crew, the old man has been bragging about that, but you probably would anyhow. Now I'll go home and make a note of things. I expect I shall need it before very long. In the meantime I wish you the best of luck and a safe departure from 'Frisco, the worst place for sailormen in the world. Good-bye."

As soon as he had gone the two officers held a colloquy, in which they decided that things were not going so bad, that nothing the vice-consul had said was surprising, and that even if he had a little axe of his own to grind they had given him no hand to use against them.

Their conference was interrupted by Frank, who came down into the cabin and said, "The men are all aft and say they want to speak to you, sir; they seem perfectly civil and quiet. I think it's about their liberty."

"All right, Frank, thank you, I'll be up directly; go and tell them so."

And with that the mate and second mate departed up the after-cabin companion, so that they might look down upon the men from the height of the poop. As soon as they had reached that vantage place they found all hands except the Kanakas awaiting them. The mate said quietly, "Now then, men, what is it you want of me?"

The foremost replied quite respectfully, "We only want to ask you, sir, if you know anything about our getting some money and a liberty day. We're sorry to bother you, sir, but we can't get to see the skipper, and so we had to come and ask you."

"Very well, men," replied the mate, "you don't want me to tell you that I've got nothing to do with your getting money or liberty; all I can say is that when the captain comes on board to-night, I'll tell him about it, and you'll see him in the morning before he goes ashore again."

"Thankye, sir," they responded, and went back to work quite cheerfully, so great was the respect and confidence that they had for and in the man that once they were ready to kill. Of course the boys, having heard all that had passed, held their consultation too, and determined that when the men had done with the captain they would have a slap at him, as Williams irreverently put it. But who could reverence such a man?

Sure enough when the skipper came on board that night Mr. Jenkins awaited him and told him of the men's request; but he was too far gone in liquor to attend to anything that night. In the morning, though, the mate waited on him before breakfast and told him that the men were waiting to see him about liberty and money. He would have burst into a torrent of oaths and threats, but he was in mortal terror of his chief officer, and after vainly trying to make excuses for not meeting the men, at last consented, and rising, came on deck.

They were waiting for him, and gave in their request civilly. He, foolish man, began to bluster, but the men feeling that they had right on their side and that they would not now have the officers to reckon with, met his threats with equally high words, saying that if he did not give them their due, they refused to do any more. At which he laughed, and, turning on his heel, gave Mr. Jenkins orders to hoist the police-flag. This was at once done, and the men retreated forward and began to pack their clothes, not caring for the consequences, after the manner of sailors.

Then the mate, following the skipper as he returned to the cabin, said, "Captain Swainson, I want to remind you that I have not yet had a run ashore or any money from you, and whatever you choose to do in respect of the men does not concern me."

The skipper stared at him for a moment, and after struggling to keep down the words he longed to utter, suddenly gasped out, "Oh, all right, Mr. Jenkins, I s'pose you'll have to go; but I haven't got any money, I'll have to go ashore and get some. Order my boat at once."

The mate smiled, and replied, "All right, sir; but won't you wait for the police-boat you've ordered?"

"Oh no," said the skipper, "you can see to that; send all the beggars ashore as mutineers. They refused to obey lawful commands, you know, and you got my orders to lock 'em up."

"No, sir," firmly replied the mate, "that's your affair, not mine, and it's for you to carry it out. I've nothing to do with it."

This was too much for the skipper's nerves, and he burst out, "I believe you're as bad as they are, and I'll make you pay dear for this——"

"Now stop right there, captain," coolly replied the mate, "before you say something you'll be sorry for. You're not drunk now, and you ought to know what you are talking about. Anyhow, here comes the police-boat, and you'll have to make up your mind what you are going to do."

Captain Swainson was now, however, to find out that the time for his choice to be exercised had gone by: having started this ball rolling, he could not stop it. The police-boat arrived, and the officer in charge, a lathy, keen-looking American, swung himself on deck, casually adjusted his revolver-belt, and advanced to where the captain and mate stood, saying, "'Morning, gentlemen, what's the trouble?"

"My men have refused duty, with a great deal of insulting language, and they are, I think, quite dangerous. But I'll give 'em one more chance before I proceed to extremities with 'em. Call 'em aft, Mr. Jenkins."

"Lay aft, all hands," roared the mate instantly, and as the fellows had been awaiting the summons all ready to go ashore, they came at once, ranging themselves across the quarter-deck and looking up at the police-officer, skipper, and mate, who stood on the poop looking down upon them, while the policemen stood by the rail, regarding with grave faces this gang of supposed mutineers.

"Now men," quavered the skipper, "you see what you've done; here are the police ready to arrest you all and take you to chokey, for that's what it means for every one of you if you don't obey my lawful commands. But if you will behave yourselves and go quietly to your work, I'll look over it this once."

"Thank you for nothin', cap'n," said the leader of the men, "but we think it's us that ought to look over what you've done. We ain't going to talk about that now, though; we want to see the consul, and then we'll have our say. And we'll see what he's got to say to you."

It was really pitiful to see the strait to which the skipper had brought himself by his behaviour. He dared not send those men to the consul with their tale, which would be corroborated he knew by his officers. And he could not grant their demands, for he had no money wherewith to do so. Had his record been clean, of course the men would have been compelled to obey him or go to gaol, but now by his own act he found himself disabled from taking advantage of the law that would otherwise have been in his favour. So he stood there disgraced and ashamed before all, and his miserably muddled brain rendered him unable to think out a plan. The silence was dramatic, and lasted so long that the police-officer lost his patience, and said in dry, incisive tones, "Well, captain, what's to be done? Does the men's bluff hold good? and what are you going to do, anyway; for I can't be here doin' nothin'?"

The wretched man, looking the very picture of pitiful irresolution, said at last, "I think I'd better come ashore with you, officer, and see what I can do; you might just try and scare 'em a bit, so's to keep 'em quiet till I come back, you know."

The officer looked at him for a moment as one boy looks at another, who, after bragging a lot, runs away as soon as he's faced. Then he went a step forward and said, "Now then, men, the cap'n is going ashore to see if he can find some way out of this tangle without gaoling you. He says you're a good lot of men, and he don't want to punish you for a mistake. But you must keep quiet, and go about your work until he comes back, anyhow."

There was a ripple of laughter from the men, and then their spokesman replied, "That's all right about turning to and keeping quiet, but what about our liberty and money? Are we going to get it or not?"

Turning to the captain, the officer said, "Shall I tell 'em you'll be back this afternoon with a definite yes or no? It's no use bluffing any longer, you can't keep it up, you know. And I don't propose to stand here shilly-shallying any longer."

"All right," said the skipper, "tell them that if they'll turn to and keep quiet, I'll be back this afternoon and let 'em know definitely."

Upon the officer conveying this to the men, they sulkily muttered "All right," and retreated to their den to get off their shore rigs, while the skipper went below to get ready for the shore.

Then the officer, approaching the mate, began cheerfully, "Well, Mr. Mate, there doesn't seem much danger after all, does there?"

The mate was almost too disgusted to reply, but managed to say, "No, officer, and there never has been except for folly. But I can't talk about it, if you'll excuse me. I hope, however, that you don't think that either Mr. Cope here or myself has had anything to do with this miserable business. We can handle this crowd all right, but—" and he stopped dead.

"Yes, I guess that's so, and there's no explanation necessary. Where are you bound from here; 'Frisco, I s'pose?"

"I really don't know for certain," replied the mate, "but I should think so."

"Ah well," drawled the officer, "you'll have no more trouble with the crowd if you're going there. You can't keep 'em whether you want or not. It's a bad place, is the city of San Francisco, for the guileless sailorman. He doesn't get any show at all. Well, so-long; here's the old man comin'."

Captain Swainson was about to leave the ship without saying a word to the mate, when the latter, stepping up to him, said, "Before you go, sir, I'd like you to arrange for my leave and some money. You do not remember, perhaps, that I have been in the ship the best part of a year, and have had neither holiday nor money."

Oh, but it was an awful face the old man turned to him. But he only said, "Very well, Mr. Jenkins, I'll attend to it." And went, a figure of fun to all hands, more despised than detested.

There was no more trouble, but of course there was very little done. In fact there was little routine work to do, for the ship had been kept thoroughly overhauled, and was now quite ready for sea. To have started other and regular work now would have been foolish, especially in view of the uncertainty. And so the day passed quietly away until the skipper returned at three o'clock, when everything tightened up once more in expectation of events. He went straight to his cabin and remained there, until the men, coming aft in a body, politely asked Mr. Jenkins if they could see the skipper. And then he was bound to come forward and tell them that he had arranged to give them a month's pay each on account of their wages, and that one watch could go next morning and the other the morning after. He did not tell them, of course, the terrible price he had been obliged to pay in order to get this money, for that would have involved too many explanations as to the way in which he had wasted his owners' money in riotous living both in Levuka and here. But he had evidently obtained sufficient for everybody, for when the officers applied to him they each received what they asked for, and even the lads got a little, as much as they could have expected.

Thus peace was preserved for the time, and with the exception of a little drunkenness among the crew, which was only to be expected under the circumstances, nothing occurred to hinder the departure of the ship four days afterwards for San Francisco. None of the lads had been allowed ashore, and they felt very sore about it, but knowing whither they were bound, they hoped to have what Johnson called a good fling when they got there.

For the first time, I am sorry to say Frank began to feel a bit tired of his position. It was one of those little eddies of reaction that occur in the lives of every one of us, and often coinciding with some other trouble, lets us in for some foolish headstrong action of which we repent for the rest of our lives. Fortunately for him, beyond being slack in his work and getting reprimanded by the mate several times, he did not do anything very bad, and help came to him in a curious way.

When a week out from Honolulu, and about half-way to the Golden Gate, a sudden and very violent gale sprang up almost without warning. It found them all more or less unprepared for it, because they had been so long enjoying the loveliest weather imaginable that they had forgotten the very existence of such things as gales of wind. However, the good seamanship and energy of the mate and second mate, coupled with the really noble way in which the ship's company worked, prevented any serious damage to the ship herself, although, being in ballast, she was so light that the handling and securing of her sails was a tremendous task, occupying all hands all night; especially as she was very short-handed, the Kanakas having left in Honolulu, and no other men being available. As usual the skipper took no part in the affair, being ill in his bunk, as he said, although it was exceedingly curious how he revived from these mysterious illnesses as soon as the vessel got into port.

A week after the gale the *Sealark* sailed grandly into the beautiful bay of San Francisco and anchored, and now Frank's love of adventure got a delightful morsel to feed upon, although it was one of those abominable acts that disgrace any country and yet is only possible in one, the country making the loudest boast of freedom of all. The sails were hardly secured when a boat came alongside with a gang of as truculent-looking villains in her as any one ever saw. Two out of the six of them mounted the rail, and, stepping on deck, were met by the mate, who inquired their business.

"Wall," drawled the leader, "I guess my business ain't with you n'r any other lime-juicer mate, an' if you've got any savvy you'll just run away an' play an' not try an' fool around where men are."

He had hardly uttered the words when Mr. Jenkins struck him full in the face with his clenched fist, and down he went like a log. His comrade whipped out a revolver, and shot the mate through the body. He fell as the other villain rose, and with a horrible oath gave the mate's body a tremendous kick.

The three boys and the second mate ran to the assistance of their officer, and were not molested or hindered by the ruffians who swaggered forrard among the men. Meanwhile the wounded mate was laid in his bunk, and the skipper called, who only said, "Dear me, what a man to get into trouble. I'll go ashore and send a doctor off. I hope he isn't seriously hurt."

"Any help, to be of service, sir," answered the second mate, "must be very soon here, for Mr. Jenkins is wounded in a very bad place, just at the pit of the stomach, and I'm afraid he'll die if he doesn't get help soon."

"Ah, very sad, indeed, very sad," replied the skipper; "I'll send some one off to him," and he sauntered back to his cabin, leaving the second mate foaming with rage, but determined that his friend shouldn't die if care and attention could keep him alive. And with the help of Frank he stripped the wounded man and succeeded in staunching the blood, also in making him as comfortable as possible.

The visitors having no other interference to look for, rounded up the crew like a flock of sheep, all except Hansen, who hid away, and did not venture into the forecastle. First of all they told the old tale about high wages, plenty of ships, &c., but when the crew evinced no disposition to come at their call, they grew suddenly fierce. Long domination over helpless seamen and immunity from justice for their many crimes, at the hands of venal judges, had made them also very bold.

So they changed their tone, and the chief, producing a jug of whisky with one hand, and a heavy revolver with the other, said, "Now, boys, it's like this. You don't know what's good for ye; I do. And I'm bound to give it yer, if I have to bore a few holes in ye to make ye take it. Get that dunnage of yours rolled up and put it in the boat an' come ashore into God's own country where there's thirty dollars a month waitin' for ye, an' two months' advance. And all the whisky, cigars, and best grub in the world for nothin' until ye get a ship. I'm in the fy-lanthropy business for keeps, I am. But if ye won't have kindness shown ye, ye've got to suffer, no question 'bout that."

His little harangue, coupled with the look of the pistol and the bottle, had an immediate effect. The bottle, or jug, as they called it, was passed round, and almost directly you would have thought they were all going ashore to a picnic, they seemed so uproariously gay. And yet they thought piteously of the seven months' hard-earned money they were leaving behind. But they dared not bemoan themselves, and in a very short time had all been cleared out of the ship by as absolute an act of piracy and man-stealing as ever disgraced humanity. We may as well finish with them at once; in forty-eight hours the whole of them had been shipped away, with two months' pay in advance in the hands of the scoundrels who had stolen them, and a substantial sum had been paid in "blood money" for each of them to boot.

So precipitate had been their departure that the skipper had not gone until they reached the shore. True, he had been very deliberate, for he was enjoying the little episode in which his mate had been such a sufferer. It was, he felt, judgment on that impetuous officer for his ill-behaviour to him, the captain, on certain occasions, and he felt quite pleased about it. Then he went ashore, and from the time he landed all trace of him is lost. Sudden, you say! yes, but not at all uncommon there, I can assure you. Whether he was shanghaied, stolen, and shipped away like his poor men, and died on the passage, or was just robbed and murdered with as little compunction as these trivial happenings are achieved in San Francisco, the great Metropolis of the West, as it is called, no one ever knew. At any rate he disappeared just as easily as that, and never was heard of again.

But so far from this sudden bereavement of the ship being any drawback to her prosperity or the comfort of those on board, it was felt as a positive relief by everybody. An exception must be made in the case of the poor mate, who lay in agony throughout that long night awaiting the help that did not come, and when the morning dawned was in a high fever. So evil was his condition that the second mate, unable to wait any longer, hoisted the signal for a doctor, which was promptly answered by an American man-o'-war at anchor near. Her surgeon, upon arriving within twenty minutes of the hoisting of the signal, and seeing the wounded man, looked very grave, and sternly asked why assistance had not been summoned before. Matters were explained to him as he worked, and he understood; but so low was Mr. Jenkins after the extraction of the bullet that the surgeon said his recovery depended entirely upon the strength of his constitution and careful nursing. Then after a pleasant chat with Mr. Cope and the lads, who were as anxious as the second mate about a man whom they had grown to admire exceedingly, if not to love, he took his leave, promising to return at any time he might be needed.

When all that could be had been done Mr. Cope turned the three lads, Hansen, and the cook, to washing decks, for idleness on board ship is fatal; but while they were in the midst of the work the agent boarded the ship in a towering rage because she had not been reported direct to him, entered inwards, or anything indeed done that is necessary when a ship enters a civilised port. It took some time to explain matters to him, and the explanation did not make him less angry, only transferred his rage to the missing skipper who had of course taken the ship's papers with him. After a brief visit to the suffering mate, who was now easier and in his right senses, the agent departed, promising that he would send a medical man for regular attendance upon the wounded officer, and also add such comforts as might be necessary.

And the little crowd resumed work in peace, being unmolested from within as well as without—word having gone round among the crimps, of course, that the *Sealark's* crew had been dealt with. Later in the day the agent returned, saying that no trace of the skipper had been found from the time of his landing, but that the police were making inquiries. Meanwhile no business could be transacted owing to the absence of the ship's papers and the illness of the mate. The owners had been cabled to, and had replied that the mate was to be confirmed in charge if he recovered and the skipper were not found. This news being told to the mate, caused the first gleam of pleasure to appear on his grave, worn face that had been seen there almost since the ship left England. No doubt he felt that he was about to receive his reward.

And now set in a weary time for the boys, all three of whom were a bit stale and wanted a change, yet were not allowed to go ashore by the second mate, in case of accidents. They went about their work in grudging fashion, quite unlike the brisk way they had been behaving, and worse still, neglected their learning from Hansen; they would only listen to yarns, or lie about and smoke, and wish for impossible things. Frank put in a good deal of time writing home a very long account of the proceedings on the voyage, and incidentally gave vent to his feelings about his letters having been kept from him. He little knew how many of those loving missives had gone astray. And then his heart was suddenly cheered by receiving a cablegram from home telling him they had seen the news of his arrival in the *Journal of Commerce*, and the other news as well, and that their letters were on the way to him. This acted as a brisk tonic upon the flagging energies of the lad, and he again addressed himself to his work, bucking up his friend too. So valuable is a message from home to a heart that is sound. And this opened the new and better era of life on board the *Sealark* for all concerned.

CHAPTER VII
HOMEWARD BOUND

Perhaps the title of this chapter may seem a little premature, since the last closed just after the arrival of the *Sealark* in San Francisco, but then sailors have a language and phrases entirely their own with regard to the events of life. For instance, when a seaman ashore has spent his money, he says he is "outward bound," although he may have no immediate prospect of a ship to go away in. So the ship he may be in is "homeward bound" when in the port where she is loading, or is to load, for home, even though her cargo may be very slow in coming. Therefore in sailor parlance the *Sealark* was homeward bound.

Everything had settled down under the rule of Mr. Jenkins, who made an excellent recovery from his wound, and a no less excellent captain. All difficulties about the loss of the ship's documents had been successfully arranged. Only the owners' persistent inquiries by cable as to what had become of all the money drawn by the skipper could not be satisfied. The new captain could only tell the story of the voyage, and leave the owners to draw their own conclusions. And when it is remembered that they had engaged him on the strength of recommendations of his teetotalism, Christianity, and ability, their state of mind upon receiving Captain Jenkins' report may be faintly imagined. But when they received from Mr. Brown his son Frank's long letter describing in boyish but graphic language the exploits of the mate, and the shocking behaviour of the skipper all the passage out, they were fain to admit that things might have been far worse; with an incompetent mate, for instance, the ship might have still been in an island harbour eating her head off and paying nothing at all back.

I was once mate for three months in a brig that had been out from home two years, and had carried four cargoes at good freight, not one penny of which had ever reached the owner, a thrifty shipwright who had saved his money and bought this vessel. Not only so, but the brig was heavily in debt for money raised solely to supply the skipper with drink and etceteras. However, on board the *Sealark* they were now fast forgetting the miserable past, and only worrying to get away from this beautiful port of unpleasant memories. As soon as the skipper was able to get about, the boys approached him, and giving him their solemn promise not to run loose as they had in Levuka, again begged him to let them go ashore. They all had some funds from home, and naturally wished to see some of the sights of this amazing city.

He heard them out, and then said, "Now, lads, I feel that you've been punished quite enough, and I certainly don't want to punish you any more. Moreover I don't want to lose you, for I doubt if I shall get three men as good as you three youngsters are now (Heavens, how their backs stiffened!) Yes, you can go ashore, but remember; dress yourself in your best, and get out of Sailor Town at once, go right up town into the respectable quarters and come back before dark, or the chances are that you won't come back at all. And I'd rather die than that should happen now."

It wasn't too long a sermon and they all took it to heart, avoiding the saloons and taking their meals in a good hotel. And as they always came on board in good time, and got into no scrapes, it became an established custom for them to go ashore on Sunday and Saturday afternoons, sometimes with the new mate, Mr. Cope, but oftener by themselves, until they felt quite at home in the Queen of the Pacific. To their amazement no one ever attempted to molest them. The only way that they could account for this was that they did not hang about low groggeries or slouch along the waterside half drunk, inviting the raids of those creatures of prey to whom every sailor is merchantable commodity. They enjoyed the city very much, and felt almost sad when the golden grain had filled their ship down to her loading marks and she was ready for sea.

Fortunately for them they did not need to worry about the providing of the new crew as their skipper did. His whole heart and soul revolted at the payment of the hideous blood-money to those fiends in human shape who batten on sailors. In vain he tried to arrange for a crew who should ship with him voluntarily, paying no more than the legal dues and getting the whole of what they earned. He was assured by everybody connected with the business, from the British consul to the seamen's missionaries downwards, that it was impossible. That if he attempted to fight the boarding-masters' ring, which really was superior to justice and the law of the United States as administered in San Francisco, he would only succeed in delaying his ship and in costing his owners a great deal more money, if indeed he did not lose his life, quite unnecessarily.

So he yielded, most reluctantly, and bought his crew as usual from the grinning scoundrels who had stolen them, and put to sea one fine afternoon with as sorry a set of sufferers as you could imagine. Not that they were as bad as sometimes may be seen, especially on board of American ships sailing from this port, or Portland, Oregon; but still they were poisoned, filthy, and sore, and of necessity quite unfit for their duty. A strong breeze awaited them outside, and when the tug cast off it was pitiful to see the efforts made by the poor fellows to obey the commands of the officers, for they did not know what sort of a ship they were in yet.

But it was a sorry business, and Frank found himself with a flush of pride mentally comparing himself at this time with the sea-sick bewildered youth, who, leaving Liverpool a year ago, felt that he did not care whether the ship sank beneath his feet or not, and doubted entirely the possibility of his ever being of any use. Now, he proudly reflected, he was able to show any of these unhappy men the way, there was practically nothing in the way of sail-handling he could not do, and that in seaman-like fashion, and if he came to anything he was not master of, he was never content until he had mastered it. So useful are the lessons learned in actual work compared with those that are based only upon theory.

The work for the lads and Hansen was of course very hard for the first few days, until the poor cosmopolitan wretches had recovered from the terrible effects of the poison they had taken in 'Frisco, but it gave them a status which they never lost again. For both Captain Jenkins and Mr. Cope (they had come away without a second mate, because one could not be obtained) were of that good stamp of man who, while they can be as kind as possible to sick men, will give no sympathy to loafers. And so when upon the recovery of all hands there were the usual attempts made to shift disagreeable tasks on to the lads, they were nipped in the bud, and the new-comers made to understand that there were no distinctions made there between one man and another if all knew their work, but if any could not do their work they would surely be put upon the dirtiest and most tiresome tasks going, not as punishment but of necessity.

Fortunately the attitude taken up and kept by the officers at the beginning was so wise and steady that there was no trouble. No men are quicker to see and take advantage of any disagreement between the captain and his officers than sailors are, and if once that evil is allowed to creep in, good-bye to all hope of discipline and comfort. And on the other hand no men are readier to see the good in a commander who knows his own mind and his work, and trusts his officers—not all honey one day and all vinegar the next. Such men, no matter what crews they have, can usually get the best out of them, although, of course, it is only reasonable that the handling of an incapable crew should give them a terrific amount of work and anxiety from which they would be free if only the men knew their duties.

There is one great blessing, which Frank and his chums now felt to the full, which is that a sailing-ship homeward bound from 'Frisco round Cape Horn has ample time before she gets down to the stormy latitudes to get her crew seasoned to what they are about to receive. All the way practically from 'Frisco to 30° S. she may reckon on fine weather, with plenty of variable winds for the handling of yards and sails, and ample opportunity to prepare for the stress of the mighty seas and the tempestuous gales of the great Southern Ocean, which must be coped with when rounding that far-reaching horn of America which stretches down nearly to the Antarctic ice.

Be sure that nothing was neglected in the *Sealark*. Her best suit of sails was bent, new running gear rove wherever needful, and all seizings, lashings, gaskets, and foot-ropes looked to in time, so that when at last the weather began to take on that stern appearance which marks the approach to the South Pole, all hands could console themselves with the thought that they were well fortified to meet anything in reason.

So they drew farther and farther south and to the westward withal, the weather becoming daily more grim and threatening in appearance, while the wind was restless and unsteady with a mournful note in it that was full of warning. Frank now began to recall some of their outward experiences in those regions, and to wish most heartily that they were well round the Horn and pointed for home. Nor was he to blame, for I never yet met any man who did not feel the same with regard to that terrible corner of the world. But whenever the subject was broached in the half-deck they always comforted themselves with the same conclusion, viz. that being homeward bound it would always be a fair wind for them.

At last in about 40° S. the wind dropped completely away, and left the good ship rolling heavily upon a black, greasy-looking swell, under a leaden sky, with a feel of snow in the air. Their thin blood felt this inclemency sorely, and they shivered with cold as well as with apprehension, while the short day drew to its dreary close and the heavy sky drooped deeper down upon them. Hour after hour dragged by in ever-growing gloom, until suddenly there was a lightening on the western horizon, a breath of colder air as if off an iceberg, and then a sensible increase in the motion of the ship, on the swell rolling up as a precursor of the storm.

"Square away the main yard," shouted the captain, and amid the weird cries of the sailors the great spars swung slowly athwart her hull, the wind meanwhile increasing so rapidly that by the time her yards were trimmed she was going at the rate of five or six knots, and the whole network aloft was complaining as the gear was being drawn into its grooves, as if preparing for its heavy task.

In all the works of human ingenuity, I know of nothing finer to contemplate at its work than the top-hamper of a big sailing-ship under all canvas in a heavy press of wind. It is all so perfectly adapted to meet the uneven strains laid upon it, the stress of the various ropes and spars and shrouds are wonderfully distributed, and it towers to such a tremendous height above the comparatively insignificant hull, reaching up into the black howling night so proudly defiant of the might of the storm—no wonder that a brave sailor loves to "carry on" as we call it.

Steadily, swiftly rose the wind, and faster went the *Sealark* until at eight bells (eight in the morning) she had nearly reached her limit, being under maintopgallant-sail, any farther reduction of sail meaning reduced speed, no matter how hard the wind might blow. She was too foul to be fast, but she did her driven best, while the wind howled its wailing chorus, the mighty seas thundered past and aboard, and the lower rigging grew white with spindrift. But all quite normal and acceptable except for the bitter cold, until on the third day just at the sun's setting there was a yell from the man on the look-out, and a sudden swinging of the vessel up into the wind with a tremendous thundering and bellowing of canvas suddenly released from steady strain, and shaken like dead leaves in the storm, and the *Sealark* surged closely past a gaunt and ghastly thing all jagged corners and covered with flying spray, the first wandering iceberg of the South. As Frank gazed at it and realised the possibilities of danger had it been seen a minute later, had in fact anything happened that would have prevented her from being sheered clear of this most terrible of all the dangers that beset the stormy ocean.

The bell struck and Frank's watch was over. He went below, and flinging off his oilskins and sea-boots rolled into his bunk, his brain surging with pictures of black seas and rolling icebergs. But the sailor's consolation, the thought of the faithfulness and ability of his shipmates on watch, came to soothe him, and succeeded so effectually that, in a moment or two it seemed, the voice of his berthmate Williams sounded stridently in his ears calling him from the depths of dreamland to take his trick at the wheel, and keep the *Sealark* on her steady course before the stern gale.

Steering away, he forgot the cold in his manful efforts to do his best. The little oval of light in the binnacle showed the heaving disc of the compass, but outside of that charmed circle all was as the outer dark, wherein nought was to be seen, and only the proximity of danger made itself felt. What a splendid education in high courage for a fine-spirited boy!

But now the gale took on a deeper note, a fiercer blast with every squall, and a blistering snow-squall came down and blotted out all things in a smother of white. It mattered little to Frank at the helm, as he had not been able to see anything but the compass for some time, except that it hardly melted fast enough off the warm glass of the binnacle to let him see clearly how her head was. There was, however, no doubt in his mind that she could not run much longer like this, for the wind had risen so much that he could hardly keep from being pressed against the wheel, in every squall the wind increased, and between them it did not take off to its former strength. So he was not surprised when he heard, like ghostly wailings in the dark, the cries of the men shortening sail, and in his heart he was glad that it was his trick at the wheel and not up *there* fighting with board-like canvas, getting thrashed black and blue, and feeling his finger-ends torn and bleeding with the struggle.

The time wore on, and still he was not relieved, still he heard occasional cries of labour, until at last, when he was thoroughly fagged, a ghostly figure glided aft and took the wheel from him saying, "Lucky young beggar. We've had a night of it and no mistake. She's shortened down to two lower topsails and foresail, an' I wish she was hove to, for I feel sure there's a lot of ice about."

It was Williams, whose young face looked haggard and worn in the fitful light from the binnacle, but who took up his task after the long fight with the sails like a veteran. He had come on a long way towards manhood since we first met with him, as some lads do under stress. Frank sped forward into his berth, and found Johnson sitting moodily smoking.

As he came in Johnson looked up and said, "Some people have all the luck. Fancy you standing quietly up there for four hours while we've been working—slaving—I feel as if my blessed arms were torn out by the roots. And I don't like the look of things at all. Why don't the old man heave to? Fancy runnin' her like this when he knows what a lot of ice there is about. What's that?"

As he spoke there was a long grinding quiver that ran through the whole ship and made their bowels tremble. Then it passed, and as so often happens all was still save for the gentle roll of the ship, as if the watchful genii of the storm were listening to hear what the sailors were doing in response to their grim warning.

Nothing happened further, it was just the ship grinding along the side of a small piece of brash ice. And Frank said, "Now, Johnson, get into your pew, we've got a watch's sleep in front of us, and the poor devils in the starboard watch have lost theirs. An' if you worry your head off you can't help things happening. We've done our bit, and after we've had some sleep we'll be ready to do it again, I hope. Well, here's luck," and with a swing

Frank flung himself into his bunk, gave one contented sigh, and subsided into sleep. He had learned well the lesson of the sailor, as you see, to take what comes of good or ill with equal nonchalance, but to be ready for any fate.

The quiet of their sleep was broken at four bells (six o'clock) by a cry of "All hands," and they bundled on deck into the piercing cold and driving sleet. It was heave-to, and no mistake, for the whole of the sea around them, as they found when day broke, was simply studded with icebergs, and to run any longer while it was dark was simply madness. I say nothing of the Providence by means of which they had run on through those black hours without mishap. But now, although the air was like liquid ice and blowing hard enough to pin a man against a rail and prevent him moving, it was absolutely necessary to get the remaining sail in, and Frank, wise through experience, only put on a suit of warm clothes with a thick sweater over all and no oilskins.

They clewed up the fore-topsail and foresail, eased off the fore-topmast staysail sheet and brought her to the wind. As she came up, the wind bore down on her like a gigantic hand, and she went over until her lee sheerpoles touched the water, and the waiting crew held their breath, wondering would she rise again. At last she reached her limit (I say nothing of the enormous seas that poured over her deck meanwhile, because that is so usual and obvious a matter that it does not deserve special notice), and all hands realised that the worst was over for the time. But oh! the capers she cut now that she was hove to. She rolled to windward until she scooped the whole ocean in, apparently, over her weather-rail, then over she went to leeward as if desiring to empty it out over the other side. Pointed her jibboom at the stars, and then aimed it at the sea-bed. And some ass said she laid to—like a duck!

Unfortunately it was necessary to get aloft and furl those sails—they could not be allowed to blow away, or breaking loose from the confining gear to endanger the masts, so, "Up you go, boys, and tie 'em up."

Frank and Johnson kept together in the assault upon the fore lower-topsail, and, as there were eleven of them at it, and it isn't a bad sail to handle after all, they soon got it snugged in and secured. But the foresail! It tore at its gear like a raving demon, and when they had got it partly in, she would lurch up into the wind on the scend of a sea, and away from their stiffened fingers it would go with a roar as if of triumph. During this conflict Frank was hardly conscious except of the necessity of keeping on until that sail was fast. His very intelligence became mechanical, and physical pain and weariness did not count as long as they did not disable him. And at last the great sail was furled.

Calling up all his energies, he descended to the deck and crept along until he reached the house, for he was parched with thirst, and felt that he must have a drink of water. There in the feeble flame of the lamp, after quenching his thirst, he had a sort of languid curiosity to see what ailed his fingers that they were so sore. And as he looked at them a sense of self-pity came over him like a wave—whoso has never felt it may legitimately be thankful—for all his finger-nails had been torn off by the desperate energy with which he had dug them into that obdurate sail. Then, with a fine gesture of contempt for bodily pain, he shook the slowly oozing blood from them and lit his pipe.

When a ship is snugged down to the limit the heart of the sailorman is freed from much care, because whatever happens there is little more "branching" possible, and that is what makes sailors unhappy. So every one was fairly content until the cold, grey dawn broke and revealed a scene that was enough to daunt the most hardy of them, not being whalers or accustomed to such sights. For all around as far as the eye could reach the sea surface was covered with massy heaps of ice, some raising their grim heads to a height of three or four hundred feet, others only just showing above the sea surface, but all tossing and heaving about in appalling confusion upon the stormy sea, and every one of them threatening destruction to the frail intruder upon their terrible conclave. The flying clouds seemed to reach down and tear themselves upon the summits of the heaving bergs, streaming off in long black lines like mourning weeds. And the furious waves dashed themselves frantically upon those icy masses as if outraged by their presence, and craving to destroy them. While in the midst of it all tossed the helpless ship, all unfitted for any such stern contact as now threatened her.

All that long weary day the seamen looked on at those heaving mountains, waited hopelessly for any sign of relief, and saw the gloomy day pass into night so black that all the horrors seen during the day were intensified by inability to see them at all. Yet men slept during their watch below as they always do, if the conditions will permit, all except the skipper, who never left the deck, so great was his anxiety for the safety of his crew. But even had he possessed the accumulated wisdom and seamanship and courage of a thousand sailors, under those circumstances he was powerless to do aught but wait and hope, and if one of those masses had collided with the ship, and penetrated her side so that she sank, the chances of saving one life would have been almost nil.

Nothing happened. The long, long night wore away, and the dawn broke with a brisk gale and a somewhat lightened sky, while to the wondering eyes of the watchers not a hummock of ice was visible anywhere. How joyfully the watch obeyed the call to loose the fore lower-topsail and foresail, and having set them, squared the yards and kept her away before the wind and sea for Cape Horn. So great was the change that all hands felt as if the weather had suddenly become fine and almost calm, the watch below turning in their sleep, and wondering at the cessation of their troubled dreams. And when the watch came on deck at eight bells, all hands were set to work to "pile the rags on her," as we say, until she was speeding away again at her utmost gait for the turning-point of the voyage.

The good breeze held by day and night, and no further trouble was experienced from ice or sudden squalls. To the delight of everybody on board she passed the Diego Ramirez Islands without losing a ropeyarn, and almost immediately afterwards the hearts of everybody were gladdened by hearing the order given to haul up three points. "Starboard fore-brace," shouted the skipper, and right cheerfully was he answered, while as the big ropes were drawn through the blocks, and the yards canted forward, the glad whisper went around the ship, "Homeward bound indeed at last."

For that is another definition of being homeward bound which I omitted in my previous chapter. When a ship is on her homeward passage either from the Far East or Far West, whichever of the Capes she must double, she is not considered by her crew to be really homeward bound until having rounded it she begins to head northward, and the reason is so obvious that I shall not add further in unnecessary explanation. Then all hands agree tacitly that they will consider the worst of the passage over, ignoring entirely what the stormy North Atlantic may have in store for them at the close of their long journey. For have they not now the sweet amenities of the Trades before them, the long genial stretch across the depth of the South Atlantic, when for a week on end you need never touch a brace nor a halyard save to freshen the nip, and may devote all energies to making your ship look as spruce and trim as paint and varnish will make her after her long, long ocean journey?

All this Frank heard with quiet appreciation, although it was outside the range of his experience. But he was altogether happy at the change from the cold stern exercises of ship-handling, of wet clothes and heavy strivings with battering sails, to the softening pursuits of smartening up the rigging, rattling down, painting and varnishing. And to crown all he felt a growing delight in the thought that each placid day's run was bringing him nearer the home which became daily a more distinct object to his mental vision, while the sense of having accomplished his first voyage with credit to himself grew with each closing day. Occasionally he felt impatient, wished that the sweet following wind would blow stronger instead of taking off as it was doing, and when at last after crossing the line the wind died away altogether, and left her rolling languidly upon the glassy surface of the ocean, he could hardly restrain his discontent. Johnson annoyed him, too, by his lugubrious forebodings of long-continued calms, of waiting about here, as he put it, until all the beautiful new paint which they had put on with so much pains should be washed off again.

The hindrance of the Doldrums, however, did not prevent their northern passage for a longer period than usual, and presently, with yards braced up on the starboard tack, the *Sealark* was stretching across the North Atlantic towards the brave west winds of the north, the last helpers on the homeward road. It was all very humdrum now to Frank, who felt quite a contemptuous indifference to weather, and forgetting, as youth will, the hard past, turned a deaf ear to the warnings of Williams and Johnson, who began to recall incidents of the last voyage wherein it seemed they had suffered more at the end than during all the previous months of the voyage.

Behold them, then, at last clear of the north-east Trades, awaiting, as they had on the other side of the Horn, the change from fine to bad weather, from light variable breezes to strong steady gales with all their concomitants of cold, wet, and other discomforts, but with the knowledge of the homeland very near to cheer them up and nerve them to endure with cheerfulness. Just in the same way began the change. Only here they were accompanied on their pilgrimage by many another ship, and occasionally a huge steamship would come gliding past, receiving with just a flutter of her answering pennant their waving signals of request to be reported all well. These passings of rival ships, although most of them were steamers, aroused the feeling of envy in Frank, who wished he were in a faster ship; he could not brook the idea of being out-distanced, although there was a little consolation in the thought that some of them would give his dear ones the welcome news that he was returning soon.

So that he was entirely glad when a strong stern westerly gale arose, and began to drive the *Sealark* at her utmost speed due east and homeward. Every day now his spirits rose, and his duties, from being irksome and burdening his mind with a sense of servitude, grew lighter and easier as he thought of the rapidly lessening distance. Just a sight, no more, of Corvo, the northernmost outlier of the Azores, and it was past. And that night Hansen, entering the house, told them tales of runs made by sailing ships home from the Western Isles, proving that with such a breeze as they now had their passage might be reckoned by hours.

It is quite vain for me to attempt any description of the state of Frank's mind just now, for I have often been baffled in trying to describe my own feelings under similar circumstances. But of all the joyful states into which we may happily come during life, I know of none more truly satisfying, elevating, and ennobling than when, having striven manfully for a certain worthy object, we get the goal in sight while yet we have the full capacity for enjoying the fruits of our labours. These fruits will never come up to the sweetness of our anticipations, but that matters nothing at all. In the whole round world there was no happier being than Frank when during his first trick at the wheel, after passing Corvo, he thought of the rapidly lessening distance between him and his home. He was full of worthy pride at his conscious ability to do anything that might be required of him, his health and strength were perfect, and he knew how he had grown by the awkward figure he looked in his clothes, and he had absolutely no misgivings about the future.

But he could not help wishing that it was a little warmer. The splendid following gale had a touch of northing in it, and the rolling mist-banks that swept over the ship every now and then seemed to soak into his very marrow, for his blood was yet thin from his long journey through the tropics. Fortunately he had a happy knack of remembering that everybody else on board was in just the same case, and felt that he could bear it as well as any of them. So although he did not "sing at the wheel" like the hero of Michael Watson's song, being far too well disciplined for that, he felt as if he would very much like to, so high did his spirits rise. For all that he was very glad to be relieved and get some scalding tea.

And when with glowing pipes he and Johnson were yarning to Hansen afterwards, and Hansen said casually, "She's pipin' oop: I hope ve don't gets any more vind as dis, 'noughs a plenty," Frank burst out indignantly, "Why, you're gettin' to be a reg'lar old croaker, Hansen. I wouldn't care if it blew twice as hard as this, as long as it doesn't shift. She'd run a good lick under bare poles now." Hansen looked at his pupil admiringly, but made no reply; he felt it was of no use attempting to damp the boy's ardour.

Still the good ship ran on, the sail being gradually shortened, as compelled by the still rising gale, until Frank noticed the change in the colour of the water, even though the heavy sky gave little opportunity for discerning the difference. The weather grew steadily worse, and the gravity of the officers' faces deepened; for since sighting Corvo they had been unable to get a peep at either sun, moon, or stars. And although a knowledge of the depth of water would have been of the utmost value, because with it and a sample of the bottom such as is brought up in the tallow at the end of the deep-sea lead (technically called the arming), it is such a terrible business, heaving to a flying sailing-ship which is running before a gale, to get that sounding that officers naturally shrink from it. They want to get home, and they feel that if they once heave to they may as well remain so, the work of shortening and making sail again being so great.

So they ran the risk with a load of terrible anxiety at their hearts, and the weather grew steadily worse, until she was under the two lower topsails and the fore-topmast staysail only, and running then at the rate of fully ten knots. No need now to tell the hands to keep a good look-out, for practically everybody in the watch were straining their eyes through the gloom and flying spray for sight of anything, and to their tortured fancy the Channel was just thronged with ships going in every direction.

At last it became intolerable to Captain Jenkins. He believed himself to be in mid-channel somewhere between St. Catherine and Beachy Head, but after five days of dead reckoning knew that he might easily be fifty miles out in his estimated position. So he decided at midnight to get a cast of the deep-sea lead, and having hove his ship to, he would let her remain so until the weather cleared. The evolution was performed most creditably, and the ship swung round into the wind quite easily. But it was then evident with what terrific force the wind was blowing.

And before the lead-line was passed along there was a yell from all hands, and a huge steamship came flying past so closely as almost to touch the *Sealark*. She seemed to leap out of the darkness and disappear instantly, but she left everybody on the *Sealark* shaking as if with the palsy. In truth it was one of those situations where man feels his limitations and his impotence, a time when the demon of uncertainty is gnawing at the very vitals.

Just at that dread moment there came out of the gloom and smother of spray a clear ringing voice, "D'ye want a pilot?"

Needless, surely, to give the answer. A boat bumped against the side, a rope was hurled, and a bulky figure swathed in oilskins clambered aboard, apparently out of the sea, for the water streamed off him at every pore.

"Good morning, sir," said a cheery voice.

"Good morning," replied the skipper. "Are you a Trinity pilot?"

"No, sir, but I can put you alongside a Trinity pilot for ten pounds."

The skipper hesitated for a moment, not knowing how far he was away; but the weather was very bad and his anxiety fearful, so he accepted.

"All right, sir," responded the pilot; "could you spare a bit o' bacca and meat for my chaps. Times has been cruel hard lately."

Several plugs of tobacco and pieces of meat were flung into the darkness and acknowledged by some invisible recipients, then the new-comer turned to the skipper and said, "Square away the main-yard, sir; put your helm up, my lad."

The change was miraculous. He seemed to have brought fine weather with him. Only ten minutes after he took charge the Royal Sovereign light was sighted, and four hours afterwards the jovial pilot, who had wrought such a change in everybody that they all regarded him as a heaven-sent benefactor, hove her to in East Bay, Dungeness; and drawing his well, if easily, earned pay, took his leave.

Five minutes later the Trinity pilot was on board, the yards were trimmed again, and under a press of canvas the willing *Sealark* was speeding around the Foreland towards London. Here she soon lost the wind, and by daylight the weather had so far cleared that the outline of the land could plainly be seen, making Frank's heart leap for joy. He noticed, too, with the utmost interest, the throngs of vessels of all kinds about, from barges to ocean steamships; but his attention, with that of all hands, was presently centred upon a small steamer, with two funnels set side by side, which ranged up alongside them, and whose skipper began a running fire of chaff with Captain Jenkins about the price to be paid for a tow up. After about half-an-hour of this and several feints to go away, the tow-boat was hired for twenty pounds to tow the vessel up to the docks, and see her safely bestowed therein. Whereupon the glorious order was given, "Get the tow-rope up," an order which is obeyed with more cheerfulness than any other given on board ship.

In a very brief space the *Sealark*, with her sails all clewed up, was travelling in docile fashion at the rear of the tug, and all hands were busy clearing up decks and getting the ship ready for dock, working as if their very lives depended upon it. I am bound to say that Frank did not do much, he was too full of the wonder of his surroundings—the bosom of Father Thames in the heyday of his traffic. It was so entirely different from anything he had ever seen before; and when the vessel paused at Gravesend to exchange her Channel pilot for a river pilot, he was literally amazed at the crowded state of the river. However, little time was wasted there, for the skipper was anxious to save the tide at the Millwall Docks that night; so they were soon off again, threading their way through the multitudinous craft in the gathering dusk.

Gradually everything around became to Frank but a hurrying horde of phantoms, and he marvelled at the dexterity with which the pilot kept clear of his competitors, and never seemed to need to slacken speed. And then suddenly it all became one babel of confusion and uproar. There seemed to be vessels so closely packed around them as to leave them no room to move. Numberless voices yelled, in all sorts of tongues, no end of conflicting orders, till Frank's head fairly whirled; and then he saw to his surprise that they were slowly passing between two walls of stone apparently barely wide enough apart to admit them. The shouting died away to a few quiet orders, and soon the *Sealark* glided gently into a berth prepared for her alongside of a stone-faced wharf. Hawsers and chains were taken on shore and secured, then hove tight on board; and when she was jammed so tight that she could not move, Mr. Cope said quietly, "Clear up decks, men." That took but a very few minutes, then the long looked-for words were heard, "That'll do, men," and Frank's first voyage was over.

CHAPTER VIII
HOME AT LAST

It was eleven o'clock at night before the *Sealark* was finally moored and the dismissal words said, but there were already those alongside of whom Dickens said "they were all waiting for Jack." Frank and his two housemates, lounging by the rail smoking their pipes, watched the proceedings, saw how earnestly the hired emissaries of the boarding-masters laboured to prevent the newly arrived men from going with the representative of the Sailors' Home; saw, too, the passing of bottles laden with the most potent argument a sailor knows as a rule. Presently they had all departed their several ways, and the boys, tired out, retired to their bunks and slept the sweet sleep of wearied youth.

They were allowed to sleep it out in the morning, not being aroused until eight o'clock, and then the captain summoned them aft and handed them some money with which to telegraph to their parents and get their breakfast, telling them at the same time that until the ship was paid off they would be required to remain by her, but as the dock rules did not allow of them getting food on board without special permit, he would see about getting them a lodging-place where they would be well and comfortably housed.

So the three sallied ashore together all unknowing of the intricate neighbourhood, and the story of their adventures before they found their way on board again at eleven would make a serious inroad upon this chapter. Mr. Cope received them on their return with a grave face, but when he saw that they were all right and sober he did not scold them; indeed, except that he reminded them that they were supposed to work, but not hard, he might have been, as far as his behaviour went, one of themselves. By noon they all had replies from home. Frank's telegram ran thus: "Dear boy, so glad and thankful; are sending money by letter; come home as soon as ever you can, we are all longing for you.—Father and Mother."

But Frank to his horror found that he could not wear his go-ashore clothes. They were shabby anyhow with mildew and other marks, but he had grown out of them so much that he was ashamed to go ashore with them on. In this plight he applied to the skipper when he came on board at noon, radiant with good news, who immediately gave him an order upon a tailor's runner who was even then waiting on board, and Frank was forthwith measured. Then the skipper thanked him for the letter which he had sent home from San Francisco describing the events on board. He said that he had reason to believe that mainly owing to that letter the owners had confirmed him in the command of the ship. And Frank felt very glad, for he knew how well Captain Jenkins deserved it.

It is perhaps unnecessary for me to say how irksome Frank found it kicking his heels about on board the ship awaiting her paying off. Neither he nor his two chums were able to settle down to anything, and they all detested, as any country-bred lads would do, the grimy, unlovely purlieus of the Millwall Dock. Moreover, they had no money to spare for sight-seeing and no one to show them around if they had, so their journeys never took them farther than Aldgate, and they unanimously decided that they did not like London, having seen nothing of it but its seamiest side. So that indeed it was a cheerful morning when Frank found himself at King's Cross boarding one of the splendid Great Northern expresses for Leeds, and a surprise so sweet that it nearly broke down his sedate air of manhood when, on the train steaming into Leeds after a journey so delightful that it seemed all too short, he saw his two dear sisters awaiting him on the platform. I am glad to say that he did not put on any of that silly public-school side that is ashamed to show any affection in public, but allowed his long pent-up love to overflow as he hugged and kissed those loved ones, who indeed were ready to eat him, as we say.

They had but a few minutes to wait after changing to the other station, and they hardly knew anything of them, in fact they were all in a perfect dream of delight, only, Frank's long training having rallied to his aid, he kept a good look-out for everything, and presently they were in dear old Dewsbury. A cab was called, and off they rattled over the cobbles *home*. Father was there from business, fearing the effect of the shock upon the mother and anxious on his own account to see his fine son. Over that sacred moment of meeting I drop a veil, for it is always to be felt only, not described. And then when the happy mist had cleared from their eyes and they saw him clearly, how deep was their joy. They saw that the boy they had sent away with trembling hearts had stood the ordeal well, had come back clear-eyed and manly, nothing of the braggart, or sneak, or cad about him. Happy parents! no wonder that down in their hearts they thanked God.

Such evenings as those stand out in the memory like the golden milestones of life, when safe back from the numberless perils and temptations of such a voyage as his had been, with all the dear ones whom he had left greeting him sound and well, Frank was able to sit and tell them such things as they had never dreamed of before. Of course they asked no friends, they wanted him all to themselves, as well they might, and so thoroughly did they enjoy one another's society that it was midnight before they realised that half the evening had gone. And oh, the delights of snoodling down into a mother-made bed after feasting upon the delicious food of home, "Why," Frank said naïvely, "this alone is worth going round the world for." And with a happy sigh the young sailor fell asleep.

Now it is my intention to pass with extreme rapidity over the events of the next month, as it is so easy to imagine what sort of a time Frank was bound to have at home. Of course all his girl friends fell promptly in love with him, much to his annoyance, and all the fellows of his own age felt their noses put clean out of joint and envied him consumedly. Indeed six of them pestered their parents so persistently that they were allowed to go to sea too, but that is another story.

Of course Frank went to Lytham to see Captain Burns and had a splendid day with him, the captain being intensely interested in his young friend's experiences, as may be supposed; also from thence he paid the owners a visit and came away from them with a full heart, for they said many pleasant words of encouragement. And then, before, as he put it, he had time to get soft, he received a summons to rejoin his ship in London, as, having discharged and ballasted, she was bound round to Cardiff to load coals for Hong-Kong.

But before he starts off again I must mention one fact which I had nearly forgotten. He had specially requested Hansen to let him know his address in London, and Hansen, being the only sensible fellow apparently of the whole crew, gave him the Sailors' Home as the place where he was going to stay. He said, moreover, that he was coming back to the same old ship again, as she suited him, and he wanted to be with his young friend.

Frank's report to his father of Hansen's inestimable services to him led that gentleman to write a private letter to Hansen enclosing an order for ten pounds, not as payment, as he put it, but as a small token of his appreciation. But his surprise and gratification were very great when he received a well-written reply from Hansen praising up his boy and returning the money, with the remark that it was a very great pleasure for him to do what he had done, so that to take money for it would rob him of most of that pleasure. He further said that he had fully made up his mind to go in the same ship again, and he earnestly hoped to be of further use.

This of course was splendid hearing for both Frank and his father, while the dear mother insisted upon sending by Frank's hands a token of her loving thanks to the man who had been kind to her boy. So after the manifold leave-takings, behold Frank off again, full of eagerness to return, for he felt somehow that all this petting-up was not good for him, and the salt having entered his blood, he was anxious to be at sea again. I know there will be many of my friends acquainted with the sea who will sneer at this, but they will surely remember how many fellows they have met who were quite like-minded, and acquit me of making any misleading statements.

He reached the ship without any incident worth mentioning, feeling strangely as if he were coming to another home as he neared her, although truth compels me to say that when he reached the deck-house he felt a cold shudder of disgust at the inevitable contrast between the sweet cosy home he had just left and this dirty, dingy hole with the bunks full of the odds and ends of all kinds that had been thrust there out of the way temporarily.

I would like to say in passing that this is one of the drawbacks to a young officer's early career which is now very much altered for the better in the steamers which carry apprentices—but then steam has ameliorated the seafarer's condition all round and there is no use to blink the fact, romance or no romance. However, Frank was not the boy to stand and look at a thing that wanted doing; so first going aft and greeting Mr. Cope, also confirmed in his position as chief officer, he asked that gentleman to excuse him while he went and made a clearance in the half-deck, which he explained had been turned into a bo'sun's locker.

Mr. Cope grinned sardonically as he replied, "Yes, I expect it looks a bit off after home. But never mind, Frank, you'll soon settle down to it again; not like last trip, eh? There's two green hands coming though, so you'll have your hands full. Williams has been sent to another ship."

Feeling rather glad that it was not Johnson who had left, Frank returned to his work and there, at the door of the house, to his intense delight he met Hansen, who had just come aboard as he said to have a look round, having signed articles yesterday morning and the ship being due away the next day. Seeing the condition of things, Hansen whipped off his coat and lent Frank a hand to get the den cleared out, both working with all the more goodwill because it was a bitterly cold day in December, only a fortnight before Christmas, and the blistering east wind whistled round that bleak deck enough to freeze the marrow of their bones.

While they were thus busily engaged they became aware of the presence of two new-comers, boys of about fourteen, in all the glory of their first uniform suits, who stood looking helplessly on at their energetic movements. And then the mate's voice in the rear was heard saying, "Frank, these are the two new apprentices, Jones and Fordham. I know you'll put them straight—they'll be better off than you were, eh?" Frank flushed with pride, and resolved that he *would* behave differently to them, remembering his own early misery, and immediately took them in hand. If he was somewhat dictatorial and patronising, I am sure he was to be excused, for his help to them was invaluable.

So stoutly did he labour and drive them too that by five o'clock the little house began to look shipshape, the new-comers' gear had been unpacked, their working rigs got ready; oilskins, sea-boots, mess-traps, all hung up and put ready for use, and they themselves were feeling more accustomed to their strange surroundings than Frank had been after a week at sea. The good it did them, too, was great, and all the more so because he was not conscious of it. Then, when all was done that he could do at that time, he sought the mate and inquired about their supper and whether they should stay ashore the night, as Hansen had offered to convoy them to the Sailors' Home. Mr. Cope thought it would be a good idea, but first he called Hansen on one side and gave him a solemn warning to look after the lads and not let them get into any mischief.

"Mr. Cope," replied Hansen, "I lofe dot boy like he bin mine own sohn, unt I rader lose mein life as let anyding happen mit him."

"All right, Hansen," rejoined the mate, "I believe you, in fact I know you're a good chap; but last night ashore, you know."

"Ah, sir," said Hansen seriously, "last night all same as fust night, it don't make no diffrunce mit me, I don't never go unt make fool of mineselluf, 'tain't good enough for me. Goot night, sir, we been abort goot unt early to-morrow."

And off went the four through the foul byways of Shadwell towards Well Street, piloted by Hansen, who seemed to be thoroughly at home. I do not wish to linger over this part of my story, but I cannot help pausing a moment to point out that on that short journey of a little over a mile, and despite the extreme youth of two of the party, they were molested several times by brutal-looking men and rough unsexed women, who were prowling about those gloomy streets like wild animals in the jungle seeking their prey. But by great good fortune they escaped, Hansen declaring that if he had to make the same journey again he would take the main road for it, he wouldn't run such a risk after dark again for anything.

It was a dreadful night, so after they had finished their supper in the Home they did not stir out again, but made themselves comfortable in one of the cosy reading-rooms, or roamed about the great building looking at the beautiful models and pictures until it was time to go to their cabins, which they did early, feeling tired out and remembering the early call that would be made on them in the morning.

And so well did they sleep that it was no easy task to get the youngsters under way again in the morning, as the steward said, the beds pulled so hard. But at seven o'clock they were all out in the fast-falling snow, which, however beautiful it is in the country, makes the poor streets of a big city dreadfully miserable, and turns the docks especially into places of horror. The appearance of the ship when they reached her sent a cold shiver through them, she looked so gaunt and wintry, and even Hansen the stolid said, "I hopes ve don't go out this morning; I don't like snow anyway."

Frank said nothing, but he thought of his last putting forth and felt thankful that he was better prepared this time. And then as he reached the snow-drifted decks he saw the crew tumbling about in their drunken efforts to reach the fo'c'sle, and looking at Hansen he said, "I'm afraid, old man, some of us'll be in bad trouble before we get to sea with this crowd."

Hansen only shrugged his shoulders and passed on, while just at the moment Frank stumbled against Johnson, who had reached the ship the night before, and had put in a rather miserable time. Their greetings were cordial if brief, for the time of their departure was at hand, and all the usual confusion attendant upon getting a sailing ship out of a crowded dock was in full swing. In addition, of course, there was the nuisance of the drunken crowd, who simply could not be got to work, being indeed so bad that it was necessary to retain the services of several riggers, who had been working on board, to see the ship as far as Gravesend. That settled, matters eased a bit, the helpless crew were left alone to sleep off their drink, and the sober workers soon got the ship pointed into the river where the seagoing tug awaited her.

Away she went at a brisk speed, while the hands laboured fiercely to get the decks cleared up and take shelter, for it was indeed, as they tersely put it, a perfect beast of a day. And now Frank recognised fully what a nuisance he must have been last voyage, for his new shipmates seemed to him to be as stupid as chunks of wood, irritating him so much that at last he drove them into the house and told them to stop there, which they were very glad to do, being nearly frozen. Yet they were really no more stupid than he was, only—well, you know now—and can yet sympathise with Frank in his annoyance.

In due time the *Sealark* reached Gravesend, where, upon an examination of the men by Mr. Cope and a consultation between the skipper and the pilot, and after receiving the mate's report upon the men's condition, it was decided to anchor for the night in order to let them sober up thoroughly.

It would never do to go out to sea with them all in that state. So she was brought to an anchor, the riding-light hoisted and the riggers discharged, and the boys and Hansen felt their minds greatly relieved at the thought that they had not to face the Channel upon such an awful night with a helpless crew.

So they retired to their house and had a bit of fun with the new-comers, introducing them to the wonders of board-ship feeding. But while they were in the midst of their fun there was a voice at the door and they saw their new second mate, a grizzled elderly man with a harsh voice, who said, "Now then, you last year's apprentices, you'll have to keep anchor watch. What's your names?"

Frank, readiest of the twain, rose to his feet and said, "Are you the second officer, sir?"

"I am just that, and my name's Jacks, Mr. Jacks," answered he, "and don't forget it. You're Brown, I know, and this other seaman here is Johnson, I suppose. Well, one of you'll come on watch at eight bells and stand till four bells, the other'll relieve him till eight bells and then call Hansen, and mind you keep a good look-out," and he was gone.

Johnson and Frank looked blankly at each other, for they hadn't reckoned on this, and were looking forward to a good night's sleep. So I won't record their unjust remarks about Mr. Jacks, who was only carrying out his orders after all, and somebody must do the work. But it was a bit rough on the boys, to be thus called upon to supply the place of men who were sleeping off their debauch in the forecastle. They were cheered up though presently by the appearance of Captain Jenkins, who came and spoke generously to them, bidding them look forward to a better time this voyage than last, and assuring them that he had not forgotten their splendid behaviour. He also spoke kindly to the two bewildered youngsters, who sat blinking at him as if he were some dread apparition fraught with terrible meaning for them. Then he departed, giving them good night and leaving them with a sense of grateful appreciation pervading their whole being, Johnson expressing himself, boy fashion, as follows: "Well, the old man hasn't forgotten us after all. He ain't half a bad sort, even if he has got to make us do men's work. I'll bet he'll make it up to us by-and-by, though. Don't you think so, Frank?"

"I do that," replied Frank, "and now we'll toss for first watch, so as one of us can turn in."

"Right you are," said Johnson, who produced a halfpenny, with which he won the toss and immediately elected to stand first watch. So it being seven o'clock they all turned in, and Frank knew no more until Johnson, his teeth chattering in his head, turned him out at four bells (ten o'clock) to watch over the safety of the ship until midnight.

It was an awful night, half a gale of bitter north-east wind blowing, with occasional squalls of blinding sleet; and certainly Frank may be forgiven if he did seek the most sheltered corner he could find, and there, with his head sunk between his shoulders in the collar of his reefer, and his pipe fiercely glowing, prepared to endure the passing of the time until midnight. It was not an ideal method of keeping anchor watch, but honestly, it was not very far removed from the way in which the vigil usually is kept. And in any case I think it was utterly indefensible for the second mate to behave as he did. He suddenly appeared before the half-dozing lad and, snatching him by the collar, flung him aside with such force as to make him fall heavily on deck, at the same time assailing him with a string of foul names for, as he falsely said, sleeping on his watch.

The half-dazed lad staggered to his feet, unable for the moment to comprehend what had happened to him. Indeed, it was nothing short of a catastrophe, for he had never been used like that in all his life. And then as the second mate, still cursing, advanced upon him again, the whole ghastly truth broke in upon him, and he went temporarily mad. He flew like a wild-cat straight at the second mate's throat, clutching it with both hands, and the weight of his body bore his assailant backward to the deck. In vain the second mate tried to beat him off, to tear himself loose; the boy held on, his one idea being to destroy his enemy.

And I think there can be little doubt but that in his mad rage he would have killed this man of nearly twice his strength, but that the skipper, who had come on deck to take a last look at the weather before turning in, heard something unusual, and came forward to see what it was. He snatched at Frank, being the uppermost, and tore the frantic lad off his foe. The second mate struggled to his feet and rushed at Frank again, held as he was in the grip of the skipper. He had been in American ships, where it is the humane custom for one officer to hold a man tightly while another batters him out of all resemblance to humanity. It is a characteristically American feat, but, fortunately for Frank, Captain Jenkins was not built that way. Holding the second mate off with one sturdy arm, he said sternly, "What does this mean, Mr. Jacks."

"I'll kill the − −" gasped the infuriated ruffian. "I'll cut his liver out. I'll − −"

"Look here," shouted the skipper, "if you don't cool down I shall heat up, and then you'll wish you hadn't. Now then, Frank, what's the matter?"

It was no easy task for Frank to reply. Rage and shame made him almost speechless, but at last he gasped out the shameful story and told just the plain truth. When he had finished, Captain Jenkins said soothingly, "There, there, that'll do, my boy, you're over-excited. Go and turn in, I'll arrange for your watch." And off Frank went, glad enough to get away.

When he had gone, the skipper turned to the second mate and said, "Now, Mr. Jacks, what devil possessed you to go and assault one of my apprentices, and one too that's as good a man as any we've got in the ship. I know the value of muscle and of a little punching occasionally, but to go and strike a lad who's doing man's work, that those fellows in the forecastle are paid for doing, why, you must be an infernal cur yourself to dream of such a thing. Now mark, that lad is in your watch and I shan't take him out of it, so as to give you an opportunity of doing the right thing by him. And you'll get a chance to win your character back as a man by the way you treat the crew. If I find you let them skulk and put their work on the lads, nothing shall save you from going forrard as one of them. You must behave man-fashion, and above all treat that good lad properly, or I'll make you wish you'd been dead before you shipped with me."

"Better let me go ashore at once, cap'n," replied the discomfited man; "there's no room for a second mate between the skipper and his favourites."

"Well, in the first place, you're not going ashore; in the next, I have no favourites. As long as man, boy, or officer does his proper work, he'll get justice from me, and if you do your duty you'll be all right. Now go and turn in, I'll see about things till midnight. Good night," and they separated.

I need not recount the eventless hours until 4 A.M., when the cook was called to prepare coffee. That comforting beverage was ready at five and all hands were called, with the warning that it would be "Man the windlass" in half-an-hour. They were all sober by this time, but in a state of abject misery, and the prospect of mounting the forecastle head and heaving up the anchor was to them a terrible one. Nevertheless the work had to be done, for the tide was making strongly and the tug was waiting.

It was now that the second mate found full scope for his evil temper, for the poor wretches were continually taking shelter below from the bitter blast, and were quite regardless of his oaths and blows until he dragged them out by main force, and then if they were not closely watched they would scramble below again. Heart-breaking work, indeed, for both sides, but down underneath, where the big muddy links of the cable were lying hauled back in darkness and filth and biting cold by the four young gentlemen's sons, certainly not less so. And one of those boys at any rate could not help feeling disheartened, apart altogether from his work. He knew—how could he help knowing?—how well he had done his work hitherto, and now to be cuffed and cursed like a dog—it made his brain burn as it would never have done had he been dragged up to it. But still he persevered with his work, for it had become a habit with him, even though he had lost heart.

In this wise, and by superhuman efforts on the part of those who really did work, the anchor was hove up and secured, and the clumsy ship, lying like a balloon upon the water by reason of her ballast trim, was headed down the darksome river again, while the miserable crew were kept going in order to prepare them for the work that would presently fall to them, when, the tug having left, the ship would need her own canvas under which to sail. The grey, dreary morning came, and a good breakfast of lobscouse was served out, which put some life into the men, and even infused a little cheerfulness into the grim forecastle whence all hope seemed fled.

But the treatment, though severe, of hard work, bitter cold, and complete stoppage of drink, was having a beneficial effect, and amid the customary growlings, mostly meaningless, men might be seen having a few draws of the pipe, and making halfhearted efforts to put things a bit straight in the forecastle. In the house the two unhappy new-comers were just quietly miserable, feeling quite unable to eat the new food, bitterly cold, and full of alarm for the future. Frank and Johnson discussed the second mate, Johnson being surprised at the change in his genial shipmate, who seemed transformed into a veritable demon of revenge. That brutal bully had done the boy irreparable harm, not so much by his action itself, but by the sheer injustice of it, for that, however incapable we may feel about arguing it out, is the craving of all of us, justice, and nothing hurts me personally more than injustice.

They were all wisely allowed a good long time for breakfast, in order to allow the good effects of the food to soak in, and then they were turned to, to prepare for the coming struggle, which, as the sky was filling with heavy, banked-up clouds in the west, threatened to be a severe one. The tug ahead went on like fate, until off Beachy Head, the limit of her contract, then signified the same by two sharp whistles which made the mate jump and shout for the fore and afters to be run up. The pilot, of course, had been dropped early off Dungeness. As soon as the fore and aft sails were hoisted and the topsails loosed, the tug gave another short, sharp blast of her whistle, and slipped the hawser, turning sharp round and pelting back for another job, all interest in the *Sealark* at an end.

Oh, it was a work to get that hawser in! Nothing for all hands in good form, but then—they felt as if it would never be done, and indeed it might well have been far easier if the tug had aided by backing astern instead of letting the gigantic rope go and trail under the ship's bottom. Being wet and stiff, it was hardly less difficult to stow it than to haul it in, and then to get sail on her. Then, too, they found how indifferently the riggers in London had done their work. It is impossible to explain in a book like this the hardships imposed upon sailors who have to handle a ship in Channel on a stormy winter's night when the work of preparation aloft, which has been done in dock by riggers, has been done so scandalously that it seems as if the ship were all coming to pieces. There has been no time to supervise these men's work, and so a lot of poor fellows, quite new to the ship and her peculiarities, have to contend with them and the neglect of the riggers at the worst possible time, and when they are in the worst possible fettle to do it.

Well, in the end they got the ship under easy sail (she could not carry much, being so very tender), and blessed themselves that at least they had a fair wind, although some of the wisest of them looked wistfully ahead at the great, gloomy banks of cloud that were piling up there, and felt in their very marrow that this slant would not last long. But it gave them a respite, and before the night fell the usual job of picking for watches took place, when Frank took the opportunity of noting his new shipmates. There were ten all told, so that as ships go she was fairly well manned. A big Swede named Ohlsen, Hansen, and a smart-looking Italian answering to the name of Natalie, with two young Scotchmen, Mackenzie and Donald, made up the second mate's watch, the mate having a fine stalwart west countryman, two Norwegians, Larsen and Petersen, and two Welshmen from Carnarvon, Davies and Evans. So that she was, although quite cosmopolitan in her crew, not so full of the foreign element as sailing ships usually are. The cook and steward were both Maltese and fairly good men, while the carpenter, about whom I had nothing to say last voyage because he was one of those self-effacing men who usually elude notice, was an elderly Finn named Stadey, a thoroughly good and efficient man, but withal so quiet and inoffensive that you would hardly know how he was on board at all. He had been in the ship seven voyages.

Remains only to speak of the second mate, Mr. Jacks. Ruffian and bully as he undoubtedly was, he was evidently a fine seaman, the combination being a very usual one in American ships, where he had served most of his time. But the same aptitude for driving men and brutally ill-treating them in the bargain, which had made him a favourite in the Yankee blood-boats, operated against him in English vessels, to which he had come when he had grown too old for the position of a Yankee second mate. And now, in addition to his naturally evil temper and cruel disposition, he was soured by disappointment, and getting on for fifty years of age, which for an executive officer at sea is fully equal to sixty ashore.

It was, of course, the second mate's first watch on deck that night from eight till midnight, according to ancient custom, and the first thing he did after the watches were set was to call Frank on the poop and tell him he would have to keep his watch there (the two new-comers were both in their bunks, helpless with sea-sickness). Very respectfully Frank pointed out (although his voice trembled) that he had been doing a man's work for some time, that he stood his regular wheel and look-out, and that while he didn't want to disobey orders, if the second mate persisted in ordering him to stay up there like a boy who could do nothing but watch the clock, he must appeal to the captain.

This new check made the officer furious, and although trying to put some restraint upon himself, he could not help rapping out a few fierce oaths, cursing the day that brought him into a ship where he could be bearded by a pack of boys, Frank meanwhile keeping a wary eye upon him. At last he blurted out, "Very well, I s'pose you must do as you like, but don't you drive me too far or you'll find me a match for you and the skipper too." And Frank got down from the poop feeling no elation at his victory, but heavy-hearted rather at the prospect of a long voyage under such a man. But he made up his mind to give no cause for offence, and to do his utmost for his own sake, even though he had no hope of ever getting into the good graces of his superior officer.

The watch wore easily on, the wind dropping steadily until it was nearly a flat calm. But the weather looked vile in its threatening appearance, the greasy, rolling, ragged, black clouds hanging low, and the sea having an uneasy chop that in itself betokened a change. That change came almost exactly at midnight, and, much to Frank's disgust, it was nearly four bells before she was snugged down to two lower-topsails and foresail, and put off the land on the starboard tack. But he could not help noticing as he had not done before what a superb seaman the second mate was at work like this, and being a lad with a passionate desire for justice, as I have said before, he determined if possible to compel this brave bully to recognise that he at least did not owe anything to the skipper's favouritism.

The next ten days were full of misery for them, for the gale blew with scarcely an hour's intermission and would not allow them to get down Channel at all, while the cold and wet and constant dread of her capsizing from her scanty ballast tried the crew severely. Still they were what you must call a fairly good crowd, and once freed from the effects of their liquor had developed into first-class seamen, working together with a will in spite of their diverse nationalities. That is not always impossible, for I very well remember being before the mast in a big barque on an East Indian voyage when my watchmates were an Irishman, a Swede, a Finn, a Frenchman from St. Malo, a Breton from Peniche, and a negro ordinary seaman. And but for the Irishman, who was the most worthless and degraded specimen of the race I have yet encountered, we were quite a happy family; indeed when we got rid of him in Hong-Kong we were entirely so. But as his principal boast was that he had been in gaol in every port he had ever been in all round the world, having commenced many voyages but never completed one, his detrimental qualities will be understood.

Still, fore-reaching down Channel in midwinter is not an experience to be desired, however much it may bring out the manliness of the sufferers. Of course the amount of suffering varies with the ship, and the *Sealark* was by no means one of the worst. There were, however, many lightened hearts on board two days before Christmas, when, having had by sheer hard labour worked her down to a position off the Bishop, the wind hauled round to the southward and permitted them at four o'clock on Christmas Eve to anchor in Penarth Roads. That was good, but better still was the blessed chance that enabled them to get into Penarth Dock early on Christmas morning, and then, having cleared up decks, to have the rest of the day to themselves, and to enjoy such a feast as only sailors could. I feel that I have grossly neglected the two youngsters Jones and Fordham, but really in the first place I am not telling their story, and in the next they had been entirely out of the picture, so to speak, since leaving Gravesend. It was well for them that both Frank and Johnson had taken pity on them and had not allowed them to endure the usual fate of first-trip apprentices, so that taking things all round they had not been very uncomfortable, although they would probably have told a very different story.

Thanks to Captain Jenkins' wisdom and forethought, they all had a splendid Christmas as far as food and pleasure went, but the weather still remaining atrociously bad, there was no inducement for any one to go ashore, more especially in Penarth, which is an out-of-the-way place affording few temptations to the sailor. Had it been Cardiff now, another story might have been told, for the shipping fraternity there are a very scaly lot indeed, and doubtless some of the men would have been induced to desert. But nothing of the kind happened, and in due course the ship was hauled under the tips, the great trucks came rumbling alongside, were swung into the air and outward withal, then lowered over the hatches and their grimy load released amid a blinding cloud of dust, to find its way into the recesses of her hold. It is a filthy job this loading of coal under tips, but it has its fascinations for a contemplative mind able to trace it from its deep resting-place in some Welsh valley through all its vicissitudes to its final destination.

What, however, we are chiefly concerned with now is the fact that owing to the despatch for which the great South Welsh coal-ports are famous, the *Sealark* was laden in two days, and, the tide being favourable, was immediately towed out of dock to commence her real journey to the Far East. At the beginning of things it seemed as if the elements had tired of buffeting the poor old *Sealark* about, for a strong south-easterly breeze held good with smooth water until she was off soundings and her voyage fairly begun.

And now, to the very great delight and satisfaction of the boys, Captain Jenkins took a step that was at once wise and kind. Calling Hansen aft, he told him that he had decided to make him boatswain at an increased wage of ten shillings a month. This meant to the good fellow not only better pay but better food and lodgment, as he would take the other berth in the carpenter's little den, and besides he would be next door to his beloved boys, in whose welfare he had always taken so keen an interest. As for Frank, he felt that this was all that had been needed to make the voyage a success, for he had quite made up his mind that he should be able to get along well with Mr. Jacks after all.

CHAPTER IX
THE TESTING OF A MAN

Very regretfully I notice how the recital of Frank's career has drawn me on to longer and longer chapters, until I hardly know where to draw the line. But then at sea, you know, as a rule day succeeds day and work flows on so steadily that, except when some sudden catastrophe occurs, the necessity for a break in the narrative is not evident. Such a necessity is now at hand. I have said that the elements seemed to favour the departure of the *Sealark*, and the elevation of Hansen to the position of bo'sun, or foreman of the crew, made Frank feel that things were going exceptionally well with him, and that this voyage was indeed a great improvement upon the last one.

And then a change took place, a change in the weather that made, as the Scriptures say, "all faces gather blackness." The wind backed round into the north-west, with an awfully hideous sea which made the deeply-laden *Sealark* strain and labour as if she would loosen her plates. (I hope I have made it clear that she was an iron ship, but I don't think I have.) Captain Jenkins, full of care for his charge, saw to it that all the sails were well secured, all the mast supports well looked to by means of preventer backstays, and, in short, everything done that a good sailor could think of for the safety of the vessel and all on board under any circumstances of weather. For he knew how low the glass had fallen, and he felt the need of preparing for the worst possible eventuality.

At last the weather grew so bad, and the wind so high, that the carrying of any sail was impossible, and so the *Sealark* lay hove-to under bare poles, with just a tarpaulin in the mizzen rigging to keep her head from falling off and leaving her in the trough of the enormous sea then running.

She lay pretty comfortably considering, but Frank, who was quite a sea-dog by this time, was much moved by the terror of his two poor little housemates, the two new apprentices. They did not know how much they were indebted to him for any comfort they had felt, yet unconsciously they clung to him in their distress, because Johnson, though a good fellow enough, hadn't Frank's sympathy with the weak. He had quite forgotten his own early disadvantages. Some men are like that, but it is a great pity, because it is a trait that rather adds to manhood than detracts from it.

And in this dread time, when the howling storm tore off the sea-crests and made them envelop the cowering ship in clouds of spray, when sky and ocean seemed to mingle, and the uproar of the elements made ordinary conversation impossible, they clung to one who, only a little older than themselves, had risen to the full stature of a man and knew how to control his natural fears. Not that Frank was in any way lavish with his sympathy; rather he evinced it by speaking and acting in the most natural and usual manner possible, as if there could be nothing to make a fuss about. This, I take it, is, in the majority of cases, far more effectual in the comforting of others than the most elaborate endeavours to do so can ever be.

Nevertheless, it cannot be denied that time and conditions were bad enough to daunt the stoutest heart. Only youngsters, not being able to see so far ahead, are able to keep their end up at such a time much better than the majority of men, that is, if they are as good stuff as Frank Brown was to start with. It was a gale that will be long remembered in shipping annals for the enormous destruction of property and loss of life at sea, a regular tropical hurricane raging in the temperate zone and just where the greatest traffic in the world congregates, outward and homeward bound. It blew so hard that the *Sealark* lay down with her lee rail under water, deep laden as she was, and refused to rise; while the sea smiting her weather side was caught by the furious tempest and hurled high over her masts' heads in great sheets of spume. Then is the time when the weak spots show and when faithful work proves its worth, for one small mishap at such a time may, and often does, lead to the loss of the ship and the lives of all hands.

So day faded into night with no relief, while all hands hung on to their patience, as it were, thankful for a staunch ship and a fairly good cargo. But oh! the weary hours of the night. A man does get so weary of the ravenous roar of the wind, the unceasing assault of the mighty sea, does long so for a little respite. Day, moreover, broke again upon an ocean that was one expanse of white, for the sea seemed mingling with the sky, its very surface torn off by the ferocious wind. It was impossible to see for any distance through the hissing spray, two or three hundred yards at the most, and yet they craved for further vision, it was so lonely. Then suddenly there was a slight lull, the ship eased up a little, and the sky cleared temporarily, although it was still blowing a tremendous gale.

And into their circle of sight there came an object of pity, awakening a passionate desire to do something at any risk whatever for the help of their fellow-men. It was a vessel of about the same size as themselves, but of wood, and by the appearance of her very near the foundering-point. Her three masts, bulwarks, and boats were gone, she was just a mere hulk upon the terrible sea; but upon the highest part of her, lashed to the stanchions of the departed bulwarks, which showed up like a set of broken teeth, were visible the cowering forms of her crew, visible, that is, at intervals, when the incessant spray which swept over them became thinner than usual. The word went quickly round the *Sealark*, and all hands rushed on deck, staring with bated breath on the pitiful sight, and glancing anxiously at the skipper between whiles to see what he might be going to do.

Poor man, it was an anxious time for him, for his ship was quite unmanageable, as he dared not make sail. True, the derelict was to leeward of him, and a boat could reach her without very great danger; but unless the wind let up soon, the getting of that boat back was an obvious impossibility. However, there was no question about the urgency of the matter, for at every scend of the sea it would be noticed that the unfortunate craft had settled deeper, had less buoyancy. So pulling himself together, Captain Jenkins shouted at the pitch of his great voice, "Who will volunteer to go and try and save those men from drowning?"

There was only a momentary hesitation, and then four men stepped forward. They were the two Scotchmen, Hansen, and one of the Welshmen, the other being at the wheel.

Then the second mate looked up at the skipper, and said quite coolly, "I shall want another man, sir."

He had hardly uttered the words when Frank, who had been watching the wreck with indescribable feelings, sprang forward and said, "Let me go, sir; I would have offered before, but I was afraid you would not let me go."

The skipper shook his head sadly, and said, "I'm afraid it's no place for you, my boy."

But Frank bounded up the ladder to his side, and said gaspingly, "I'm as strong as any of those men, sir, and you know I can pull a good oar. Besides, I want to show the second mate, sir— —"

That was all, but the skipper nodded "All right," and immediately all hands were busy getting the boat out, a difficult and heavy task in a ship like that, where the boats are seldom carried ready for launching. But by dint of hard work and eagerness, she was got all ready for lowering in fifteen minutes.

"Now, Mr. Jacks," roared the skipper, "all I've got to say is, keep your eye on that ship that she doesn't go down while you're alongside, and take you all with her. As soon as ever I see you have reached her, I'll keep away and run down to leeward at any risks, so that you can run down to me as you are going to do to her, and may God grant you save 'em all and yourselves too. Off you go."

The six of them got into the boat as she hung by a single bridle from a main-yard tackle, a steady shove off and she touched the seething surface almost instantly. The man at the tackle fall let go, and, as the barque heeled over, one hand in the boat unhooked the tackle and hove it clear, while the sea surging up beneath the vessel's bottom bore the boat a hundred yards to leeward at a single sweep. The second mate at the tiller kept her off before the wind, ordering his men to ship their oars and hold the blades high out of water by depressing the looms, with the effect that the boat sped away as if under a press of sail.

There was no time to be afraid had the crew been ever so fearful, and in addition they all felt at once that they were being steered by a master in the science of boat-handling. It seemed but a minute or two before she reached the wallowing vessel, and as she flew under the stern the second mate shouted to his port oarsmen to pull for their very lives, starboard oarsmen to ship their oars and watch for a rope. The boat spun round right up into the smooth, and at the same moment a coil of rope was hove into her from the derelict, which was caught and held.

But now the boat's position was full of peril, for the derelict's decks on the lee side were under water, and some ugly fragments of spars, still attached by the lee rigging, were tumbling about and threatening the boat with destruction. It was quite impossible to get close alongside, and yet every moment was precious, while the poor fellows, so close to rescue, and yet confronted with that terrible few feet of boiling foam and jagged tumbling spars, were in an agony of doubt. But their natural hesitation was solved by a huge sea which, bursting over the weather side, washed full half of their number overboard, as they were not then on the look-out for it; and before even they themselves had realised what had happened, they were clambering into the boat.

The rest were emboldened by what had happened, and jumped into the foaming vortex at the same moment as the second mate screamed, "Let go that rope, she's going." Happily one of them managed to reach the boat's side, and clung to it with desperate tenacity, as the heavily laden craft, caught by a swell, was swept away clear of that brutal entanglement alongside. Only just in time, for, as the boat swung off the wind, those in the boat, in spite of their efforts to get the struggling men who were hanging on to the gunwale inboard, could not help seeing the defeated ship give one throe like a Titan in his death agony, and, her bow rising high in air, she slid down a yawning gulf into darkness and peace, never again to be seen by the eye of man.

It was a splendid rescue, nobly planned and carried out, and all the more impressive because of the scanty sum of the moments during which it had been effected. And now the heavily laden boat must needs be brought to the wind and sea, which latter was getting up at a most dangerous rate, because it was evident that otherwise she would go as fast to leeward as the ship to which she belonged. It was most fortunate, therefore, that the second mate was so skilful, and calling upon his men to stand by, one side to pull and the other to stern on the word, he watched the smooth when a big sea had passed, and then shouting fit to crack his throat, "Pull port, stern starboard," he swung the boat up into the wind, and she was safe for the time.

But she rode very deep, and threatened every moment to swamp, only the most energetic baling keeping her afloat. In addition, the air was so thick with spray that they could see nothing of the ship, and they could only hope that from her superior height their shipmates were able to keep sight of them. They all looked wistfully at the grim face of Mr. Jacks, which showed no trace of his great anxiety, and took comfort therefrom.

On board the ship they had not yet kept away, for a tremendous squall had blotted out the whole scene, and when it had passed and vision was restored for about a square mile, there was nothing visible but the small circle of white sea and black sky, although all hands were straining their eyes to leeward through the clouds of spindrift, for sight or sign of the devoted little boatload of beings who were at present all in all to them.

Suddenly there was a scream from forward heard above the monotonous growl of the storm. It was from Johnson, who had climbed up inside the lee fore-rigging, and had just caught a glimpse of something, he knew not what, a black patch on a hill of white. But the skipper had heard, and saw his pointing arm, and, focussing his glasses on the spot for a moment, shouted, "Run that fore-topmast staysail up."

All hands flew to obey, and steadily the small triangle of sail rose, carefully attended as to the sheet, until without a shake it was set. "Hard up with that helm, stand by your weather braces," were the next orders, while springing into the weather mizzen-rigging the skipper tore the tarpaulin down which was holding her up to the wind. Slowly she paid off, and gathered way as the yards were checked, and presently, to the almost hysterical delight of all hands, they saw the boat, a tiny spot in that snowy waste, being tossed like a chip in a torrent, but looking staunch and seaworthy still.

Down towards her sped the ship now, although only that rag of sail was set forrard, under full steerage control, with the skipper clinging in the weather rigging like a bat, and conning the vessel with waves of his hand, for his voice was useless in that uproar. Down past the boat they swept, high on the crest of a gigantic wave, while the tiny overloaded craft seemed to cower in the valley between two wave-crests as if she were sheltering there.

Then at the skipper's beckoning hand some of the fellows rushed aft and hauled out the head of the mizzen. Down with the helm, no time to watch for smooth seas now, let go the fore-topmast staysail halyards, and up she comes into the wind, receiving as she did so the full impact of the terrible sea that seemed as if it must crush her into fragments. She shuddered in every rivet, but survived, the drivers of those rivets in some far-away shipyard all unconscious of this life and death testing of their work.

And there, hove to again under bare poles with just the tarpaulin spread as before, she lay with all hands straining their eyes for the coming of the boat. Mr. Jacks, watching with stern-set face the manœuvres of the ship, followed her passing with orders to stand by the oars so that at his word the boat might be swung off again, and driven before the wind and sea, and got under the lee of the waiting ship.

It was boldly, gallantly, successfully done, but not one of them failed to note how hungrily the mighty seas roared around their insignificance, but while some felt their hearts shrivel within them at the immediate prospect of dissolution, others, among whom was Frank, were elated as the old Vikings at the prospect of battle, and would fain have shouted for joy. But the weary time of watching, and waiting, and noting the onrush of each awful sea had tested them to the last fibre, and they felt infinitely relieved at the change of action for passive endurance.

Away she sped, flung from crest to hollow of the seas, but steered so splendidly by the second mate that, although the foam seemed to stand above her gunwale in wreaths, nothing but the spray came over. And they all watched the face of the steersman, who looked, as indeed he was, a tower of strength, confident and able. Just shaving the stern of the *Sealark* by, as it seemed, a hand's breadth, he shouted, "Pull port, all you know," and the boat shot up alongside, to receive a line and be secured.

Then as she rose and fell, kept away from being stove in by the eddying seas coming under the ship's bottom, one by one, watching their opportunity, scrambled on board until, all but the second mate and Frank having left her, the bridle was hooked on and many willing hands swung the gallant craft up into her place again. A splendid feat nobly performed, and one that all those engaged in it would ever remember as making an elevating epoch in their lives.

No sooner was the boat secured than the weather broke, and before midnight the *Sealark*, under topsail, foresail, and lower staysails, was plunging away on her course again as if rejoicing in her victory over the hungry sea. Meanwhile all the heroes of the adventure had slipped back into their grooves again, Frank especially treating the whole affair with a lofty nonchalance as if it were hardly worth recalling, but secretly enjoying an uplifting sense of having done a good deed.

The saved crew were distributed according to the barque's limited accommodation, and made as comfortable as was possible under the circumstances, none of them, fortunately, being injured or so exhausted that they needed special care. The skipper, entertaining the rescued officers in the cabin, learned that the lost ship was a soft wood ship hailing from Frederikstad, laden with coal from Newport, and bound to Rio Janeiro. That she was leaky when she started from port, and never from the first coming on of this frightful gale had she possessed the faintest chance of living through it.

The Norwegian skipper further told them that towards the last, when the enfeebled rigging had given way and the rusted-through chain-plates had been broken off or torn out of the rotten topsides, letting the masts tumble over the side, the overstrained hull just opened out like a basket, and pumping became useless. The boats went early in the fight; in any case they were of very little use, all of them having the dry-rot. He finished his account by saying, "And but for you coming just when you did, Captain Jenkins, sixteen of us some hours ago would have been deep below the surface of this rough sea, all our troubles over." Thus the Norwegian skipper, one of nature's gentlemen, as with eyes humid with gratitude he grasped Captain Jenkins' hand. Jenkins, confused, changed the subject, and pointed out that he must land them all at Las Palmas as his commissariat, to say nothing of his accommodation, was entirely unequal to the strain upon it. In which the Norwegian entirely agreed.

This little episode in a sailor's life was full of interest for Frank, and did him no end of good, but strange to say he did not once associate his part in it with his folks at home until Sunday, when, to his immense surprise, he received a summons to dine in the cabin. Now in many fine ships I knew when I was at sea this was quite usual, but it had never happened in the *Sealark* before, and Frank hardly knew how to contain himself at the prospect of having a decently-laid meal.

So he dressed himself as if for going ashore, to the undisguised amazement of the two youngsters who had already begun to feel as if they never had worn decent clothes and never would again, and then waited most impatiently the tinkle of the steward's bell. When he got to table he was introduced to Captain Rasmussen, the rescued skipper, as "One of your rescuers, sir, a lad on his second voyage," and the big Norwegian, taking both the lad's hands in his, solemnly blessed him, and predicted a splendid career for him if he lived. Poor Frank could not speak, and wished himself anywhere else, but still the praise was very sweet, and I am glad to say it did not spoil his appetite for dinner.

But far beyond all praise, or even the satisfaction of his own mind at what he had been able to do, was Frank's gratification at the difference in the second mate's behaviour towards him. There was nothing said by either of them bearing upon the subject, but Frank noticed with the utmost pleasure that he was now treated by Mr. Jacks with a courtesy and consideration greater than that offered to any other man on board, and this made him not only happy but more and more eager to justify the position he had won.

And as an outlet for his energies he took upon himself the training of the two youngsters Jones and Fordham, who were now fully recovered, but extremely loth to begin work. Frank, however, roused them out and drove them like a regular taskmaster, fully explaining to them that it was all for their good, and when they rebelled and told him that he was only a boy like themselves, and they weren't going to be bullied by him, he took unto himself a bit of ratline stuff, and laid it about them sharply. Of course they did not appreciate this one bit, but as Frank blandly explained to them, it was better that he should chastise them for their good than that they should suffer the loss of all their best days. I know there are many good people who would condemn Frank for this, but I don't, especially as I know there was not a bit of the bully in him.

The run down to Las Palmas was quite a lady's trip, steady gentle Trades, bright beaming skies, and smooth sparkling seas. The kind of weather, in fact, that Frank had grown to regard as leaving the sailor free to do his repairing and reconstruction work without bothering his head about the ship's progress at all, she attending to that with just a hand at the wheel to steer her. But when the bold outlines of the beautiful Peak of Teneriffe rose up sharp and clear against the horizon, all his interest in the external surroundings burst up like a suppressed spring suddenly let loose, and he was as eager as possible to see all that could be seen. That is a good sign in boy or man. I have this opinion because I have known men who after voyages to the same port still retained their interest in its approaches, still maintained that every hour of the day, to say nothing of the wizard-like changes of the night, added to the interest of the place. The *Sealark* coasted the beautiful island of Teneriffe, and Frank saw with pleasure the dull drab of the land change into a curiously irregular series of lines like a checkerboard made of paper and twisted a bit; then the sun shone out and the checkers began to glow with many tints of green creeping up the side of the mountain, until they reached barrenness just below the line of snow, whence the pure white cone soared into the blue.

Past that wonderful scene they sped with a splendid breeze, and across to Gran Canaria, arriving off the port of Las Palmas well before sunset. The port official's boat came off, and finding that the captain was unwilling to anchor, tried, as is their wont, to make him do so. But Captain Jenkins was not inclined to waste his owners' time under any pretext. So he would not anchor, just lying hove to until a boat came off, in which he was able to tranship his involuntary passengers. They bade him farewell with heartfelt gratitude for his kindness; and as they left the side he shouted "Square away," and off went the *Sealark* on her long journey, leaving the shipwrecked men to be dealt with by their consul. It was a splendid experience for Frank, and one that left its mark upon his life; but he could not help wishing that the skipper had not been so obdurate, and had allowed at least a day's stay in this wonderfully beautiful island. That, however, to a careful skipper was out of the question; and so the shades of night falling saw the dim outlines of the Canary Islands fade away into the distance and become but a memory.

And now, as in many respects one voyage is the counterpart of another in certain parts of the world, I propose to pass by without comment the next fortnight, wherein day succeeded day in orderly sequence. The Trades were lost, and the calm belt passed, while the ordinary duties of the ship, like those of a house that is well managed, succeeded one another in unfailing procession—a slipping by of unhistorical days, wherein the commoner souls who are part of them just stagnate and think how wearisome it all is, while those who count in the scheme of things are ever growing in all those details that go to make up the sum of life.

How happy in these halcyon seas is the youth who is not afraid of work, and who is fully equipped mentally and physically for that work; to whom the sweet first breath of the new day arouses in him a desire to do, and whose heart is too high to be daunted by any suggestion of monotony. If in addition he is a reader, and can compare present-day sea-life with the past, he will in addition be inclined to thank God that his lines are cast in pleasant places as compared with the bad old days of seafaring, when even the finest of days were lingered out amid scenes of such horror as make the flesh of a modern creep to think of, especially when he knows how much of this misery was entirely preventable.

These are the reflections which often give me pause when endeavouring to call attention to conditions which might be made so much better than they are in the lives of our sailors. It is impossible for any one who knows to ignore the wonderful advance that has been made, that is still being made, in the amelioration of the lot of our seafarers, even compared with the conditions of thirty years ago. But if we go back for a century, and tear aside the veil of romance which distance and fine writing has woven around the lives of those earlier seafarers, we shall, if we possess any human sympathies at all, be nauseated, horrified, made profoundly sad, to think of what poor human flesh and blood has been called upon to endure for the benefit of us who live in these luxurious days.

I often wonder how many of those who revel in the beauties of Kingsley's "Westward Ho!" stop to think of the meaning of the short sentence or two in which he describes the arrival of Amyas Leigh and his companions at Barbadoes. The length of the passage from England is not given, but it could hardly at the outside have exceeded forty days. Yet in that brief space we find that many of the crew are almost at death's door with scurvy and other foul diseases, which were then regarded as the inevitable concomitants of life on shipboard, a life whose only parallel apparently was to be found in our loathsome gaols at that date, and even there, if the prisoner had friends or money, he might be well, even luxuriously fed, and far from badly lodged. Such necessities could not be had by the sailor at sea though he possessed the treasures of Midas.

To-day we are fast approaching the maximum of comfort possible in a seafaring life and compatible with the earning power of a ship; that is, in the best type of ships. Of course there is a wide range, and undoubtedly there are still many vessels afloat in which the food and accommodation and the conditions of labour are no whit better than what was the rule thirty years ago, and is happily the exception now. There is, notwithstanding all this, much still to be done in order to bring the lot of our workers at sea up as nearly as possible to the standard obtaining on shore, and it is pleasant to know and realise that some of the most strenuous efforts in this laudable direction are being made by ship-owners themselves. Officers and seamen, too, are doing their share; and when once we can get the press generally to take an interest in our splendid mercantile marine, and deal with its stirring story from the point of view of knowledge, I believe that sea life will have little to fear by comparison with any other calling, as far as the lot of the seafarer is concerned.

With none of these matters, however, did our hero trouble his head. He was in the happy position of being in love with his work, healthy, full of energy, and of a temperament to make the best of everything. Added to this he was fortunate enough to be with men who appreciated him, and to be free also from the continual croaking of those confirmed human ravens so often met with on board ship, who take a sinister pleasure in dinning into a boy's ears what a silly ass he is to come to sea. Soured in temper and stunted in mind, these old "growls," as we used to call them, are undoubtedly the means of spoiling the promising career of many a bright young seaman, by making him feel that it is useless for him to go on with a profession which is being continually represented to him as the worst paid, and as having the least consideration of all open to a lad who wants to make his way in the world.

Moreover, in great contrast with the last voyage, everything seemed to go on greased wheels, as we say. The crew had settled down to their work in splendid fashion, the weather was all that it should be, and the *Sealark* came bowling along round the Cape in fine style before a steady, strong succession of westerly gales, never too strong for her to carry her maintopgallant sail. A deep content was visible on the face of the skipper. He was indeed a happy man. He had nobly won his position, and he was fully justified in the way he was holding it, while the elements themselves seemed to conspire in the determination to do him good. And so in comfortable fashion they ran down the long stretch of lonely ocean until they came in sight of the tiny island of St. Paul's, and hauled up for the passage up the Indian Ocean.

CHAPTER X
A CATASTROPHE

When we consider the illimitable stretches of ocean over which a sailing ship has to work her way by grace and favour of the winds, and the innumerable possibilities, not merely of disaster but of adventure, befalling such a ship on account of the well-known variability of those invisible aids of commerce, it is nothing short of marvellous that there should be so many men afloat who will tell you with perfect truth that they have been sailing for so many years and have never met with an accident of any kind, nay, that they hardly know what bad weather means. To a man who can scarcely cross one ocean without meeting at least a heavy gale, and who looks for trouble as a necessary adjunct to his profession, this is a strong reason for belief in luck, since he cannot disbelieve that what so many of his co-workers tell him is true.

So far, I think Frank's experiences had been about the average, but he was now to meet with something that some men who go all their lives to sea know nothing of—an East Indian cyclone. These terrific disturbances of the atmosphere are not peculiar to the Indian Ocean, but are also met with in the Atlantic and Pacific within the tropics, and are called cyclones, typhoons, or hurricanes, according to their locality. But the word hurricane, like "awful," "shocking," "terrible," &c., has nearly lost its meaning owing to its being improperly applied very often by some excited passenger to what is really only a moderate gale, and thence getting into a newspaper. It has become suspect, like the oft-repeated phrase met with in print, "The captain said that in all his experience of — — years he had never known such a storm." Captains may say that with a definite purpose in view to a persistent questioner whom they think will report their words, but if it were only partially true it would argue that storms were continually becoming so much more violent than of old that we are in danger of being swept off the surface of the globe altogether.

But the language of exaggeration can hardly be applied to a typical East Indian cyclone, because it is one of those appalling manifestations of Nature's energy when man is made to feel his physical insignificance in the scheme of things, so that it is beyond all extravagances of description, which indeed only tend to disfigure and misrepresent its real proportions. So I shall endeavour to be quite simple in my description of the experience which Frank was now called upon to pass through. It began very quietly. They were just about in the heart of the Trade Winds, or about half-way up to Java Head from St. Paul's, when one evening in the first dog-watch Frank, being at the wheel, noticed that the sun at setting had lost his usual splendid lustre, and seemed of a sickly greenish red. At the same time the steady genial breeze which had sent them speedily northward began to falter and die away.

Mr. Jacks lounged over the lee rail, his eyes fixed upon the western horizon. There was a profound silence only punctuated by the flap of the sails and the creak of the ropes as the ship rolled lazily on the swell in the dying breeze. Suddenly the skipper appeared up the companion and cast a comprehensive glance around and aloft. His face was set and stern, but showed no trace of hesitation such as he must have felt. Then he strolled over to where the second mate stood and said, "Looks queer, Mr. Jacks."

"Yes, sir," responded that officer, "very queer. If the glass— —"

"Yes, it does," sharply interrupted the skipper, "it's away down ever so low; 29.34 already, and it only started to fall at noon. But this last hour it has been going and no mistake. Well, you can start and get the kites in, and at four bells we'll put all hands on it. There isn't much time to lose, I'm sure, and anyway there's little or no wind to waste."

Thenceforward until eight o'clock the Sealark was a scene of the most violent activity, every rag of sail in her with the exception of the main lower-topsail and fore-topmast staysail, both of which were fortified with additional gear for securing them in a hurry, was not only furled with the utmost care, but extra gaskets were put on, and no corner of canvas allowed to show that might invite the grip of the cyclone fiend to seize it and rip the whole sail adrift. Every article that could be moved on deck or below was fortified in its position by additional lashings, preventer backstays were set up and life-lines were stretched fore and aft in case of the bulwarks going. Finally the ship was put upon the starboard tack in order that when the wind began to haul she should come up to it, and not be liable to the great danger of being caught aback. And then, with the exception of the man at the wheel, all hands were dismissed to rest and a good meal to fortify them for the coming event.

There was a long and very painful period of waiting, during which it was perfectly calm, and the air was hot and oppressive. But the sea gave evident signs of the approaching storm by its steady rise into an enormous swell, long hills of glassy water rolling in upon the ship in solemn orderly succession from the westward, conveying in the most unmistakable language to all what a tremendous force was being exerted upon the sea far beyond the horizon. The sky above grew black and near, and there was a strong smell of sulphur in the air. And the mercury in the tube of the barometer fell steadily, palpitating meanwhile in its glass prison as if in sympathy with some disturbance in the atmosphere as yet unfelt by human sense. At last, when it was close upon midnight, the pitchy heavens began to show tiny trickles of light, fairy-like streakings, such as one may see at almost any time by closing the eyes and pressing the fingers on the lids. Then a hot breath of wind, which made every one on deck start and stare in the direction from whence it had come. Another and another, fiercer and fiercer, until in five minutes from that first sultry zephyr the tempest had begun.

It only remained to them now to hold on and endure, hoping in the staunchness of their ship, which was tested to the utmost, and thankful to know that all they could do by way of preparation had been done. For in that gigantic conflict of the elements wherein for a time the wind was so far victor that the sea was held flat as by the pressure of the hand of God, no man might expose himself and live, much less do anything, even if aught remained to be done. Indeed it was difficult to breathe anywhere except shut up within bulkheads, not merely because of the amazing commotion in the air, but because that air was so mingled with water torn from the surface of the defeated sea that it was almost like inhaling water.

But the skipper and his two faithful officers watched compass and barometer with intense scrutiny, noting with the most jealous care how she lay with regard to the wind, how it was hauling, and hoping that the cyclone would at least obey the regular law, and not complicate matters by any recurving owing to their being so far to the eastward. Suddenly the sympiesometer (a more sensitive kind of barometer) began to rise, followed more sedately by the mercury, and the skipper sighed, "Thank God, there's one half of it over anyway." Only the clock warned them that eight hours had passed since the cyclone first struck them, for it was still dark as the pitch lake of Trinidad.

And now the floodgates of heaven opened as the wind slowly eased its awful force, and it was difficult indeed to know whether the vessel was still above water or below it. Moreover, as the wind fell the sea rose, and she began to tumble about in truly horrible fashion, making it a most difficult thing to maintain a position by holding on with all one's strength. And this condition of things grew steadily worse, until it seemed as if the two poor boys on their first voyage would die with fright. Small blame to them. If ever fear is justifiable, and I hold it most certainly is, it is at such a time as this, when sky and sea meet in the utmost outpouring of their powers.

Frank and Johnson felt many qualms but said nothing—it was no time for talking anyhow, but like good sailors they just held on to their patience and hoped for the best.

The wind still dropped, and the sea rose higher and higher. The roar of the storm had died down, but was succeeded by the immense crashing chorus of the thunder and the falling masses of water—it is absurd to call it rain. It was impossible to feel any lightening of anxiety, although the wind had taken off so greatly, because the pressing dark and hideous tumult forebade the uprising of hope. All felt bound and depressed beyond measure, but also mercifully beyond the reach of fear, for they had passed the limit of human capacity for being afraid. But still they held on mechanically as the staunch ship was flung from sea to sea like a tennis-ball between rackets, only with much more irregular motion. And the one idea predominant in all minds but that of the two youngest boys was, "How long can she possibly endure?" As for the top-hamper, that spread of yards and towering masts, they had forgotten it, or if they did remember it for a moment, it was with an incurious detachment of mind as about something which no longer concerned them, over which at any rate they had no control.

It was almost calm, but the infernal tumult was at its height when suddenly there burst upon them, like the crack of doom, the other half of the storm. It struck them with the impact of an impalpable mountain, irresistible, and over she went. All their senses were merged in one effort to hold on wherever they were, and had she then gone down to the bottom quickly I doubt whether any of them would have suffered more than a momentary spasm of pain. But she did not go farther than over on her beam ends, and then almost as suddenly she righted again. And even then the sufferers noted a certain definite change in her movements, a change for the better, but one for which they could not account. However, it was soon evident that the worst was over, and that they were still alive.

And, as the rain and thunder ceased, a dim light began to struggle through the rifts in the pall of driving clouds, revealing to them the reason of the sudden change in the feel of their ship. That amazing blast had made a clean sweep of her masts above the tops, and only a few remnants of what had been a far-spreading entanglement of topsail, topgallant and royal yards, with their accompanying masts, dangled pathetically downward from the deserted lower masts, while the gear, like a drowned woman's hair, was wrapped about and mingled with the remaining wreckage, forming a snarled-up mass which appeared only open to one mode of treatment, namely, that of being chopped clean away. Men thought grimly of their careful labour in furling those sails so securely which had now gone, yards and all, and then as the claims of their life again began to assert themselves, they thought of what lay before them in the bringing of their ship to some place where she might again be made fit to do her work.

The weather rapidly improved, and Captain Jenkins, able to walk his quarter-deck once more, looked sternly at the wreck and said to his mate, "We've got our hands full here, Cope."

The mate shrugged his shoulders and replied, "No doubt of that, sir. But what are you thinking of doing, working back to Mauritius or going on to Anjer? Seems almost a pity to go back now, doesn't it, when we are so well over?"

"Oh," hastily answered the skipper, "I had no idea of Mauritius, might almost as well abandon her at once; she would cost a jolly sight more than ship and cargo are worth by the time the Port Louis folks had picked her bones and we'd got her to Hong-Kong. No, no, we'll go on, anyhow. As soon as ever the boys have had a feed and a smoke, turn to and clear away that raffle o' gear. We'll save all we can of it, for the Lord knows we've little enough to make shift with, and I very much doubt the ability of Anjer to supply our needs. It's never been much since Krakatoa."

So after about an hour's spell, behold all hands toiling like beavers, led by Mr. Jacks and Hansen, who seemed suddenly endowed with the ability to do impossible things, and were seen hanging in the most precarious positions, hacking, shouting, pushing, and infecting everybody with their own feverish energy, the energy of men who had got a task they felt supremely capable of performing, and one moreover entirely after their own hearts. Again and again the skipper thanked his stars he had not lost the second mate at Penarth, for he knew that such a man as this splendid type of seaman was one of the rarest jewels, and literally priceless in an emergency of this kind.

Such was the enthusiasm engendered among the crew by this splendid example that there was no need to enforce labour—every man did his very best, while Frank and Johnson, their young hearts fired by this splendid opportunity of showing how they had profited by the lessons they had learned, worked so hard that it was necessary to restrain them, lest they should forget their limitations and lay themselves up.

The old carpenter, too, who might have been considered by unthinking folks ashore as almost past his work, wrought steadily with his broad axe, adze, and topmaul to fit the jury spars for their service aloft, muttering congratulations to himself all the while that the lower masts had stood the strain and left a good foundation whereon to erect topmasts and topsail yards at least, with which no ship can be considered helpless.

None of them gave a second thought to the grim fact that all of the boats were gone or else driven in like a bundle of slats, either by force of wind or weight of sea; but then your sailor is apt to think little about boats until the necessity comes to use them, and even resents the good rules that make him in a passenger ship handle them periodically to see that they are all in order.

But on the third day of this great work, when they were saying one to another that they had done so well that another couple of days would see them under as good trim as possible—able at any rate to compass four knots an hour with anything like a decent breeze—while they were in the middle of their multifarious activities, the attention of all was suddenly arrested by the appearance of a thin blue spiral of smoke arising from one of the ventilators and lazily curling upward into the blue above. No word was said, but instantly the heads of all on deck were turned towards it, the minds of all traced it to its origin, and the bowels of all began to heave with that indefinable sense of the imminence of an awful danger, a sensation like that upon first experiencing a shock of earthquake.

This pause only lasted a few seconds, and then the clear, quiet tones of the skipper were heard: "Mr. Cope, come aft here a minute."

"Aye aye, sir," replied the mate, mechanically reaching for a wad of oakum and wiping his hands, but without haste, and following the skipper's steady steps into the cabin. As soon as they entered they felt that their worst anticipations were realised—the cargo of stern coal was on fire by spontaneous combustion, for the smoke was filling the cabin.

"Now, Cope," said the skipper quietly, "this is a bad business, especially coming on top of the other, but the first thing is to locate the fire without alarming the chaps. They're pretty good, but this is calculated to put the fear of God into the best of men who cares what becomes of him. You see the hold's full of smoke by the way it's pouring into the cabin, and going down to see is out of the question, so now the only thing to do is to bore through the three hatches, after plugging up all the ventilators, and then lead the monkey pump down the hole that the most smoke comes out of, and try and drown it out. Updraught is what we have to fear most, as long as we can keep it smothered it will only smoulder, and we may drown it; of course, we can't do anything with the gas—as far as that is concerned we must trust to God's mercy. Luckily she's an iron ship. Can you fasten off aloft so as to keep the bit of sail we are carrying safe, and set all hands free to pump for their lives?"

"Oh yes, sir," cheerfully answered Mr. Cope, "a couple of hours at the outside will enable us to carry the fore and main lower-topsails and the lower staysails and spanker. With this breeze she ought to make Anjer in a week like that."

The skipper sighed heavily as if seeing nothing at Anjer but safety for his crew, for there was little hope there of saving his ship, he felt, and that is always the chief concern of every skipper worth his salt. But he only said, "All right, Cope, make all the haste you can to get finished aloft, while Chips and I will see about these hatch-holes."

The absence of any fuss or symptoms of alarm did just what was needed to prevent any undue worry on the part of the men, although they could not help casting an occasional regretful glance to where the boats had been, and it was equally impossible for them to help now and then looking at the spiral of smoke still ascending, a symbol of the most fateful significance. But they worked with the utmost docility, and Frank could not help remarking to Hansen, "What a wonderful adventure we are having, to be sure." Hansen only grunted and looked pityingly at the eager face of the youth apparently so unable to realise the danger of the situation.

Very soon the loose ends had been secured aloft, and the men coming down were called aft to rig the hand-pump, a quaint old machine used for washing decks, but capable of throwing a good stream of water with four hands to the brakes. The skipper and carpenter had found that a much fiercer volume of smoke ascended from the hole they had cut in the main hatch than anywhere else, and, moreover, there, as they well knew, the coal rose nearer to the main deck, being as usual piled amidships for stowage purposes, making the ship easier in a seaway. So with the suction-hose trailing overboard and the discharge-pipe pointed down the small hole bored in the main hatch, the weary task of pumping water into the ship was begun, and before long the escape of steam from various places showed that the incoming water had reached at least a portion of the fire.

Then the most careful stoppage of every outlet was effected, and the skipper said with an air of relief, "Well, the steam will help to choke the fire anyhow, although Heaven knows how much there is of it." Except for this quiet remark to the mate, Captain Jenkins might to all appearance have been dealing with one of the most ordinary incidents of a sailor's career. He felt rather than knew how closely he was being watched by his men, who at a time like this reflect in a remarkable degree the character of their commander.

Now, of course, all work that could be avoided was stopped in order that the labour of all hands might be concentrated upon the one needful thing, subduing the fire. It was found that one watch could manage to keep the pump going and do the steering without undue pressure on the men, while the boys and the officers could do a little aloft in adding some lighter sails to those they had been able to set. So that for two or three days the water was steadily poured into her until she began to settle so low that the captain decided it was dangerous to flood her any more.

And yet the fire was obviously not subdued, for, as soon as the ventilating hole was opened, smoke as well as steam burst forth, and, moreover, the ship felt dangerously hot. However, the weather remained beautifully fine and the sea quite smooth, with steady Trades, before which the waterlogged *Sealark* crept gradually northward, and the crew, released from the pump, were kept busy adding to their makeshift appliances aloft, but without affecting her speed much, she being now so deep in the water.

But for the whole week never a sail did they see. Then there crawled up to them a vessel which had evidently been through a similar stormy experience to their own, for she looked very much as they did aloft. Slowly the new-comer ranged alongside of them, revealing herself as the four-masted barque *Windhover* of London, having lost fore and mizzen topmasts and maintopgallant masts, also a goodly portion of her bulwarks, but having all her boats.

She came near enough to speak through the megaphone, and condolences were duly exchanged, while the new-comer naturally inquired whether the *Sealark* had sprung a leak. When he was told the dread truth he immediately offered one of his lifeboats, for, as he said, "You never know what may happen in a case of that kind, and at present you're very like rats in a trap. Without a boat or anything whatever on deck that you can make a raft of—it's too bad."

So the two cripples were hove to, and very curious they looked, recalling almost the old battle-pictures of ships after an action; while the crew of the *Windhover*, feeling full of sympathy for their unfortunate sea brethren, worked with a will. They did not at all realise how familiarity with the awful danger beneath the feet of the *Sealark's* crew had blunted their sense of its terrors, and so were full of wonder also that all the apparently doomed men should be taking things so calmly.

As soon as the boats were ready, the captain of the *Windhover* paid a visit to the *Sealark*, and was of course warmly welcomed by his brother skipper, who took him below and offered such hospitality as he had at his command. Then the new-comer did the only thing possible, offered to take them all off the ship if Captain Jenkins should feel so inclined, knowing at the same time that were their positions reversed he would never dream of accepting such an offer.

"Thank you very much," said Captain Jenkins, "but I think we'll see her through. I've got as good a crew as a man could wish for, from the mate downwards, and if the worst should come—through your kindness we have now got the means of escape—all I'll trouble you for is that you'll report me at Anjer and see if they can rake up some spare spars for me. I don't want to be detained there any longer than I can help."

"Right you are," replied the skipper; "I'll see to it, and now with all my best wishes I'll bid you so-long and hope we shall meet all square in Hong-Kong. You may be there as soon as I am, unless my coal takes it into its head to combust spontaneously too."

And off he went, having rendered the only assistance in his power. But he could not help looking wistfully back as he regained his ship, and feeling an overwhelming sympathy for that brave little crowd so quietly doing their allotted duty under circumstances so difficult and dangerous.

It is always pleasant to record success, and so I rejoice to say that after eight days of the strong steady suasion of the kindly Trades the look-out at the fore-topmast head of the *Sealark* sighted Java Head, and the next day the good ship crept quietly up to her anchorage at Anjer, still seaworthy and mutely testifying to the faithfulness of those in charge of her. She was immediately surrounded by a horde of touts, all eager to share in the plunder of an unfortunate ship. Men to whom the advent of a vessel in distress is a boon, a feast, an occasion of great rejoicing, people who, however necessary, feed fat upon the misfortunes of others, and whose rapacity knows no limit except the impossibility of getting more.

Very few indeed are the ports of the world into which a ship can enter in need without being immediately the prey of men like this, whose only but all-sufficient excuse is, when they condescend to make any, "that the underwriters can well afford to pay." And indeed in these days of scanty earnings and absence of perquisites, a skipper must needs be made of stern stuff who can resist this, practically the only opportunity he ever gets of "making a bit" by standing in with the gang who are making a great deal.

They anchored without any incident worth recording, and, as soon as ever she was well cleared up, the skipper chose his agent and demanded a gang of labourers to investigate the condition of things below. Off came the main hatches and up shot a dense cloud of smoke, steam, and gas almost like the first ejection from the crater of a volcano. All the Javanese fled aghast to the rail, prepared to dive overboard, and gazed awestricken upon the open mouth of the ship from which she was vomiting the elements she had endured so long.

But after an hour or two it became possible to get below and ascertain the extent of the fire. And it was found that there was still an immense heap of coal forward of the main hatch which had been as yet untouched by the water, and which on being disturbed glowed fiercely. The pump was at once brought into play, and amid blinding smoke and suffocating gas the lively Javanese toiled manfully through a day and night until it began to be evident that the fire was under control. Meanwhile the water was pumped out of the lower hold, where there could no longer be any danger of fire, since she had been practically flooded up to her 'tween-deck beams for three weeks.

It would be sheer waste of words to say how anxious and worried Captain Jenkins was all this time. His first command, surrounded by a gang of foreign harpies who looked upon his ship as their legitimate prey, but could not work their will upon her without his signature, the one vestige of authority left to a captain in a foreign port where there are no accredited agents, and, above all, his high desire to accomplish his voyage, he, like any other man in a similar position, must demand all our sympathies. His men, on the other hand, were quite happy. They felt like conquerors who in the face of fearful odds had succeeded in overcoming the most terrible forces of nature, and were now reaping the rewards of victory.

Especially was this the case with Frank. He literally grew with the occasion, felt proud of his ship, his shipmates, and himself with a grand and legitimate pride, and yet went on learning in the great business of re-rigging the ship and preparing her to resume her voyage. This is no place to talk technicalities, or I would like to tell of the stupendous labours of Mr. Jacks and the crew, all of whom were given over to him to work aloft, while the mate superintended the work of the coolies on deck and below.

Well, in the end the *Sealark* regained her normal trim appearance under the hands of Mr. Jacks and his hard-working crowd, and the captain, chafing with impatience as day succeeded day and the prospect of his leaving seemed as remote as ever, at last began to see a possibility of getting to sea again, where he would be free of those landsharks who made life a burden to him. It is of course impossible in a book like this to give any detailed account of his adventures, every day of which would furnish materials for a most exciting story, but I may go so far as to give his conversation of a few minutes with Mr. Cope when at last the ship was considered ready for sea.

"Cope, I'd rather face the cyclone again than deal for another day with these fellows. They smother me, they make me doubt myself, make me feel that whatever I want to be I am bound to become an infernal thief and liar such as I am sure the majority of them are by choice. They are like the villains

I have met in London and Liverpool, ready to curse or bless anybody and everybody for payment. Yet they have never lost sight of anybody they had a down on, while it was safe they'd do their best to ruin him, or her, it didn't matter which, for their price could always be paid and the payer passed at once from being an unspeakable villain to an angel of truth and, especially, of financial rectitude. I'm choking to get out to sea again, Cope. If I stay here much longer I shall lose all faith in either God or man. It isn't right that we should fight the sea and winds as we do to conquer them only to become the prey of a gang of beach-combers like these, for that's what they are, I don't care what swagger names or offices they put up, they are even less reputable than the pukka beach-comber."

"Never mind, sir," replied Cope, "you have fought the good fight."

"At a price, my boy, at a price," interjected the despondent skipper.

"Anyhow," continued Cope, "we are all right again after as hard a time as a man can have. The owners will have a nice letter to cheer you up in Hong-Kong. But apart from all that, sir, what a good sturdy crowd we've got, haven't we? And those two lads, Frank and Johnson, they'll make splendid officers if they'll only stick to it, I think they're the right stuff."

"Yes, Cope, they're good, I know, but I'm dead tired of the whole thing, and wondering whether the game is really worth the candle or not. I know I'm a bit out of sorts with all these bloodsuckers hanging on to me; perhaps I'll feel better when I get out on the clean sea again. We'll get under-weigh to-morrow morning at daylight, and before any of this nest of liars and thieves are awake we'll be well on our way to where it's clean. Good night."

From all of which it may be inferred that alone among his whole crew Captain Jenkins was despondent, unsatisfied, his victory having brought him no joy. You can see why for yourself. Everybody else who had no thought of financial details, and who when their work was done had nothing else to think of until turn-to time again, was supremely happy. Especially as within certain limits Captain Jenkins had ordered them a free bumboat, that is, fruit and eggs and vegetables and soft-tack for nothing.

And Frank had bought a monkey, a furry gentle thing black as Erebus, but with a pathetic expression upon its furry flat face and in its big eyes that touched him strangely. He had never had a pet before, although often conscious of a strange need which he could not name. It was time that need was supplied, for he was growing up curiously unsympathetic, from the absence of anything or anybody whereon to lavish the affection which is possessed by all of us, but in the absence of the opportunities for its exercise almost certainly dies away, leaving in its place a cold heartlessness and selfishness which is dangerous. From this Jacko came just in time to save

Frank, although it must be confessed that his advent was not altogether an unmixed blessing, seeing that his native predilection for mischief kept most of Frank's shipmates wondering what he would be up to next. But after all he was a healthy stimulant to the activities of the crew, who, after their late strenuous life, were in danger of stagnation.

By this I wish to convey that having got clear of Anjer the wind and weather were so uniformly kind to them as to reduce the absolutely necessary work to a minimum. The navigation of what we always call the China Sea, meaning the Indian Archipelago, after passing through either the Straits of Sunda or Malacca from the westward, is difficult and dangerous, especially for a sailing ship, but the weather is often perfection itself for a week at a time, and so it was now. True, the ship was in a parlous state as regards cleanliness of paint, &c., but her skipper being a just man, could not see the force of harassing his boys with work that the first day of discharging cargo in Hong-Kong would undo.

So all hands had a very easy time, only just doing enough simple tasks to keep the devil out of their minds, as we say. This they all fully recognised and accepted as their due, although, of course, nothing was said upon the subject by anybody. And so the much-tried ship with her doughty crew crept slowly northward through the tortuous ways of the China seas, until one morning there rose before their delighted eyes the towering mass of Victoria Peak, the culmination of the British island of Hong-Kong. It was a triumphant sensation which they experienced then, remembering all the struggle they had waged to this end, followed by deep satisfaction as steering up towards Green Island Pass they received on board the queer slant-eyed pilot, just one hundred and fifty days from Cardiff Roads, a passage which under all the circumstances might be looked upon as highly meritorious.

CHAPTER XI
THE IMMUTABLE EAST

Under the able guidance of this impassive pagan, who merely waved his hands in the direction in which he wanted the ship to go, she was brought gently to her allotted moorings in the splendid harbour, amid the great crowd of cosmopolitan shipping which is the outward and visible sign of this mighty seaport of the Far East. Down went one anchor after another in orthodox style (which beautiful manœuvre I would like to explain, but dare not for fear of being tedious), the sails were clewed up or hauled down, and the deed was done.

"Give the sails a harbour furl, men," shouted Mr. Cope; and lovingly they rolled and patted into regulation shape the great squares of canvas, whose precision of outline when fast owed nothing to painted coverings put on afterwards, but were the hall mark of good seamanship. Then the yards were trimmed and squared, the ropes coiled up, the decks swept, and at four o'clock, "That'll do for to-day, men," sounded gratefully on the ears of the crew, who sauntered towards the forecastle with the air of men who had earned their reward.

In the next berth lay a big Yankee ship, the *Colorado*, of New York, which had come in almost side by side with the *Sealark*. But what an amazing difference in the methods followed on board of the two ships! In the English vessel, an occasional quiet order which was just sufficiently loud to be heard; in the American, a very hurricane of oaths and yells which raged incessantly, no matter how well and rapidly the work was done. Of course it was done well, slipshod seamanship in a Yank being quite unthinkable; but at what a price! Then when the *Sealark's* crew received that consideration from their commander to which they were really entitled, the crowd of the *Colorado* seemed only just to have begun their work. Frank watched, fascinated, the tremendous energy of the mates, the desperate efforts of the men, heard the ghastly chorus of profanity by which the whole work was accompanied.

As I have said, the work on board the *Sealark* ceased at four o'clock, the ship being made snug and harbour-worthy for the night; but on board the

Colorado there was not one moment's respite from labour until everything on board was as if she had been in harbour a month—sails unbent and stowed away, running gear stopped up, cargo gear prepared ready for the morning, and a host of other things, leaving the hapless crew, when they entered the fo'c'sle at eight o'clock, relieved at last, so weary as to be almost unable to crawl when the relief came. I believe in work, and hard work, but a feeling of utter disgust comes over me when I see how men are driven under the flag of the great Republic. Nowhere in the world is the last ounce so mercilessly extracted from poor flesh and blood as it is there, or less concession made to human weakness or limitations.

I said that Frank was fascinated, and with reason, for he could hardly tear himself away from the rail to his supper. But when the second mate sauntered up to him and said, "That's the way to get a ship's work done, my lad; no crawling there," Frank looked quickly round and said, "I see they're smart, sir, but it isn't necessary to work them so long or curse them so hard. The work is not so pressing as all that, surely." The old black scowl came over the second mate's face as he muttered, "You so-and-so lime-juicers don't know what a man is," and turned away.

For which sentiment I cannot help hating him and his like, while fully appreciating their splendid seamanship. The sight not only held Frank fascinated, as I have said, but it fired his blood; and he made a mental vow that whatever happened he would, if ever he had the power, treat his men as remembering that they were made of the same material as himself.

He was drawn from the contemplation of brutality by one of the small boys calling his attention to a sampan, or a Chinese boat, which had stolen up alongside. It was not much bigger than a large rowing-boat, but rising in a graceful curve at the bow, and completely decked over except for a domed cabin aft. In this craft there were obviously three generations—grandfather and grandmother, father and mother, and a family of five children of varying ages, the youngest being a toddles of about three, who staggered about the deck with a big bladder attached to its waist by a stout cord.

The use of this appendage bothered Frank very much, until he saw the tiny creature stumble, and take an involuntary dive over the unprotected side of the boat. As coolly as possible the mother, who was standing at the big steer-oar, lifted a boat-hook from the deck, and hooking the child by the bladder cord as it floated quite safely, hauled it on board, and, giving it a shake, set it on deck to drain, at the same time scolding it in what seemed a very discordant, loudly-sung song.

Meanwhile all the other members of the family were begging with eloquent gestures, pointing to their attenuated bodies and their mouths alternately. Frank went and fetched some bread, and was about to give it to them, when the mate espied him, and calling him said, "Now remember, Frank, you must never give these people anything; if you do, the ship will be surrounded with sampans from morning till night, and there will not only be annoyance but danger from them. There are 30,000 people like that living upon the waters of this harbour, who do not know from whence their next meal will come, and who are consequently pressed so much that they will stick at nothing to get plunder of any kind. They must not go ashore, and every boat is registered and numbered, as you see; so that if a crime is committed they are easily traced, but that is like locking the stable after the horse is gone. The only wise thing to do is to keep them at a distance."

And so saying he mounted the rail, and in a fierce voice with violent gestures made the boat clear off, the head of the family looking at mate and ship alternately with utterly expressionless face, as if nothing in life interested him at all.

"I can't understand," said the mate, turning away, "why they don't make an organised raid some night upon a ship like this, and steal or murder as they like. But I suppose they've got no power of combining for a purpose of that sort, besides having, as a race, a tremendous respect for the law. Hello, here comes the skipper."

He went to the gangway to receive Captain Jenkins, who had been ashore in the agent's smart little launch, and was now returning with a promising little bundle in his hand that said "Letters from home." In five minutes Frank was transported from all his surroundings by the magic of the written word, was oblivious of strange sights and sounds and smells, and actually listening to the well-remembered tones of the dear ones at home.

There was quite an accumulation for him, for his people were wise, and knew how eagerly prized were their letters; so they all wrote to him once a month, and consequently, owing to their long long passage, there were at least a dozen letters. No more getting a word out of Frank that evening, or claiming his attention even for meals. He was perfectly happy, for the letters breathed only love and the calm, even flow of a prosperous life, which he could not help mentally comparing, to its disadvantage, with the stirring times through which he had just passed, or feeling that a special Providence had watched over him in answer to his mother's tender prayers.

I am glad to say that he immediately set about writing a long letter of reply, that is, as soon as he had mastered the contents of his budget. It was boy-like, and glossed over many of the thrilling incidents of the passage in curt, careless fashion; but it must always be remembered to a young man's credit who occupies a position like Frank's, that such letter-writing as he does is pursued under great difficulties in the matter of position and light. There is no comfortable table for him to spread his materials upon, and there are usually many interruptions; so that, when the parents get a good letter, they ought to bear in mind that it means much perseverance against odds.

Next day they commenced to discharge, and this was also a revelation to Frank. For the appliances were of the simplest—just shallow, saucer-like baskets and spades, and a hundred or so sturdy Chinese to handle them. A huge scow-like junk came alongside, a tarpaulin was carefully stretched between her and the ship to catch any falling lumps, and gangways were laid, along which, when once the business was started, there went a never-ending procession of naked men bearing baskets full of coal, which, as they reached the side, they emptied over into the junk, and then returned by another route to where they found full baskets awaiting them. The air was full of coal-dust, the heat was melting, and the noise bewildering.

In the midst of it all stood a spectacled Chinese, a wadded teapot by his side, from which he continually refreshed himself with tiny cups of straw-coloured, tepid tea, as impervious apparently to the discomfort and din of his surroundings, as if he were carved out of wood. Overside the scene was stranger still. There were at least twenty sampans, the occupants of which were diligently engaged in dredging the bottom for such small fragments of coal as, in spite of all care, would occasionally bounce overboard. And these energetic snappers up of unconsidered trifles conducted all their operations amid a deafening uproar of languages that sounded quite uncanny, and made Frank wonder whether such a queer concatenation of sounds could in any possible way serve to communicate thought. In which he was only following a line of fancy trodden by very many before him.

There was, however, one cry which, especially in the evenings and early mornings, resounded over the waters of the harbour and puzzled Frank a great deal. He had considerable difficulty in locating its source, but did so at last. He found that it proceeded from the solitary occupant of a small canoe-like boat that was apparently drifting aimlessly about the bay doing nothing at all.

And then one night there suddenly broke out in the forecastle a furious and exceedingly bloody fight, in which the good, peaceable men who composed the crew were changed into devils incarnate, with a mad lust to rend and tear each other to pieces. The skipper and two mates rushed forward to quell the frightful outbreak, but soon found that they were not dealing with sane men, but with raving lunatics, and were bound to retire and leave them to fight it out, since to persist in the endeavour to separate the warring fiends was only to court destruction themselves. They waited outside, though full of anxiety, and wondered mightily whatever could be the meaning of it all. Drink, of course, but whence obtained, and what kind of drink that could thus change this peaceable crew so entirely?

Neither the skipper nor second mate had ever been to China before, and so they were inclined to believe that the bumboatman employed to supply the crew with fresh fruit, bread, eggs, vegetables, &c. was guilty. But Mr. Cope, who had made one visit to Hong-Kong before, scouted the idea. He said that he had heard that the bumboatmen were above suspicion in that direction, knowing that they would certainly be found out, and when that happened they would forfeit all the money due to them from the crew, for such was the law, besides getting a long term of imprisonment. Mr. Cope, however, could find no reasonable explanation of the source whence liquor could have come.

Then it was that Frank bethought him of the weird cry and the drifting canoe, and going up to the skipper he told him of what he had seen, and suggested modestly that there might here be found some explanation. At that very time, and just as Frank had finished speaking, the cry was heard again, quite softly but clearly, close under the bows. The skipper rushed forrard and nipped over the bows, where he struck a match, held it blazing for a moment, and then extinguished it. There was silence for a moment or two, and then the grating of a boat against the cable below, while a soft voice called up through the darkness, "Wanchee samshaw, Johnny?"

"Yes, yes," hurriedly whispered the skipper, "What thing wanchee for one bottle?"

"You no catchee dolla, my takee shirtee, Climean shirtee good one, shabee?"

"All right, John, I catchee," whispered the skipper, lowering the end of the jib downhaul; "you makee fast one bottle, I bring shirtee chop chop."

And away he went, hurriedly explaining the situation to the two officers, and telling them to get each as big a lump of coal as they could handle and bring it forward to him when he had got a shirt ready. Then the obtained shirt was exchanged for a bottle, but as soon as the latter was safely hauled up the two masses of coal, each weighing at least half a hundredweight, were hurled down through the darkness on top of the purveyor of madness. There was an awful crash and a yell, then all was silence, as the skipper said with a sigh of relief, "I hope there is one villain less in the world." Indeed it seemed so, for their utmost peering through the gloom could not descry a trace of anything, even wreckage.

The bottle was taken aft and opened. Its contents stunk of all the foul things imaginable, while as for the taste, no description of it would be adequate.

"And this was the stuff those unspeakable asses forward have been poisoning themselves with after buying it at such a rate. Well, well!" said the skipper, "the folly of sailors is surely without limit. But, thank God, that infernal devil will never poison a poor fool of a sailor any more."

"Indeed I don't know so much about that," said Mr. Cope. "It's harder to kill a Chinaman than a cat, and I shouldn't be a bit surprised if that fellow isn't about again plying his vile business in a day or two. But at any rate we know now, thanks to Frank's keeping his weather eye lifting, and others are not likely to come along here any more without getting their due."

"Yes," went on Mr. Jacks, "that boy gets smarter and better every day. I never saw a more likely lad, or one that shaped for a first-class seaman more steadily than he does."

"I'll have a talk to him presently," said the skipper; "meanwhile let's go and have a look at those poor fools in the forecastle, they seem to have quieted down a bit now."

So they went forward to the forecastle, and hearing only groans and heavy breathing went in, to find the place a very slaughter-house, reminding one more of a Roman arena after a gladiatorial show than anything else. Fortunately no knives had been used, so that although blood had flowed in a ghastly manner the wounds were only superficial. But the bodies were nearly all naked, the clothes having been torn off them in shreds, beards and hair had been torn out by handfuls, and—but you can imagine what *would* happen if a dozen homicidal maniacs were suddenly turned loose upon one another, and further attempts at description would be disgusting.

Captain Jenkins turned away from the miserable spectacle with a sigh, feeling that he could do literally nothing at present until the fumes of that horrible poison had died out of its victims. But he went and found Frank and thanked him warmly for his help in locating the source of the evil.

Then, as a sudden idea came to him, he led the young man forward and showed him the forecastle, "Look at that, Frank," he said, "and remember it all your life. The poor sailor has many drawbacks to a comfortable existence, but he has none greater than himself. And yet he is much to be pitied. Don't forget this when you come to be in command, as I feel sure you will be; always remember that a sailor, in a ship like this at any rate, needs to be protected against himself in spite of himself, and, if you find a man who is all right, he deserves and should get every encouragement that you can safely give him, and you needn't patronise him, which is of all things the treatment which disgusts him. Now go and turn in, and don't forget that what you have done to-night has saved more trouble and suffering than you have any idea of, to say nothing of the expense to the ship."

And so they parted for the night, Frank feeling at least an inch taller. But when Johnson asked him what on earth the old man had been gassing about for so long and he told him, Johnson replied discontentedly, "Some people have all the blessed luck." As if luck could have anything to do with the matter.

Oh, but she was a sad ship the next day. The condition of the crew was too pitiful for words. Their injuries, severe as they were in many cases, were as nothing compared with the state of their brains and stomachs from the poison. The doctor paid his usual visit in the morning when the forecastle had been cleansed a little and the sufferers had got into their bunks. He gave it as his opinion that, despite the proverbial toughness of the sailor, it would be fully a week before any of them were fit for work again.

The skipper asked if nothing could be done officially to prevent the possibility of such horrors. The doctor shrugged his shoulders, saying, "The policing of this great harbour with its 30,000 of a floating population ready for any deed of darkness which they may do with impunity is hard enough, especially when you remember that one side of it is Chinese territory, and the only thing that can be done is to keep a good look-out. But I admit that all captains that are new-comers should be warned of the possibility of such an occurrence as yours. Which you certainly were not." And he went away, leaving Captain Jenkins both angry and sorrowful, but, with all a sailor's cheery optimism, ready to admit that it might have been a good deal worse.

Fortunately the ship was in very good order aloft, as the crew had been employed there out of the way of the smother on deck since she came in, and therefore the loss of their services was not so much felt. The discharging went on steadily, and the ballast came in natural sequence without any disturbance, so that by the time the crew were all fit again the ship, except for the bending of her sails, was ready for her passage across to Manila, where she was to load hemp for New York.

But as soon as it was evident that she was ready for sea, those men, only newly risen from their bunks of pain, came aft and demanded the usual twenty-four hours' liberty and a month's wages. This presented a cruel problem to Captain Jenkins. He was no admirer of the system by which alone among workmen the sailor is kept out of his money for a period sometimes of two years, and then, getting it all in a lump, is liable to be robbed of it in a lump, but he saw a great danger ahead now. These men were obviously unfit to be trusted, for, if he was any judge, he felt sure they would not profit a bit by the awful lesson they had received.

But he felt bound to make the attempt, so he said, "Now, men, I am quite aware that a day's liberty and some money to spend is due to you by the usual custom, and if you are bent upon having it I don't feel justified in driving you into any foolishness by refusing it. But you know very well how ill you have all been through that filthy liquor you bought so dearly. Now the same kind of stuff is obtainable ashore, and if it drives you mad as it did before, you'll get locked up and have a very bad time, while I shall lose the services of as good a crew as I've ever had. Don't you think you'd better wait until we get to Manila and have your liberty there? You'll have had more time to get thoroughly well."

The two Britons at once growled out a reply that they wanted their liberty, and the skipper, looking round upon the rest of them, saw only sullen insistence upon their right in every face, so, angrily, but feeling deeply sorry for the foolish fellows at the same time, he said, "Very well, then, the starboard watch can go ashore to-morrow, and the port watch the day after, Saturday. Come to me in the morning, you starboard watch men, and I'll give you your liberty money."

The only reply was a series of satisfied grunts, conveying the idea that he had tried to bluff them out of their rights, but he had found he couldn't do as he liked with them, and so on. So they parted, and the skipper returned to his cabin and held a consultation with his officers on the immediate probability of their having to get a new crew of such wastrels and loafers as Hong-Kong usually affords. Nothing could be done, though, but hope that the men would come aboard again not more than ordinarily drunk; in their then surly condition of mind evidently too much to hope for.

Why prolong this pitiful part of my story, the starboard watch went ashore the next morning in the best rig they had, and although they certainly did drop a few of their hard-earned dollars in the curio-shops, it was not long before they got to the bad end of the Queen's Road, and had commenced an orgie which finally landed them all in the lock-up in a most deplorable condition, the more so because their stamina was still very low.

The news was brought off to the skipper, who received it with an outburst of keenest sorrow, and immediately called the port watch aft to hear what had become of their shipmates. And so far from it making any favourable impression upon them, it seemed as if it only spurred their appetite for such fearful joys, and a spokesman stepped forward saying, "I s'pose you ain't goin' to stop the port watch's liberty because the starboard watch 'as got into chokey, sir?"

"Since you ask me," responded the skipper, "that is just what I am going to do. As I told you yesterday, I don't want to lose a good lot of men like you by giving in to your foolishness, and until I see whether I can get the starboard watch back there's no beach for you, make up your mind to that. You're just a pack of fools and idiots, and must be treated as such."

"All right, sir," answered Micky, "that's what you say; what I say is that I don't do another hand's turn aboard this hooker until I have had my liberty, and my watchmates say the same; don't ye, boys?"

A fierce growl of assent clinched this outburst, and, turning sharply round, the watch went forrard into the fo'c'sle.

I must digress for a moment to point out that such an occurrence as this was by no means uncommon in the days I am writing of, twenty years ago, and is certainly not unknown to-day. It serves to show the peculiar character of the "deep water" sailor, and the difficulty of dealing with him. The *Sealark* was certainly not a bad ship, and the crew were, as we have seen, very good men, but whether it is the sight of land and the thought of its allurements, a sense of irresponsibility, and an impatience of the long confinement, or some such kindred feeling, I know not; I can only say that, incredible as it must appear to landsfolk, men will and do act as I have described without any provocation or other inducement than the prospect of a debauch. And nothing is more likely to stir up this tendency to revolt than the stoppage of liberty for any cause whatever.

The next morning the skipper went ashore, having first ascertained definitely that the port watch were firm in their determination to do nothing more unless they had their liberty, he being equally firm in his refusal to grant it to them. He interviewed the authorities, who informed him that his men had been so savage and had so severely injured several Sikh policemen that fines would not satisfy justice, and they must be imprisoned. Then he laid the case of his mutineers on board before them, and it was decided that he must take a posse of police on board and put the mutineers in irons if they still persisted in their refusal and he was determined to take them to sea. So he returned on board with the police, and the foolish men, after being almost implored to be sensible for once, and being told of the condition of their companions, and still remaining obstinate, were ironed and placed in the after part of the 'tween decks with all sorts of evil passions raging in their hearts at what they considered the gross and shameful injustice of their treatment.

Then he had to go ashore again, taking with him the effects of the men who were in prison, go through all the formality of paying them off after duly deducting the charges he had been put to, and then go and hunt up some more men. But here he found a difficulty, men appeared to be very scarce, and in the end he was fain to be content with eight Lascars, natives of India, who had been landed as shipwrecked men from a sailing ship. He was distressed about this, but his duty to his owners in the matter of getting the ship away compelled him to leave no stone unturned for that purpose.

In the result he sailed on Monday morning with his swarthy recruits doing very well, and the second mate was duly warned not to be too severe in handling them, while the stubborn men down below aft, with a spirit that nothing seemed able to quell, munched their bread and drank their water of affliction and made no sign of being discontented therewith. The ship, being in ballast, was fairly tender, and so he (the captain) did not dare to carry a press of sail to the strong breeze blowing, even had he been efficiently manned.

But a smart passage was quite out of the question anyhow, and he felt a glow of satisfaction as he saw how capable were his Lascars and how ardent his two senior apprentices. The two younger boys, unhappily, were neither of them at all adapted for a sea life, and regarded every opportunity afforded them for acquiring practical knowledge as a hardship and an additional outrage upon their already offended sensibilities. Which was a serious loss to them as well as an annoyance to other people.

So the passage across progressed most favourably for the willing workers, and Captain Jenkins' hopes rose high that he should after all be able to make so successful a voyage as would justify his appointment, a matter that is usually, or was usually, a serious consideration for every new-fledged skipper in those days. And to crown his satisfaction, the day before they sighted Luzon the mate came to him and said that the recalcitrant watch confined in the 'tween decks had at last weakened, and expressed a wish to see the skipper.

He went down at once, and addressing them said, "Well, men, I hear you have something to say to me. What is it you want to say?"

There was an uneasy movement among the pathetic little group, and then the young Welshman, who had been the leader of the party of revolt, said, "Beg ye pardon, cap'n, we're ready to turn to."

The skipper waited a few moments in case there should be anything else, and then replied, "I'm glad to hear it. Don't think I've had any pleasure in seeing you suffer as you must have done, but if you had gone ashore and behaved as the men of the starboard watch did you'd be far worse off than you are. Now, I want to make a bargain with you. If you'll only go back to your work, and behave as you did on the passage out, I promise you that neither my officers nor myself will make any difference in our treatment of you from what you received then, treatment that you said you were perfectly satisfied with. More than that, although I have of course entered all this affair up in my official log, I promise you it shan't be mentioned again or charged against you. But you must not think of going ashore at Manila, and you must treat these Lascars properly whom I have had to engage instead of the starboard watch, and who have behaved splendidly. I've put them all on the starboard side of the fo'c'sle so that you needn't mix, but I will have them treated like men, for they are quite worthy of it. Is it a bargain?"

"Yes, sir," was the simultaneous answer. Whereupon the skipper, raising his voice, shouted, "Mr. Cope, bring the key of these irons. The port watch is resuming duty."

So for once a difficult and dangerous situation was ended in a way entirely satisfactory to all concerned. Alas! the causes where such temporary aberrations of intellect on the part of our sailors have led to widespread misery and awful crime have been only too common. And most of their horrors might have been averted if only those in command had been fully competent and firm. In such a case weakness is a crime, but few there be among men who are judicially convinced of this most fundamental fact or believe that justice impartially administered is the truest mercy; or indeed know what justice is. But I must not pursue this subject further. I would not have trenched upon it now but to show how entirely good was the schooling my hero was receiving thus early in his sea career, as I hope I have shown how capable he was of acquiring the same.

Now all was peace and satisfaction on board the *Sealark*, for the skipper gave orders that the released watch should be furnished with an extra good meal before resuming duty—well he knew how gratefully it would come to men who had been champing the dry biscuit which used to be the sole bread of the sailor. And when they came on deck in the afternoon, eager to take hold again, glad to feel the fresh breeze blowing upon them, and glad also to sniff the briny air, they were delighted to get the order from Mr. Jacks to make sail.

They sprang to his call, giving him as much pleasure as his saturnine nature was capable of feeling, for he, like many others of his class, had a positive hatred of niggers, as he called them all without distinction, and preferred the rowdiest, most undisciplined crowd you could find anywhere to a gang of willing, subservient dark men, who had to be pushed and pulled and handled generally like a flock of sheep by a shepherd without a dog. The chief officer, on the other hand, was quite contented with his docile crowd, who not merely did the best they were capable of, but were really good specimens of the seafaring Indians, whose capacity is always highly spoken of by those who have had the opportunity of commanding them.

Only twenty-four hours afterwards the good ship *Sealark* sailed into the bay of Cavité with as favourable wind and weather as could possibly be desired, and anchored off the old city of Manila amid a goodly company of sailing ships of all nations, and one Spanish steamer. Here she lay in the most comfortable quarters, except for the fact that, with the well-known carelessness and freedom from provision on the part of the Spanish authorities, she was left alone for the remainder of the day, until her skipper had almost fretted himself into a fever, knowing well that he dare not go ashore until the authorities had given him permission. But some men are like that, great emergencies find them prepared and able, little things get on their nerves, irritating them almost beyond endurance.

I feel, however, that of late I have been letting my favourite slip into the background too much. He has been accorded his proper place in the scheme of things though, occupying as he does an entirely subordinate position in the ship, having a minor part to play, and although playing it extremely well, not being of any supreme importance to any one except his own immediate family and himself. Fortunately Frank was one of those well-balanced youths who was not always dwelling upon his position and wondering whether other people thought as well of him as he deserved. And this freedom from introspection stood him in splendid stead both at this time and afterwards, saving him much mental trouble.

As regards his actual duties, I doubt whether he had ever been so happy in his life. For the skipper had rigged a boat with a suit of sails with that loving care that only a good sailor bestows upon a pet hobby. Having made her complete, he asked Frank and Johnson whether either of them knew anything about handling a boat under sail, and Frank, who had been taught at Lytham, after waiting for Johnson's denial, modestly said he thought he would be able to do so now, having done it before he came to sea.

So the skipper, to his intense delight, gave him charge of the boat, with the two junior apprentices to teach also, and set him free of all ship work whatever. It is a good long distance from the anchorage off Manila into the "Canash," as sailors will persist in calling the carenage, and sometimes there is a very strong breeze, necessitating three reefs, but Frank rose to the occasion and, like a veteran boatman, handled the craft of which he had suddenly been made commander. Moreover he drilled those two slack youngsters ruthlessly, making them dress neatly, keep themselves clean, and practised them at rowing until they behaved themselves in the boat as if they had an object in life.

Now there may be better ways of making a boy self-reliant and resourceful than giving him a boat to handle under sail where he is likely to meet with bad weather occasionally, but I do not know of them. And if in addition the boy is passionately addicted to the sport, the rapidity with which he will acquire those qualities to which I have alluded, and others, is amazing. The beauty of boat-sailing is that the novice there learns that difficult art of feeling the direction of the wind, that impalpable force which means so much to the sailing craft in proportion to her size.

Hitherto, of course, Frank had been obliged to gather what little knowledge he possessed of how to trim the yards to the wind by what the second mate did while he was at the wheel. Now he was learning practically, finding out how when he jammed her up into the wind she drifted crabwise to leeward, and how he who was not too greedy of stealing to windward, and never let his craft shake a stitch, was sure, so long as he was not lavish, and let her swagger off the wind, to get to windward of those would-be smarties who were always fancying they could reverse the laws of mechanics, and imagining that they could outpoint the wind.

Nor was this all. He learned here by practice how the trim of a vessel affects her sailing powers, a law which applies equally to the ship's boat under sail and the 3000-ton four-master; learned how to dispose of his crew of two to the best advantage, and to study the effect that even their slight weight had upon the weatherly qualities of his boat or her speed with a free wind. Also he learned to command; to give no unnecessary orders, but to have such orders as he did give carried out instanter, or else to visit with condign punishment the slack offender.

But there is no doubt that he was heavily handicapped by the character of the two boys placed under his charge. They did nothing willingly. The only thing that appealed to them was fear of a punching from him, or of being reported to the skipper. Ideas of honour, truth, or honesty they had none, and Frank, who could not understand them at all, had to watch them like a warder watching convicts, or, when the boat was waiting at the bund in the Canash for the captain, to exercise constant vigilance lest they should run away into some of the filthy native quarters and get into serious trouble.

By all of which I do not mean to suggest that Frank was anything of a prig or a prude. He was essentially a manly boy, with a high sense of trustworthiness, and while, if he were on liberty with fellows of his own class and age, he would doubtless kick up his heels like a young colt in a meadow, yet when in a position of responsibility he was as sternly bent upon doing his duty to the best of his ability as any man old enough to be his father. Of course captain and officers noted this, and enjoyed it quietly, but after the manner of their kind said nothing, only occasionally showing by their actions how much they trusted him. And this only on his second voyage. True they were long voyages, and the circumstances highly educational, but still we must recognise the rapidity with which a lad of Frank's type will rise, given fitting occasion.

The time spent by the *Sealark* in Manila was almost idyllic in its peace and simplicity. The weather was all that could be desired, the men were most tenderly handled by way of compensation for their enforced abstinence from the dubious delights of what sailors always term "the beach"; and owing to the complete division of the white portion of the crew from the Lascars, there was no friction there either. True, they had never yet been called to work side by side in a position of danger or emergency, but in the daily work of the ship harmony reigned. The ballast was discharged by native labourers, and the hemp began to arrive all in most leisurely fashion, for when did ever a Spaniard hurry except to fight.

But the chief thing was that no trouble ensued from either end of the ship; and when at last the flag was run up to show that the last bale of hemp was rammed into its place, and all that now remained was to carry it to New York, although some of the white men forward did certainly look longingly at the shore, there was no word of grumbling at the inevitable decision of the skipper that no leave should be granted. Johnson growled consumedly, telling Frank what a shame he thought it that his junior should be so privileged, just because he possessed a little knowledge of boat-sailing; but Frank speedily appeased him by repeating his asseverations of the absolute unattractiveness of the place, as far as he had been able to see it. Besides, the cholera was raging, and it would have been constructive murder to send fellows ashore on liberty in such a reeking hole.

Therefore, without any difficulty whatever, behold the *Sealark* at daybreak on a lovely Monday morning getting under weigh for her long long passage, her crew singing lustily at the windlass brakes, but without much concord, because the Lascars could not savvy English singing, and yet would try to assist, with the strangest and most unmusical results. The wind blew fair for the passage down the bay, and the men, if not exactly satisfied, were at least resigned to what they considered their loss of the pleasures (?) that Manila could afford. And such good progress did they make that before dusk they had passed out between the heads of the great bay, and saw the island of Luzon fade away like a huge blue-black cloud in the dim and indefinite distance. They got a fine offing, then the wind faltered and died away to a dead calm. The vessel lay listlessly rolling upon the black expanse of waters under a sky of deepest violet, while the stars shone down upon the unreflecting waters like pin-points of white-hot metal without a twinkle.

Then a strange transformation took place in that dark, placid sea. It began to be streaked with greenish lambent light in ridges, and little pools of glare appeared to rise from the inscrutable depths, so uncanny that it seemed impossible to give them the name of light. There was also a faint suggestion of rippling sound, as if the silken surface of the ocean were being disturbed by sudden currents. This extraordinary glare grew in intensity, until the awed observers noticed that the lustre of the stars paled to a dead white, and the beautiful violet of the sky, with its soft suggestions of after-glow, became of a velvety blackness, such as those who sail in far northern seas are wont to associate with the middle of the auroral arch.

Then through and through the growing whiteness of the sea there began to run bands of brighter light, that marked the passage of the sea creatures as they came and went in their never-ending quest for food. And occasionally a series of ripples, untraceable to any cause, would break against the vessel's side, lighting it up with a ghostly glare, and reflecting upon the faces of the onlookers with something of the same effect which may be observed in a darkened room from the flare of burning spirit in a dish. This wonderful appearance of the ocean, which is known by the entirely inadequate name among sailors of a "milk sea," lasted about four hours, and then passed away as suddenly as it had come, with no atmospheric disturbance following it except that there was a gentle breeze sprang up from the northward, which gradually freshened into a wind that carried the good ship along at the rate of five knots an hour directly on her homeward course.

And now, as I have the interests of my young readers at heart, I must pass very rapidly over the easy, eventless course of the next fifty days. They were easy days, for the winds blew generally fair if light, and the passage through the Sunda Straits, except for one terrific thunderstorm, was unmarked by any difficulty. The crew were contented, not too hard worked, but still kept fully employed during the watch on deck in the daytime, and the upper gear of the ship was put in as good repair as was possible to conceive of, the white men doing all the sailorising, sail-mending, &c., and the Lascars doing all the cleaning, scraping, &c., which demands not so much manual skill as patience and a complete indifference as to the nature of the work the man is engaged upon, an indifference which it is hard to find among men who put their brains into their work, as good sailors should.

So that there was absolutely nothing worth chronicling throughout the passage of the Indian Ocean, and even getting round the Cape was unattended by anything more exciting than a strong wind, not amounting to a gale. The only fact that I am obliged to record is that Captain Jenkins took it into his head to invite Frank and Johnson into the saloon in the second dog-watch to study navigation, and was immeasurably surprised to find that they knew the theory of it almost as well as he did. So he set them to practise with the sextant and chronometer, until, as he declared, they were as well able to navigate a vessel as he was.

CHAPTER XII
FRANK GETS HIS OPPORTUNITY

I hope I have made it clear to my readers that Frank, although now barely seventeen, was a fine specimen of a young man both in physique and in morale or mind. For sheer love of his profession he had learned all that there was to learn about it as far as his opportunities went, and above all he had acquired the habit of self-reliance, which is a mighty factor in advancement at sea. For no matter how clever the man is in theory, if, when the time comes to act, he is ever looking round for some one else to rely upon, has a certain and deep-rooted distrust of himself, that man is debarred from obtaining an early command, or if he does obtain it, he generally loses it painfully soon, because he cannot trust himself.

Of course practice is essential to prove theory, however certain we may be of the theory, and Frank as yet had only been able to prove his learning in minor things, such as his boat-handling, his steering, his watching the trimming of the sails, and comparing his working of the ship's position with the skipper's when he and Johnson had been allowed to take and work up observations of the sun, moon, and stars. But in spite of his limitations he was far above the average of his years; he already had that steadfast outlook upon the world of his profession, that fearless grasp of its details that go to make up the complete seaman even in these so-called degenerate days, when conditions have so changed that we may, and do, find men of the highest education and refinement in charge of our merchant ships, and especially steamships.

However, I must not now spend more space in describing Frank's mental and physical condition, as I need to get on with the consequences of their high development. The *Sealark* rolled comfortably along up the pleasant stretches of the south-east Trades, with all hands busily engaged in the commonplace duties of painters and house-decorators.

It was an easy, happy time. Captain Jenkins was far too genuine a man, and also far too just, to keep his men out of their honest watch and watch in the senseless Yankee custom. He hated the sight of those dazzlingly white bulwarks, shining black topsides, and glistening spars, knowing how much human agony it represented of absolutely useless and grotesque brutality practised by armed, well-fed officers, upon cowed, bruised, and demoralised men, such as was the rule in the "smart Yankee fliers." So all hands were happy, cleansed and painted the white work, scraped and varnished the bright work, and did all those minor things that go to make a ship look beautiful, with a meticulous care and pride in her appearance that was quite absurd when you come to look at it, since probably not one of those poor sailors would be in her again either next voyage or afterwards.

She glided by St. Helena with its many memories; by Ascension, that naval rock which is borne upon the books of the Admiralty as if it were a man-of-war; on, on, gently, certainly, and almost unknowingly across the line until, in 7° N., the faithful south-east wind faltered at last and left them to wallow in calms for a day or two, watching the dank sea-grass on her bottom spread like a dead woman's hair as she rolled listlessly on the oily swell. There was little really left to do by this time in the decoration and smartening of the ship internally—that is to say, on deck and aloft, but outside she looked rusty and unkempt, and Mr. Cope cast longing eyes upon his pots of black paint, imagining how splendid a thing it would be if he could only complete his work by spreading them upon her outside. For although it may sound trivial to the ordinary reader, the appearance of his ship to others is a very serious, and, in fact, an all-important matter in the eyes of a good seaman. And when you come to consider it, rightly so, for it reveals the character of those who have had charge of her.

But before anything could be done in the matter of external painting, the pleasant north-easterly breeze, the first breath of the Trades, came down upon them, freshened, and in three or four hours from their first feeling it they were bowling merrily along on the starboard tack "full and bye" for New York. The easy home stretch of their voyage, unless indeed they met with abnormal weather in the Gulf Stream, had begun. Frank was already looking forward with pleasurable anticipation to his visit to America's greatest city, the second greatest in the world, and half wondering to himself how it was that he did not feel annoyance at the thought that he was not bound home direct, as Johnson did.

The latter young man was dragged on by the sheer force of Frank's example, but, as he often said, he had no real love for the profession, and if a chance offered as soon as he was out of his time, he would be content with a very subordinate position ashore rather than ever go to sea as a sailor again. He, like so many others, had discovered too late that he had made a leap in the dark, had mistaken his vocation, could take no pride in his calling despite its many disabilities, difficulties, and dangers, and consequently would never make a *good* sailor, and would only swell the ranks of the passable and disappointed ones.

The days now sped rapidly on as the ship, with every stitch set and drawing, made splendid progress across the Trades, with the wind steadily strengthening as she made northing. But she was barely clear of the tropics when the weight of the wind increased so much that they were fain to reduce sail, much to Captain Jenkins' disgust, the wind being nearly due east, and consequently allowing him to make his course good going free. He hung on as long as he could, but was gradually compelled to shorten down until the *Sealark* was tumbling about in a most tremendous sea, hove to under a patch of tarpaulin in the mizzen rigging; and Frank, vivid as were his recollections of the cyclone, felt as if he had never till now realised the deep, steadfast malignity of wind at the height of its power. For it was not squally, its force was persistent, massive, terrible, having in its roar a note of doom.

But yet there was an amelioration of the conditions as compared with the lurid horrors of the cyclone. It was light, and often the sky was quite clear until, with a speed that was appalling to witness, a mass of cumulous cloud would hurtle across the ether, torn into a thousand fantastic shapes in its passage. And rage the gale never so furiously, rise the sea never so high, the tiny pretty petrels, Mother Carey's chickens, still flitted unconcernedly over the mighty corrugations of the deep, even nestling to all appearance in the most perfect confidence under the over-curling head of some awful billow as if it were a shelter from the fury of the storm. And though I suppose he should by this time have lost such a boyish illusion (alas that we should ever lose them), he could not help feeling a renewed confidence in the successful issue of the great fight between ship and sea on witnessing the easeful security manifested by those wee birds.

Three days that gale blew, then died away to a gentle series of "cat's paws," which failed to steady the ship in the still gigantic upheavals of the so lately tormented deep. One other vessel was in company with them some five miles distant, and as she was behaving strangely to a seaman's eye, backing and filling and manifesting all the motions of an unmanageable vessel, Captain Jenkins used all his endeavours to get nearer to her. But owing to the lightness and variableness of the wind he was only able to approach sufficiently close by nightfall to make sure that from some cause or another she was really at the mercy of wind and wave. Her masts were intact, and so were the yards, but from them there dangled long streamers as of sails blown away and running gear flying adrift. She was a barque of apparently the same size as themselves, and setting fairly deep in the water, in great contrast to the *Sealark*, which being loaded with hemp was in excellent trim, not down to her marks by a long way.

A very careful watch was kept on her all night, during which the weather was almost perfectly calm. But now and then a light air would come along, which was utilised immediately to get nearer to this mysterious ship, and with such good effect that about two hours before daylight they were almost within hailing distance of her. She showed no sign of life in response to repeated shoutings through a speaking-trumpet, nor was there a light visible anywhere on board of her. Intense curiosity was manifested by all hands in the mystery, so much so that the watch going below at 4 A.M. could not sleep, but sat anxiously awaiting the dawn.

This, however, must not be put down to any philanthropic desire to save life or to assist distressed fellow-seamen, ready as they all would have been to do their utmost in such a cause, but because every man on board was imbued with the idea that she was a derelict, or an abandoned vessel, still manageable and likely to afford her salvors a rich reward. Such golden prizes are, of course, far more usually the prey of the steamboat man, for obvious reasons, but still the sailing-ship men do occasionally get a look in, and the present encounter promised well at any rate.

At last the glorious dawn flushed the whole sky with rosy light, the great sun leaped into the firmament, and the lonely barque was fully revealed in all her pathos of abandonment only about five hundred yards away. There is no inanimate object in the world that seems to demand our sympathy so imperatively as a deserted ship at sea. She is so helpless, all her powers are so utterly unavailable, she is a gigantic, unburied corpse, terrible, obstructive, dangerous, yet full of deprecation, as if she would implore the crowning mercy of destruction before she has become potent for harm to her still man-energised sisters passing by. And this ship was of the saddest class, for she had obviously been abandoned so short a time ago, most probably in the very last gale; everything about her except the shreds of her destroyed, wind-riven sails dangled from yards and stays, and entangled in the rigging seemed to ask piteously why she had thus been left to encounter the ocean unaided, unguided, alone.

No sooner had she become fully visible in all her pathetic helplessness than the captain gave orders to get the boat out, an order which was obeyed with the utmost alacrity, so much so that one might have imagined it to be a matter of life and death. As soon as she was in the water, the skipper and four hands went off to the derelict, passing under her stern and noting her name, the *Woden* of Stavanger. She was manifestly an English-built vessel of the best type, composite, that is, with an iron frame and hardwood skin, with wonderfully good-looking rigging, not at all neglected-looking; indeed she appeared to have only recently changed hands, as the word "London" was plainly visible under Stavanger, and she had not yet shipped a windmill pump, the distinguishing mark of all Norwegian and Swedish sailing vessels.

The derelict.

The skipper climbed briskly on board by the aid of one of the loose ends which trailed over the side, and looking about him was struck with the small amount of damage which appeared to have been done to her. True, several panels of the house on deck were smashed in, the front of the full poop was also damaged, and she looked as if her decks had been swept continuously by heavy seas for a long time, but she was very far from presenting the appearance of the usual derelict ship. Finally, and presenting the most puzzling problem of all, her three boats, obviously all she carried, were in their places on the skids, the biggest of them having her bottom stove completely in as if by a gigantic sea.

Below, or in the cabin, there were the usual poor signs of occupation common to Scandinavian ships, which are never given to luxury in any form, and from the presence of food in a still eatable condition, it was certain that she had not been abandoned for a longer period than two or three days. The men's quarters confirmed the idea, there was nothing alive on board except the rats, although how or why the crew had gone was a profound mystery. Finding the sounding-rod, the skipper tried the well. There was a depth of four feet of water in her, which afforded no reason why she should have been left.

After a few moments of intense thought, Captain Jenkins made up his mind what to do, and with an air of relief went straight to the captain's cabin, noted that the chronometer, an eight-day one, was still going, and finding the ship's papers, saw that she was from Tonala, Mexico, bound to London with a cargo of mahogany. A shade of wonder crossed his mind as to why she had none of it on deck, as is usual, but that was so trifling a matter as compared with the main problem that he did no more than note it. Then, jumping into the boat, he returned to the *Sealark*.

As soon as he reached the deck of his own ship he called his two officers to him and said, "Now, here's a prize worth making a big effort to secure. I think we can, and we ought, to secure it, if we have anything like decent luck. It's not too late in the year to expect middling fine weather, in spite of that tremendous snorter of a gale we had the other day. I propose that you, Jacks, take charge of her with your watch of white men, if they'll go, that is, and make the best of your way home with her to London. We'll work our way under easy canvas with the Lascars to New York. What do you think?"

Seeing that Mr. Cope remained silent with a somewhat discontented look on his face, the second mate replied, "I'm ready and glad of the chance, if you can spare me that youngster, Frank. I've watched him carefully for a long time now, and I feel sure that he can be trusted to keep a watch, and as for navigation, I've found that he's a jolly sight better at it than I am."

"Ah," murmured the skipper, "that wants thinking about. However, we'll call 'em all aft and see. Mr. Jacks, call all the white men aft, there is a Lascar at the wheel."

The order was given and obeyed with exceeding promptness, all the white men striding up to the quarter-deck, and the four lads gazing wistfully in the background.

"Now, men," said the skipper quietly, "there's a ship and cargo there that's worth, at the lowest estimate, £15,000. And if we can get her safely to her port, which is London, since her own crew has entirely disappeared, we'll get two-thirds of her value as salvage, say £10,000, which will mean more money than we could earn in several years of hard work. It will be a big job and a hard job for you white chaps, only six or seven of you altogether with Mr. Jacks here, to get her to London, but its like has been done before, indeed harder jobs than this. Anyhow, if you are willing to take this job on, I am willing to risk getting our own ship to New York with Mr. Cope, the bo'sun, the carpenter, and the Lascars. You can take the cook, too, if he'll go. What do you say?"

There was not the slightest ambiguity about their answer. In fact their eagerness was almost pathetic to witness. For the average sailor in ships of the *Sealark* type welcomes almost anything as a relief to the monotony of his life, a monotony that would not exist to a thoughtful, observant man with books to read and facilities for reading them, but does certainly press with iron ruthlessness upon most men of the sea during long passages.

"All right," responded the skipper cheerfully, "now go and get your dunnage together as quick as you can, we don't want to dawdle away this fine-weather slant."

The men rushed forward with the utmost alacrity to obey, while the skipper called Frank to his side and said kindly, "Frank, my lad, would you like to go with Mr. Jacks? He has said that he would rather have you than any one else in the ship to be his relief. You'll be able to keep a watch, and it will be grand practice for you. But if you have any scruples about going, only say so. Or if you think your people would not like you to take the risk. Although, I am bound to say, that I think there will be no more risk in her than there will be here."

He paused a moment, and Frank, his eyes sparkling and his whole frame quivering with delightful excitement, cried, "Oh, Captain Jenkins, I feel it will be the chance of my life! I am *so* glad to go, I can't tell you. I would have begged you to let me if you hadn't said anything about it, but I felt sure you would. I'm immensely thankful to you, sir. Shall I run and pack up, sir?"

The skipper merely nodded, for his heart was full as he noted the eager joy in the dear lad's face, and saw how whole-hearted he was in the matter. And a fervent hope filled him that nothing would happen to mar or stop so promising a career.

The next couple of hours were tremendously busy ones, for two or three trips had to be made between the ships before all was ready. It was found that she was exceedingly poorly provisioned, but she had plenty of water and spare sails; in fact she was fairly well equipped for any moderate passage, except that her stores of all kinds were poor and scanty. By dint of hard work, however, midday saw all the necessary transhipments made, the chronometer had been compared, and two or three sails, just sufficient to give her steerage-way to the light south-westerly breeze which was just springing up, were bent and set. Then the flag was found and hoisted, dipped three times, and the two ships drew slowly away from each other, one for London and the other for New York. By nightfall, the breeze having increased, they were hull down apart.

And now we must leave the *Sealark* to pursue her legitimate voyage towards America with her largely reduced crew, and follow Frank's fortunes in the *Woden*. The first few hours on board were of furious toil, for, fine though it was, that part of the ocean is proverbially unstable in its weather, and they were liable at any hour to find a gale beginning. So that they all worked their hardest to try and get the running gear in its place and fit for service, and also, a far heavier task, to get sufficient sail bent to take full advantage of the present slant of wind. So hard did they work that when, amid much astonishment, eight bells (midnight) was announced, all hands, though feeling desperately weary, realised gratefully that as the result of their toil the *Woden* was once more fit and ready to be handled, and that they might safely take a little rest.

So Mr. Jacks, having previously ordered the cook to prepare as good a meal as possible, called his little crew together, numbering five, not counting the man at the wheel and the cook, or seven all told. He then divided them into two watches, taking himself two hands and the cook, and appointing the other three men, two Scotchmen and a Finn, as the starboard watch.

"And now, men," he said, "Frank here is going to stand the watch, and I want you to remember that although he is young he's a clever fellow, and fully capable of handling the ship, besides knowing all the navigation necessary. So in spite of his youth I hope you'll all do your best for him and yourselves, and I feel sure we shall rub along splendidly. The grub isn't up to much, but we'll all fare alike and do as well as we can on it. Now you, Bill and Tom, of my watch, go and get some grub as soon as you can, so as to let the watch below go to sleep. I'll go down and relieve August at the wheel."

Then turning to Frank he said, "Tell the cook to bring something aft for us as soon as he has given the chaps theirs. You don't want to waste any time in getting to your bunk. When you're as old as I am you'll wonder how people can sleep as they do."

When at 4 A.M. Frank heard Mr. Jacks' gruff voice calling him to rise, he sprang up as usual, but his brain was in a tangle of conflicting recollections. But as he dragged on his clothes, one fact began to separate itself from the rest—responsibility. And it was with a novel sense of trepidation and a certain diffidence and distrust of his own powers that he hurried on to the poop, and approaching the *captain* said, "Good morning, sir."

"Good morning, Mr. Brown," replied the skipper pleasantly, without the slightest suspicion of sarcasm, and Frank felt a glow of satisfied ambition pervade his whole frame. It did more, that simple little salutation, to nerve him for his duty and to dispel his distrust than any long address could have done. But the skipper went on to say, "Now, Frank, don't be afraid of yourself. I'm not afraid for you. I've watched you close ever since our first unfortunate meeting, for a long time trying to find fault with you, and you've made me more fond of you than I've ever been with a shipmate before. Now I'm going below, tired out, but quite satisfied to leave her to you. And I don't want you to call me unless you are absolutely obliged to. I can trust you fully. Oh, you might give her a sluice down, easily you know, nothing elaborate, and then if you have any time, see if you can find any topgallant sails in the sail-locker. If you can, get 'em up ready for bending. Course is E.N.E. and the weather's steady. Good morning." And away he went below, leaving Frank in charge.

I am not going to attempt any elaborate analysis of Frank's feelings as he stood there, the autocrat of the quarter-deck. But certainly the paramount sensation was one of perfectly legitimate pride, happy pride in the result of honest endeavour allied to the eager hopefulness of youth that it would be still better further on. And so the time flew rapidly until the cook shouted "Coffee!" and that ever-welcome reviver with its aromatic smell was dispensed, Frank taking the wheel while the man whose trick it was went forward and got his coffee without delay.

A curious little incident occurred here. One of the Scotchmen, called, as usual, Mac (and the other was of course Scotty), said to the Finn as he was knocking the ashes out of his pipe preparatory to going back to the wheel, "What r'ye doin' that for? Just tak' yer pipe along. Ther's naethin' severely against smokin' anywhere the noo."

But the Finn said mildly, "I like fine t' schmoke at de veel, but I ton't like to begin id mit de poy in charge. Ef de olt man schmoke all right, nodt ellas," and aft he went. Mac muttered something uncomplimentary, and that suggested little breach of discipline was not committed either then or subsequently.

As soon as ever four bells sounded, Frank, who had been nerving himself for the effort, shouted, "Wash decks!"

"What's that?" said Mac angrily. "Wash decks! What th' 'ell's the meanin' o' this anyhow?"

"Oh! think shame o' yersel'," answered Scotty. "This 's th' second time you've been sejestin' kickin' at the laddie aft. An' it disna maetther a snuff anyway, fur it's yer wheel. Why shudn't the decks be washed, though, ye bletherin' cauf? Hev we changed into pigs all in a minnut?"

There was no answer. Mac went to the wheel, and never again was any attempt made to resent Frank's authority, while he, happily for his peace of mind, never knew that any such attempt had even been in contemplation. The deck-washing was a very perfunctory performance, and was finished by six bells (seven o'clock). Then Frank, full of zeal, suggested—I can't say ordered—that it would be a great idea if they could get the two topgallant sails up.

Immediately all the watch and the cook, who had got his breakfast well under way, sallied below and turned out the sail-locker, finding two good topgallant sails. They dragged them on deck and actually succeeded in getting the main topgallant sail bent and set before eight bells, quite a feat remembering their small numbers, but one that I fear will not appeal to the shore readers of this book, who cannot possibly be expected to understand the technique of the sea.

The beautiful southerly breeze still strengthened, and the *Woden* began to give them a taste of her quality. She was a really fast ship, and greatly superior in every respect, save one, to the *Sealark*. That one was in her power of keeping out the water below. It was really quite time that she was "sucked out," as we call it, and as soon as the morning sights for longitude were taken and Frank had gone to his well-earned sleep, the flywheel pumps were overhauled and set in motion for the purpose of getting her free of an element that, however useful outside, had no business within, although fortunately it could not do her cargo any harm.

Thenceforward for two days, during which the steady clankety clank, clank, clank of the pumps became horribly wearisome to listen to, nothing was done but pumping, so anxious were all hands to get a suck out of her, and find out whether the leak was of serious dimensions or not. At last that welcome sound was heard, and the good ship was herself at last, careful calculation showing that a few minutes' spell in every four hours would keep her free.

This again aroused the question, Why did the crew leave her? how did they leave her? what had become of them? and there was no answer. It was of all mysteries one of the most profound. And none of them had ever heard of the exactly similar case of a barque which was seen yawing about in the Straits of Gibraltar one brilliant day, and on being boarded by a boat from the guard-ship, was found to be abandoned without any apparent reason. Her boats were all in their places and in good condition, and the minutest search failed to reveal the reason why she should be thus deserted. My own theory, in which I am supported by Dr. Andrew Wilson, is that she was boarded while becalmed by one of those terrific nightmares of the sea, the gigantic decapoda, vast creatures with gelatinous bodies, from twenty to sixty feet long, and tentacles extending like an immense network of living wire, gripping and holding with most tenacious clutch everything they touch. It is certainly possible, even if only remotely probable, that such a monster, prompted by some incomprehensible desire, may have risen alongside of her, and extending its enormous arms over her, have gathered the terrific crew, one by one, into its capacious maw. The imagination recoils before the spectacle of those long snaky arms, apparently irresistible in their power, searching out the remotest corner of the ship, and collecting the horror-stricken crew in a hasteless, fateful way, and one can only hope that so awful a trial never did fall to the lot of any man to endure. But I confess that it is the only possible solution of the problem which occurs to me.

The ship having been pumped out, all the necessary sail bent, all the running gear made as fit as possible, Captain Jacks said to Frank, "My dear boy, we'll devote all our energies now to getting her home. She's doin' splendid, but there's a tough time coming. With all luck we shall fetch the English Channel just as the winter is beginning to try its hand at a few gales to start with, and we can't be too careful to save ourselves up for that. I don't mind telling you that I'm mighty anxious over this; if it comes off all right I'm going to quit the sea for good, and settle down on a tiny little farm somewhere in England. I'm done up, sick to death of the constant brutality that I've always practised up till now, and also sick to find that if I hadn't learned a little better this voyage, I couldn't go on doing what I have done in that line, because I'm not strong enough now. I'm fifty years of age, and sometimes I feel a hundred. Do you know, Frank, I feel as if I'd like to be a good, quiet, religious man, and forget all about the old roaring, fighting, cursing life I've led. And, please God, if this adventure of ours pans out all right, I'll have a tremendous go at it."

Frank will never forget that conversation. The ship, carrying as much canvas as she could stagger under, plunged forward over the rising sea with a gallant, easy motion, and the great grey masses of cloud came rolling up from the southward in majestic battalions, ever reinforced from the gloomy horizon. The cold light fell full on Mr. Jacks' face as he stood speaking, and Frank, looking earnestly at him, noted that he seemed to have suddenly aged, the hard lines of his features had softened, and the grim look of determination, almost ferocious in its expression, was replaced by an almost pitiful appearance of weakness.

So forcibly did this strike Frank, that he said anxiously, "Are you quite well, sir?"

A ghost of a smile curled the corners of the hard mouth as the skipper replied, "Oh yes! I suppose I am. Nothin' the matter with me that I know of, except that, as I said, I'm tired, feel I want to take things easy. Well, I hope I can look forward now to as long a rest as I want. In the meantime, here goes for what I can get now. Carry on as long as you can, but don't carry anything away if you can help it. Call me if you feel you must, but not unless, for I think that you can handle her now as well as I can, and I want you to feel all confidence. Keep her as she goes, it's a good course enough, N.E." And down he went.

Left to himself, Frank began to meditate with a swelling heart upon the wonderful change in his prospects. Mr. Jacks no longer filled his thoughts, but he dwelt with perfectly legitimate pride upon the fact that he, a youth not yet eighteen, was in a position of great trust and responsibility. Of profit in a commercial sense he had no idea; probably he was the only person on board of either the *Woden* or the *Sealark* who had not as yet bothered his head over the possibilities of money-making presented in this latest adventure of his.

Lest it should be accounted as too offensively heroic on his part thus to ignore the financial side of things, let me remind you that he had as yet never known the need of money. Never had he felt that craving for those few coins that are as absolutely necessary for satisfying the gnawing needs of the stomach as for clothing the body. Nor had he, because of his happy youth and keen love of the sea, yet had time to realise the bitter anxiety about the future, which haunts men who work hard for their living and are yet entirely unable, owing to the scantiness of their pay, although always at work, to make provision for the old age they see dogging their footsteps like some dread spectre.

At present he was free from all such sad prevision, free to let his fancy soar into contemplation of himself, as a great commander of men, doing things upon the deep that should cause his name to be spoken of all over the world. Again, fortunately for his peace of mind, he did not realise that unless something extremely sensational happens, the greatest men of the

British mercantile marine—and they are on such a high level of excellence that it is difficult to fix upon any as higher than the rest—may pass their lives of splendid usefulness to their country and their fellow-men without any recognition by either state or public. Their own cloth know and admire them, and with that they must needs be satisfied.

And so Frank paced the deck, manfully keeping his watch, and staggering now and then as the driven ship began to leap and roll to the rapidly rising sea, through which she was being driven at an ever-accelerating rate. The wind came in fierce snarling gusts, making every portion of the great framework of masts, yards, sails, and rigging crack and complain, while the Finn at the wheel began to glance uneasily at the young officer who strode to and fro in such apparent unconcern.

At last, when it wanted about an hour to eight bells, Hans could stand it no longer, but said sullenly, as Frank neared him in one of his turns, "You goes to blow de masts outen der ship, ain't it?"

Frank flushed up, but wisely did not answer. Only he wished now for eight bells to come quickly, as he could then hand over his charge without the danger of coming into collision with this man, who was either frightened, or else afraid that after he was relieved it would be "All hands shorten sail," and he would be let in for a lot of work, instead of standing quietly looking on.

Eight bells, and Frank immediately plunged below to call the skipper, and tell him that in his opinion sail should be shortened at once, for she was carrying all that she could bear with safety, and the wind was increasing so fast that it was becoming dangerous. But there was no answer to his voice, although he raised it to a shout. He went and shook the shoulder of the still form, and the chill struck through his hand to his very heart. Mr. Jacks was dead.

CHAPTER XIII
"CAPTAIN" BROWN

For a moment Frank stood speechless with that deadly chill creeping round his young heart, and his bowels all awork with dread and sympathy. But with a rush there came to him the full sense of his responsibility, the pressing need for immediate action, and the fact that he had now no one upon whom to lean. It was then that, for the first time in his life that he ever remembered, he murmured, removing his cap, "God help me!" Then, released at once from the numbness that the touch of the corpse had brought upon him, he bounded up the companion to the deck, shouting, "All hands shorten sail."

It was a tremendous task for the handful of men, but each one was good and earnest in his work, and besides, the careful way in which the "spilling" or gathering-up gear of the sails had been arranged was an immense aid to them. So furious was the struggle that the warriors had no time to observe the absence of the skipper, and even Frank, although conscious of a curious dull pain at the heart, was far too busily employed both in mind and body to dwell upon his immense loss.

At last the ship was snugged down to two lower topsails, a reefed foresail, lower staysails and spanker, under which easy canvas she was still making good progress. Then Frank called all hands aft and made his first speech.

"I hardly know how to speak to you," he said, "but I've got to. When I went down to call Mr. Jacks at eight bells I found him dead." Here he broke down, and burst into a perfect flood of passionate tears. The men gazed at him sympathetically and silently, so he recovered himself very rapidly, almost immediately in fact. He resumed: "I can navigate the ship all right, I know, and handle her too, but I'm only a boy, and I want all the help you can give me. We've got another fortnight before us yet, I'm afraid, before we can possibly get home, and I want you, if you will, to try and forget my age and do just as you've been doing all along. And if one of you can keep a watch I hope you will take it on, because I must have some sleep."

Then up spoke Mac, the man who had shown such signs of resentment at the beginning of this curious passage, and said: "Look here, Frank, not one of us will give ye any bother. If one does, the rest of us will trouble him properly. And for a mate you'd better have Scotty here. None of us are much of a hand at what you want, but he's the best; don't you think so, boys?"

There was universal assent to this; and Scotty, as sheepishly as if he had been nominated before a vast crowd, slouched forward and said: "A' richt. I'll keep the first watch, then, so as to let Frank go below and get some sleep. It was my watch below, but that doesn't matter now; I'll stick it. Relieve the wheel, and I'll go and get some canvas, and be sewing him below there into his last suit, puir fallow."

And with this they dispersed, Frank merely asking Scotty to call him if there was anything wanted, and remembering with a sharp pang how short a time ago it was since that cold body down there had said those words to him, and how grateful he had been to know that there was a strong man to fall back upon. But he was young and weary; and so, in spite of the tremendous burden that had been thrown upon him, in five minutes he was fast asleep.

So fast, indeed, that when Scotty called him two hours after, he could hardly believe that he had more than just closed his eyes. But he sprang up and washed his face, coming on deck to find the ship still plunging gallantly forward under the same canvas and with about the same weight of wind. The stern, drab day had broken, the cold light fell upon the torn and troubled sea, making it look grim and cruel and ravenous; while the buffeted ship doggedly held her way through those fierce masses of foaming water, as some men from whom all hope has departed still battle on by some sort of striving instinct against the waves of misfortune that continuously thunder on against them.

There at the gangway lay an oblong white parcel neatly stitched up in canvas, the sight of which made Frank's young heart grow cold as if an icy hand had grasped it. And then the merciful reaction came, and the relief sometimes afforded to men of great minds, and so frequently to weaklings and women. His whole frame shook as if with ague, and hot tears forced their way through the fingers tightly pressed to his face.

That storm passed rapidly over him, and lifting his head bravely he said: "Scotty, will you call the other fellows aft, and we'll put the body overside. I don't know the service, and I haven't got a Prayer-book, but I'll say the only prayer I know."

So they came, the little crowd, and stood around Scotty and Mac, balancing the remains on the rail, while Frank, kneeling on the soddened deck, repeated, with feelings I dare not attempt to describe, the beautiful "Our Father." As he rose to his feet Scotty and Mac, looking at one another fixedly, launched the body overboard, and the splash, plainly audible to them all above the bruit of the storm, acted like the release of an intolerable tension, a relief that was grateful beyond their simple powers of expression, so not mentioned at all.

They came back to their labours almost with a bound, having buried their dead out of their sight. And it was well, for the gale immediately began to take off, and it was necessary to set sail rapidly in order to keep the *Woden* steady in that great sea. As it was she tumbled about so horribly that several old leaks opened, and gave them much severe labour at the pumps, in addition to their exhausting work of making sail with such a crew. But it was really beautiful to see how the rough, toil-hardened, and ignorant men gave Frank their entirely loving and loyal support, never once alluding to his youth or inexperience, but obeying his lightest wish with cheerful alacrity. Nor did they in any way resent the sudden rise of Scotty to the lofty position of second in command, except by way of a joke, and even then only while Frank was absent.

The result of this tacit recognition of Frank's abilities and fitness to command was that he acquired a gravity of demeanour and a steadiness of eye which made him look ten years older, while at the same time, to his secret delight and amusement, he noticed that he was growing a beard, and all boys will realise how gratifying that was to him. It saved him also from becoming too staid, of losing altogether that boyish delight in life which is so beautiful to see in youngsters who are in their work-time tremendously in earnest, and is, to me at any rate, so painful to miss in young men who reserve all their energies for play, and all ability to shirk for their duty.

The work of the ship, apart from the handling of the sails, steering, and pumping, was purposely reduced to the vanishing-point almost, except what was voluntarily undertaken by the men in the way of keeping the vessel clean. And as the good breeze that grew out of the gale carried them north as far as the Azores without ever rising to the force of a gale, they had a fairly easy time of it but for the pumping, twenty minutes of which were now required every two hours to keep the vessel free of water. At this Frank took his full share at his own urgent wish, the men having protested against his doing so, and he insisting that the energetic work was necessary to his well-being, and for the sake of exercise.

Which was undoubtedly a fact, for nothing can or could be more debilitating to a young man, or any man for the matter of that, than to eat well, and perform mental toil, and have no physical exercise. And Frank's mental toil was severe. He knew theoretically and practically how to navigate a ship; but if and when he made a mistake in his calculations on board the *Sealark* it did not matter in the least, for the responsibility was somebody's else's. But now, and this I consider more important still, he had no one to check his work, so that, work as carefully as he would, he could not feel that confidence in his figures that brings an easy mind. Finally, it must be remembered that he was not absolutely certain of the correctness of his chronometer.

So that we must sympathise with him if, when looking upon the vast expanse of trackless ocean, he sometimes felt a youthful thrill of apprehension lest he should have failed in the correctness of his working. But relief was near, a relief that amounted to a positive triumph, and one which remained with him in pleasant memory all his life. The wind had gradually hauled round to the westward, and so gradually put on strength until the *Woden* was racing along at a good thirteen knots an hour, to the unbounded joy of everybody on board.

One day, by Frank's most careful calculations, it appeared that, with the wind holding good, on the present course they should sight Corvo, the most westerly of the Azores, soon after daybreak in the morning. He mentioned the fact to Scotty immediately the sights were worked up at noon; and that genial soul, looking, as men of his stamp will, almost awestricken at the chart, said, "Ay, we're haein' a grand run." Had he made the least demur or questioned the correctness of Frank's calculations he would have given the dear boy a good deal of pain. But such a thing never occurred to him. He accepted those lines upon the chart as if they were the lines of fate laid down by unerring wisdom, which was of course flattering to Frank, who could not however help wishing that he had some one capable of criticising. But he preserved a nonchalant demeanour over his real anxiety, and waited as patiently as might be for the coming dawn.

Before light he was aloft on the fore-topsail yard straining his eyes ahead for the sight of his first land-fall. It was a grey, overcast, and stormy morning, the kind of weather when land is most difficult to pick up, but happily just as the sun rose there was a temporary break in the clouds around him, and there loomed up in grim majesty the mighty rock of Corvo, precisely at the time when and in the quarter where Frank expected and hoped to see it. The clouds sped over it again almost instantly, but the vision vouchsafed was sufficient. A great wave of satisfying certainty, of exultation in his work and pride in his undoubted powers, swept over Frank, making him completely happy. And with a firm step and erect bearing he descended and walked aft, feeling every inch a man.

When Scotty came on deck at seven bells, the island was very plainly in sight from the deck, in spite of the unpleasant weather, but Frank could not somehow help feeling a little disappointed that Scotty did not make a little fuss over this (to Frank) stupendous event. Yet had he known it, Scotty's taking the occurrence quite as a matter of course was far and away the highest compliment that he could pay. It really showed that as far as he was concerned Frank was as much to be depended upon as any officer could be, the fact of his youth being entirely lost sight of in consequence of his ability.

Then the sun came out, and Frank got some good sights for his chronometer, which he carefully verified by bearings of the land, finding to his delight that it had kept a good rate, and was substantially correct. Later at noon, when he got a good meridian altitude, he took a fine bearing for departure, and set his course direct for Falmouth. He did everything, of course, as usual, with the greatest care, but with a newly-acquired confidence that amazed him when he hazily thought about it. But he was now to be very severely tried indeed. A strong westerly gale set in, before which the *Woden* dashed along under almost all the canvas she could spread, and it brought with it a great increase in the gloom of the weather, so that all Frank's anxious watching failed to get him a sight of the sun or stars either; not that he would have been able to do much with the latter, having had no practice at either finding them or taking their altitudes, although he could work the problems.

So he was fain to depend upon his dead reckoning, or position by account, and, as the fleeting vessel surged along before the wild howling of the gale at what was for her a tremendous speed, all hands became increasingly anxious. For this is a point that sailors of every grade fully appreciate, the danger of being unable, from the veiling of the heavenly bodies, to get an accurate position when nearing the land, especially in a sailing ship when running before a gale.

No relief came, and the universal anxiety increased, until, on the fourth day from Corvo, Frank felt that he could bear the strain no longer, and, calling all hands, proceeded to shorten sail down to the two lower topsails and fore-topmast staysail. That successfully accomplished by dint of three hours' tremendous labour, the *Woden* was brought to the wind, and a cast of the deep-sea lead was taken. The result was sixty-five fathoms of water, and the "arming," or tallow jammed into the hole at the bottom of the lead, brought up grey sand and broken shells. It was good enough to keep her away again to her original course, for it coincided with the soundings and bottom given on the chart. So they put the helm up again and away she went at a greatly reduced rate.

And all through the hours of darkness the young commander remained on deck full of the most pressing anxiety, yet consoled by the knowledge that he had done his very best. At every change of watch they went through the terrible toil, under this short-handed condition, of heaving the ship to in order to get soundings, a proceeding which made the men curse bitterly the necessity, although they took care that Frank should not hear them.

When morning broke, Frank's eyes felt as if they were burning out of his head with incessant staring through the darkness, and he was weary beyond words. But all his weariness and pain fell from him like a shed garment at the sight of a small vessel, a boat, in fact, under two shreds of canvas, apparently making straight for the ship. He had her immediately hove to in order to await the coming of the stranger, who proved to be a no more romantic messenger than a Falmouth tailor, one of those enterprising tradesmen who hover off the harbour, and as far west as Scilly sometimes, in the hope of getting a substantial order from the sailors of a ship coming into Falmouth for instructions where to proceed with her cargo.

The skipper of this small craft gladdened Frank's heart by telling him just where he would find the pilot-boat, a position only a few miles away. Again the heavily-burdened boy felt refreshed, relieved, and grateful as he kept his ship away on almost the same course which he had been previously steering. And then, as a sort of crowning mercy, the beautiful shores of Cornwall suddenly became visible through a huge lifting of the massy clouds. For the life of him Frank could not help lifting his cap, and muttering with a lump in his throat, "Thank God."

There lay the pilot-boat calmly awaiting him, and soon he felt that the terrible weight of responsibility, which was making an old man of him long before his time, would be lifted. When near enough, he hove to, and the pilot came on board. His astonishment at discovering the state of affairs I shall not attempt to depict, but as soon as he had got over it he did his utmost to persuade Frank to come into Falmouth, and await instructions from London before proceeding any farther. In this difficult position Frank took what I consider to be the very wise step of consulting his crew as to their views on the matter. To his surprise and secret gratification they unanimously decided to go on to London.

After that it was vain for the pilot to coax, threaten, or bluster, all Frank would do was to insist upon getting a Channel pilot (a suggestion from Scotty), and the rest he and his crew were prepared to risk. After long consultation the pilot admitted that he was not qualified to take the ship up Channel to London, but promised to get a man out of the cutter. In about half-an-hour the other man was on board, a grizzled old sea-dog who looked at Frank with that cruel contempt that the old school always used to exhibit towards the rising generation. Frank, though nettled, preserved his courteous behaviour until the vessel was once more speeding up Channel with additional sail set.

Then when the little bustle was over, he approached the pilot, and said, "Do you take the ship right up to London or only to the Trinity pilot at Dungeness?"

To this the pilot replied with a deep note in his voice, "You needn't trouble your head about that, I'm in charge now, and I shall do just what I think is best for the benefit of the owners and underwriters. And understand, I want no interference from you."

Frank turned round immediately and hailed Scotty, who was smoking the pipe of peace in front of the cabin. "Scotty," he said, "the pilot has informed me that I am not to interfere with anything connected with the ship, that he has all the control now. What do you think of that?"

Scotty spat comprehensively over the side, took a fresh pull at his pipe, and then drawled out, looking fixedly at the pilot meanwhile, "I think he's building on salvage, but he won't get it. You've brought the ship home, and engaged him as pilot. As long as he takes the ship up nothing will happen, but if he comes any of his nonsense over you or tries to rob us of any of what we have worked so hard for, we'll talk to him. Mister Pilot, you keep a civil tongue in your head towards our young skipper, one of the best that ever lived, and you'll be all right. If you don't you'll be in deep waters at once, now I tell you. We're not goin' to have any bossing of him by you, understand that."

The pilot, who had quite naturally scented a splendid job for himself in this, was in a parlous state of surprise. He did not know what to do, especially as he noticed that the rest of the crew had gathered around with rather severe looks towards him. A moment's hesitation and then, being wise enough to appreciate the situation, he turned to Frank and said, with a note of irony in his voice which he could not suppress, "All right, sir, I can take you up to the Trinity pilot at Dungeness, and we'll leave the question of what I am to be paid to the authorities in London."

To which Frank, feeling highly indignant of course, but wisely curbing his temper, replied, "Very well, pilot, I hope this breeze will hold, so that your job will be an easy one. And now I'll leave you in charge. I've had an anxious time lately and want a good sleep."

As Frank disappeared down the companion the baffled pilot muttered, "Silly young ass, thinks he's a man, I suppose, because he's brought the ship in from sea somehow. But I'd give a sovereign to know all about this business."

Then he turned and devoted his attention to the steering of the ship, entirely unconscious of the utter injustice and shallowness of his remarks. The egotism of many youths is unpretty, but the arrogance of age and its refusal to recognise any merit in the young man is often quite as pitiful and annoying a spectacle.

Below, in spite of his weariness, Frank set himself deliberately to compose a long letter to his owners. He had sent them a long telegram from Falmouth informing them of what had happened in as few words as possible, but now he felt that he must give full detail, and he had found it the hardest task he had undertaken yet. So engrossed did he become, however, in his work that it was four bells before he had finished it, and then realised that he was dead beat. So he stretched himself out on the settee and slept like a log until he was awakened by Scotty at daylight.

He sprang up, gave his hands and face a rinse, and ran on deck to find the ship under all sail, the wind having taken off very much during the night and the lightship off Selsea Bill, *The Owers*, only about five miles off. There was also a tug (by all appearance) creeping steadily up on the port quarter, and concerning her Scotty said quietly, "If she speaks us, don't you think you'd better take her? He'll open his mouth pretty wide, but, after all, it'd be a pity to spoil the ship for ha'porth of tar, wouldn't it?"

Frank replied as quietly, "Well, Scotty, if he comes up and asks for a job I'll agree to his price, but you do the talking; if he sees me, and this old pilot man gets a-talking to him, they may hatch up some devilment between 'em."

Scotty was delighted, and went below at once to rig up a bit less like an old tar-pot, as he put it, while Frank, coffee-cup in hand, walked up to the pilot and said, "Good morning, pilot."

"Good morning, sir," replied the pilot; "the wind is dying away and looks like getting into the east'ard. Don't you think you had better take steam if you can get it?"

To which Frank answered, "My mate and I have just been discussing the matter, and we have agreed to take that tug that's coming up if we can get him on any sort of reasonable terms, but I must ask you not to interfere. You will please remember that you are the pilot, and I, boy as I am, am in command. I don't say this to make a quarrel, but you must admit that I have some cause of complaint over the way you treated me yesterday."

Poor old pilot, he was bursting with curiosity to know the ins and outs of this mysterious case—an English crew of less than half the usual number on board a Norwegian vessel, and in charge of a boy of eighteen—but in his eagerness to take charge of things generally he had spoiled all chance, he now plainly saw, of dipping into the rich dish of salvage which he scented somewhere near.

While he mused thus Frank moved aft and, with Scotty by his side, awaited the oncoming of the tug, which Scotty pronounced to be one of the best of Watkin's lot that had evidently had a long tow of some ship as far as the Wight. Nearer and nearer she drew until she ranged alongside, and the burly skipper on the bridge shouted, "Good morning, sir, where are you bound?"

"London," roared back Scotty, in his most important voice.

There was a prolonged pause, for the tug skipper was meditating many things. Norwegians don't take steam until they are driven to it, and unless utterly disabled it is not to be imagined that any ship of that flag would take steam to the westward of the Foreland anyhow. But the tug was really bound to go up for coal—they often use this as an argument, regardless of truth, but now it really was a fact—and he felt that even a very low rate of towage was better than going up empty-handed. So, while entirely unwilling to give himself away, he knew it was of no use beginning a bluff here, as she was not an English or an American ship. And he shouted back, "Do you want a cheap tow up, captain?"

"What do you call cheap?" answered Scotty.

Another pause and weighing of probabilities, then loudly, defiantly almost, "Forty pounds."

Now Frank and Scotty had made up their minds to go to any price that did not mean salvage, and so the extreme modesty of the demand almost startled them. But they waited a little for form's sake and a mischievous wish to prolong the tantalising of the pilot, who would have given his fee for ten minutes' conversation with the tug captain.

At last Scotty lifted his head and roared back, "All right, skipper, if you'll lend your towline in the bargain."

The skipper of the tug was so astonished that he nearly fell down. He had figured on being bated at least fifteen pounds, but to be accorded his first demand, and by a Norwegian too, almost made him faint. And he felt that something must be queer, but as he could not tell what he just nodded, "All right," spoke down his tube and kicked ahead, the heaving-line was flung, and in ten minutes the big string was passed and secured, and the

Robert Bruce, with the Norwegian barque *Woden* in tow, was ready to be signalled at the first station as proceeding to London.

The only work then necessary was the furling of all the sails, as the wind was rapidly drawing ahead and falling light. After this heavy task for the small crew was successfully achieved, they found themselves gently rounded to under the land east of Dungeness, and when their pilots were exchanged Frank signed the Channel pilot's note with a polite but unreciprocated farewell. Then away they sped again towards their goal under the guidance of the new pilot, who was so genial and so generally nice that Frank was tempted to tell him the story of their adventurous voyage. He listened with gasping interest, and at the close of it seized Frank's hand, saying with tears in his eyes, "Young man, if I had a son like you I'd be the proudest man in the world. I am an old sailor, of course, and I can appreciate to the full the value of your work. But how do you feel about it yourself?"

"Well," stammered Frank, "I—I feel very glad of course that we've got safe home, for I have been very anxious, because I had no one on board to back me up or correct me if I made a mistake. But now it's all over I see that I haven't done anything different from what I did in the *Sealark*, except, as I say, I had to depend upon myself here. And the men have been so jolly good, they have helped me so much, you can hardly believe how kind and willing they have been, obeying my orders as if I had been an elderly man. They are the best of men, especially Scotty, and I do hope they'll be well rewarded. But somehow I feel unhappy to think that Mr. Jacks did not live to share the happiness of to-day. It meant so much to him, for he intended to retire after this voyage on his share of the salvage, and now he is dead before he could get it, and I shall get a lot that I don't really want."

The old pilot turned away muttering, "Ah well, for once fortune has struck the right man; he'll go far and do much, I can see, if God spares him."

And so she dragged along at a clinking rate to Gravesend, where, to Frank's intense delight, there came off in the boat bringing the river pilot, the owner of the old *Sealark*, Mr. — —. He seized Frank by the arm and congratulated him most warmly on his wonderful achievement, telling him that immediately after the arrival of the *Sealark* in New York a week before, he being advised by Captain Jenkins of the adventure about which, when he had read the news, he had many doubts and fears until he received the wire from Falmouth. He had brought with him a budget of letters for Frank from home, and, after his greetings were over, despatched the lad to his berth to read them, only waiting long enough to be introduced to Scotty.

Must I say it? Yes, in spite of the fear of my hero being misunderstood, I must set down that he scanned those dear letters without any great amount of feeling, except that he was contentedly glad to know that all was going well at home. Even the owner's gracious praise did not give him anything like the sense of exultation that he felt over the finishing of his job for its own sake. Nor, I think, would coldness or even blame have unduly depressed him, for the doing of the thing well had been its own exceeding great reward. I have several times met his like, all of them unhappily compelled to look very keenly after the reward, because it was needful to their living. That part of the business had never cost Frank a thought, so that he was happiest of them all, inasmuch as the doing of the work well was all he thought about.

Therefore he returned on deck in a very few minutes to find Mr. — — and Scotty deep in conversation about him, which ceased immediately he came up. The owner had engaged a couple of watermen to steer the ship up, so that the small crew were free to get their few belongings packed up and smoke placidly, none of the usual unbending of sails and stopping-up of gear being indulged in. Frank and the owner paced the deck discussing the voyage, which enabled the young man to indulge in his unstinted, outspoken admiration of the *Sealark's* captain and officers, praise which the owner heard with grave approval, glancing now and then admiringly at the fresh, animated young face beside him.

Then Mr. — — asked that the hands might be called aft. When they came he invited them into the cabin, and said, "Now, men, will you take a word of advice from a man who knows a good deal more of the world than you do, and also who knows sailors pretty well? You will probably have the biggest sum you have ever handled in your lives out of this business, for I find that the vessel and cargo are insured for £20,000, and that will probably work out, at salvage of two-thirds, at about £350 apiece for each of you, if not more. Will you be wise and go straight out of Sailor Town, living somewhere quietly and soberly until you get it, and then putting it away carefully somewhere where you can always lay your hands on it when you want it? I'm prepared to advance you money now, in order to enable you to get away at once to some cheap hotel out of Sailor Town, and I will see that you get your wages due up to the time of leaving the *Sealark* to-morrow."

They all thanked him, and promised to do as he said. So he gave them £5 apiece on account, and dismissed them to get the mooring gear ready, as she was drawing near her destination, the Southwest India Dock. There she was speedily moored, and the men, shaking hands warmly with Frank, jumped ashore, to be surrounded at once by the usual gang of harpies, who lie in wait for the sailor homeward-bound off a long voyage. But Scotty, who had received the address of a nice little moderately-priced hotel just off Oxford Street, took the lead of his little crowd, and commissioned a boy to go and fetch two four-wheeled cabs, in which they took their departure, and amidst a round of cheering which sent that queer creeping feeling all over Frank's body, they drove away through the shoal of discomfited sharks.

The ship was duly handed over to the representatives of the owners, and Mr. — —, taking Frank under his wing, drove off to his comfortable hotel, where his wife was awaiting him with a warm welcome for "the dear boy," as she said, who had shown himself to be such a brave sailor and a man. And there, over a dinner which seemed to Frank to be a heavenly dream, after his long course of the ship's poor grub, well above the average as it had been, Frank had to tell the story of the second voyage of the *Sealark* over again. And then to a beautiful bed and the sweet sleep of the untroubled young, although, to say truth, he wakened several times during the night, and found himself listening to what was a-doing on deck, as he thought. For we do not shake off responsibility such as his had been so easily. But each time he thus roused and listened, the blissful remembrance of his successfully accomplished feat came over him, and he sank to sleep again with a contented, happy sigh.

CHAPTER XIV
TO SEA ONCE MORE

The process of adjudicating the reward due to the successful salvors of a ship is a very complicated one, and any description of it would be calculated to tire the most enthusiastic reader of a sea story. Wherefore I do not propose to touch the subject further than by saying that the value of the *Woden* and her cargo was adjudged to be £17,500, out of which Frank was awarded £2500, and a most flattering testimonial from the underwriters engrossed on vellum, which I am sure pleased him much more than the money. The other members of the crew were duly awarded their shares by the court, and, as far as I have been able to learn, were not only satisfied but sensible in the way they disposed of these well-earned gains.

And now we must return to Frank for a while, who at the earliest possible moment hastened home to dear old stony Dewsbury, and was received, as you might expect, by the admiring crowd of friends and relatives with immense enthusiasm. But his mother and his sisters felt at once that the boy was gone for ever. In his place had returned a man with clear untroubled sight and firm voice, accustomed to command, and with confidence in his own power to *do*. His mother shed a few tears, as women will, but secretly worshipped him; while his sisters hung upon his lightest word, and looked with scorn upon all the other young men they knew as utterly unworthy to compare with their stalwart brother. Only his father of all the family now met him as an equal, and talked about men and things with him as one man to another, feeling his heart swell with pride as he looked upon this grave and self-possessed man of eighteen.

Only a few days, however, had elapsed before he began to grow restless. He wanted to be off again. The company of the youths of his own age did not either interest or amuse him; they bored him with what he considered their inane, incessant conversation about cricket and football. Had they talked business, he could have understood them and learned from them, but that topic they shunned as if it were the plague. The serious side of life appealed to him, and while his sense of humour was as strong as possible, and his enjoyment of life very keen, he turned with positive disgust from people who thought of nothing with any interest except games, and only thought of work under compulsion, taking no pride in it at all. As a result of this he was in an entirely receptive mood for the owner's letter from Liverpool, received after he had been at home a month, although one part of it disappointed him bitterly. It informed him that the *Sealark*, having secured a good charter to carry case oil from New York to Hong-Kong, would of course not be coming to England at all until the close of the present voyage, if she did then. And by the same post came a farewell letter from Captain Jenkins, full of heartiest congratulations upon his success, and keenest regrets at being compelled to sail without him.

The consolation, however, came in the postscript to the owner's letter, which informed Frank that he had been appointed third mate of the *Thurifer*, a very large and fine steel ship, for those days, of 2000 tons register, and carrying twenty-two A.B.'s and eight apprentices. He would, of course, be an apprentice still, not a great deal more than half his time having been served; but he would live in the cabin, and be treated in every respect like an officer. This news caused Frank's heart to leap for joy, and he was especially elated at the prospect of having a cabin to himself; for although he had endured it cheerfully, the dog-hole of a place which he had been compelled to share with three other inmates on board the *Sealark*, had always been his greatest hardship at sea.

And the fact that he had successfully striven to learn his navigation and do all the writing that it demanded was the best proof possible of his sterling quality of dogged perseverance. Moreover the owner informed him that, in consequence of his proved ability, he would be paid a small wage of £3 per month, although, of course, he was not really entitled to any until the close of his indentures. The ship was loading salt in Liverpool for Calcutta, and was due to sail in a week's time, so the sooner he joined her the better.

This summons drove all other thoughts out of his head, and he became immediately like a keen hound straining at the leash, never even noticing the wistful looks cast upon him by his mother and sisters, and, it must be confessed, by several young ladies of their acquaintance also, who were piqued, as well as amazed, by his undisguised indifference to their charms and arch glances. No one mentioned the matter to him, but if they had he would certainly have retorted at once, "I have no time for silly spooning around at my age, nor inclination either." Yet there was not the slightest fear of his developing into either a prig or a superior person, his work was the thing, that's all.

Two days after he received the summons found him speeding towards Liverpool, full of eagerness as well as curiosity to see his new ship. He had rather a hard parting from his people, for, besides their sorrow at losing him at all, they had hoped to keep him at home until after Christmas, the great family festival being due in about a fortnight. But once away he speedily forgot all about that part of his life, and counted the stations with the utmost impatience until his train steamed into Lime Street.

In twenty minutes he was alongside the *Thurifer*, and his heart swelled with pride. He had expected a grand ship, but not one so splendid as this. Her mighty masts towered into the sky full 200 feet from the waterline, her lower yards were over 100-feet spread, the fore and main, that is; and although the jibboom was rigged in, he could see what a gigantic spar it was. Moreover the extraordinary number of her yards delighted and awed him, for, while the *Sealark* and *Woden* had only carried ten yards altogether, two masts each, being barques, the *Thurifer* carried seven on each of her three masts, and Frank could just imagine what a mountain of white she would appear at sea with all her great area of canvas spread and drawing. But he was specially charmed with her figurehead. She had been named by a man who had been attracted by the sound of the word without knowing its meaning, but when the carver was asked to design a figurehead for her, he, being an artist, made a splendid figure of a priest in full canonicals, who held a thurible on high by its triple chain, and the effect was exceedingly grand, especially when, as now, it was properly painted and gilded in its correct colours.

All this observation of his took but very little time, and he soon called a couple of idlers and bade them carry his traps on board. He was met at the gangway by a huge forbidding-looking man whom he instinctively recognised as the mate. This gentleman, although I strain courtesy in calling him so, with a deepening of the set scowl on his heavily bearded face, growled out in a deep voice, "Well, what do *you* want?"

"I am the third mate, come to join the ship, sir," replied Frank, looking him squarely in the eyes.

"Ho, ho," retorted the mate with a very definite sneer, "you're the sucking skipper we've been hearing so much about, then, *Captain* Frank Brown, I presume," with an ungainly bow of mockery.

Poor Frank flushed crimson and stood irresolute, not knowing what to do. Go forward he could not, for the mate barred the way, and he had never felt so awkward since the day he joined the *Sealark*. Suddenly the mate seemed to notice that he was blocking the gangway, and moved aside, saying as he did so, "Ah, well, I s'pose you think yourself a little tin god on wheels now, and it'll be my painful dooty to put you in your right place again. And I won't have any third-officer nonsense either, mind you; you're

Brown, senior apprentice, that's all, and don't you forget it. Go and get your dunnage stowed away as soon as you can, I've got a job for you."

And Frank, feeling dazed and cut to the very soul, hastened into the half deck like a man in a dream, while the mate stood and chuckled to himself over the impression he had made on the boy who, as he thought, needed taking down a peg or two.

Frank's first impulse was to sit and be sorry for himself, but happily his natural strength of spirit and determination came to his assistance, and he hastily unpacked such of his traps as contained his working rig, and in ten minutes appeared in a well-worn suit of dungaree, from which all its original blue had faded, looking eminently fit and workmanlike. Going up to the mate, who was standing picking his teeth in front of the saloon, he said, "I'm ready for work now, sir."

"Oh, you are, are you? Very well, just go into the saloon there and see the captain, he's waiting for you."

Frank turned at once and entered, doffing his cap as he did so, and walking up to a keen-looking, clean-shaven man of about forty who sat there writing, he said respectfully, "I'm the third mate, sir, Frank Brown. I've just come aboard, and the chief officer has told me you want to see me."

The skipper, looking up, laid down his pen and stared steadily at his interlocutor without speaking for about a minute. Then he said, "So you are the lad that brought the *Woden* home, eh? Well, as long as you don't suffer from swollen head I daresay you'll do very well, but understand once for all, I'll have no owner's favourites in any ship I command. You are nominally third mate, and on the articles as such, but you are really only the senior apprentice, and if you want to be treated properly you must remember that. Another thing, you are in a very different ship to that old tub the *Sealark*, and will have to learn to do things big-ship fashion. If you behave yourself you'll find me what they call a decent skipper, but if you put on any frills I shall have to put you in your proper place in two shakes. Now go and do what the mate tells you."

He turned to his writing, when Frank, stepping a little closer, said, "Beg pardon, sir, but it seems to me that the fact that I have done my best successfully has made me enemies already. I'm sure I don't want to put on any frills, as you and the chief officer have termed it, but if I am to be the third mate and given any responsible duty to perform, I shan't be able to get anybody to obey me, if it is seen that my superiors have a dislike to me from the outset. Please give me a fair trial before you make up your mind to dislike me."

The skipper rose to his feet and thundered, "Get out of my cabin, boy! how dare you bandy words with me? Mr. Vincent" (to the mate), "give this fellow something to do, he wants employment."

"All right, Captain Forrest," answered the mate, "I'll set him goin'. Come along here and get to work stowin' the stores in the lazaret. You'll find some of your fellow-apprentices there. It's aft, not forrard."

For one wild moment Frank felt impelled to throw up everything and go ashore without considering what his next step would be afterwards. But a sudden fierce determination seized him to show these cowardly bullies, as he thought them, that he was not to be driven out of the ship or out of his chosen profession by any such accidents as they were, and he choked his rage down, merely replying in stereotyped phrase, "Very good, sir," and walking out of the saloon.

Now of course it will be asked by every one unconnected with the sea, "Whatever could such extraordinary conduct mean?" Alas, although I will admit that this was an extreme case, it is a type of conduct towards subordinates that is, or used to be, exceedingly common on board ship. It is the outcome of one of the lowest and most despicable passions in our nature, "Envy, the eldest born of hell."

Viewed in its baleful light, Frank's offence was indeed unpardonable. He had distinguished himself as no boy could be expected to do, and would naturally be exceedingly puffed up in his own estimation, according to their narrow ideas. Besides, he had been very strongly recommended to the captain by the owner, which, to some men, is an almost inexpiable offence in itself, and one that causes more ill-feeling on board ship than enough. And as both the captain and chief officer were men of an exceedingly suspicious and resentful, as well as envious, turn of mind, their treatment of Frank was only to be expected. I could give instances of similar behaviour, which have come under my notice, and which I myself have experienced, but will refrain in order to get on with my yarn.

Frank strode aft to the lazaret hatch and lowered himself down promptly into the midst of four youngsters of about sixteen years of age, who were busily engaged in roasting one of their number, a boy evidently somewhat younger than the rest of them, and obviously about to make his first voyage. Three of them were certainly experienced to the extent of at least one voyage, and it was a great game for them to break Johnny Newcome in. But they all desisted from their sport as Frank dropped among them, and stood half on the defensive, like hens when a strange fowl is introduced to them. Frank just smiled cheerfully upon them and said, "All right, boys, I'm one of yourselves, don't mind me. But the mate'll be here in a minute or two, if I don't mistake, and I don't know how you stand with him, but I don't want him to find me one of the unemployed. What are you supposed to be doing?"

The eldest boy present piped up, "We're supposed to be stowing the stores, but, as we don't know anything about it, we're not getting on very fast. We heard that the third mate was coming to-day, and then I s'pose we shall be all right."

Frank laughed, but with a supreme effort, for his heart was very heavy, and said, "Well, I'm supposed to be the third mate, so I'd better start in, I think. But first of all, what's your names?"

"Mine's Thompson," piped up the first speaker.

"Selden me," chipped up another.

"Fitzgerald," said a third.

The new-comer, who had not settled yet after his ragging, sullenly mumbled, "My name is Reginald Percy Smith, and I want to complain to the captain."

There was a short, violent burst of laughter from the other young rascals at this, and Frank, tapping him kindly on the shoulder, said, "All right, Reggie, we'll see about complaining afterwards. At present what we've got to do is to get these cases and bags and barrels stowed away snugly, so that they won't get adrift when we are at sea. So here goes," and seizing one of the cases he up-ended it, and worked it into a vacant space which gaped to receive it.

In five minutes the whole of them were labouring energetically under Frank's direction to get the chaos of packages reduced to something like order. And then the mate came down with words of snarling disparagement of Frank's ability as a stevedore, made them do most of the work over again, while Frank set his teeth and said nothing. But even the new-comer could see the purposeful malice in the mate's behaviour, and, although he could not understand it, he dimly resented it, for it reminded him of the bully at school.

Now I do not care to dwell further upon the way in which, during the remaining days of the ship in dock, the mate endeavoured to make life a burden to the young third mate, and succeeded in making him nervous and diffident about his work, anxious as ever to do that work well, but doubtful of his ability. Still I must record one fact that commends itself to me as being the act of a brave man, to say nothing of a youth. In the midst of this sore trial Frank allowed no word of complaint to escape him to his father or the owner. And this he did knowing as well as possible what a voyage was awaiting him. I feel that he was quixotically heroic, but there it is, he made up his mind that he would go through this thing no matter what the cost might be. And out of this grew one good thing. The other lads, three of whom were new and the other four all second voyagers, grew to admire him immensely, some of them to love him, and of course that helped.

Then came sailing day, and with it a crowd of wasters, the dregs of Liverpool, there being a dearth of foremast hands just then, and skippers being glad to take what they could get. Only three out of the twenty appeared to be good sailormen, the rest looked as if a tramp steamer was the only kind of craft they had ever known, and in consequence they were almost as much out of place on board of a ship dependent for her motive power upon the wind as a landsman would be, except for the matter of sickness.

The second mate, who joined late, was a splendidly clean-built young fellow, who looked not only the highest type of seamen, but bore unmistakably the hall-mark of a gentleman; and, as like cleaves to like, he soon found Frank out, and took to him at once, uttering a few kindly words in appreciation of his late feat that gave Frank the first sensation of pleasure he had known since he came on board. He had served his time in one of the splendid ships of Messrs. Patrick Henderson & Co., the *Oamaru*, on the long trail from England to New Zealand, being third mate on his last voyage, and this was his first essay as second. His name was James Wilson, an Englishman from the Midlands.

Precisely at noon on a grim December day, the 13th of that stern month, the *Thurifer* was seized by the tug and dragged out into the river, looking most ungainly and helpless among the huge trim liners lying easily at anchor on the bosom of the grey Mersey as she submitted clumsily to the fussy efforts of the great Jolliffe tug. No sooner was she in the river, and the mooring gear cleared away, than the big business of rigging the jibboom out was taken in hand, and here the mate got the first taste of the quality of his crew. Fortunately he had as a bo'sun a huge Londoner from Blackwall, one of those splendid seamen of the old school who, although he could hardly write his name, could do anything with rope and wire and canvas that was possible, having been, as he was wont to say laughingly, almost born in a rigging-loft. In addition he was immensely strong, and stood well over six feet.

This worthy seaman, under the orders of the mate, marshalled his motley gang, who tumbled over one another, got in the way of the good men, and showed conclusively that they were hopelessly bewildered at the vast entanglement. There was much shouting and cursing and objurgation generally of men who sign on as seamen and are only labourers, the mate being almost beside himself with rage. Frank was in the thick of it toiling like any beaver, and by his intelligent seamanship completely winning the heart of the bo'sun, who, being so good a sailor himself, was fully able to appreciate Frank's ability, smartness, and industry. But even Frank was amazed at the magnitude of the spar which they were handling, and the complication of gear attached to it, for, as he afterwards said in conversation with the bo'sun, the *Sealark's* jibboom was only a walking-stick compared with it. And as the number of really useful hands engaged upon it was limited to four men and two lads, the work proceeded but slowly, while the mate raved and swore like a man possessed of a devil.

Steadily seaward went the ship into a rising gale, a nasty sea, and the coming night. Gradually she began to dip and curtsy to the seas as she was dragged to meet them, adding to the immense difficulty of the work being performed by the devoted handful of workers, because of the great showers of spray that were continually breaking over the bows. But at last the mighty job was finished as well as it could be under the circumstances, and wearied to the very bone, the workers' thoughts were turned to rest. But in cases of this kind, especially leaving Liverpool, where a ship is on the high sea so soon, those that have knowledge have the burden laid upon them of using that knowledge, with generally the added satisfaction of finding that the wasters and loafers have a far better time all round.

However, respite came at last, and all hands, with the exception of those at the wheel and look-out, went to supper, with the prospect of presently being started at setting the great sails and proceeding independently. Frank went to his cabin, which he was to share with the second mate, and while waiting for his call to supper prepared to have a wash.

But he had hardly entered before he heard the harsh voice of the mate shouting, "Brown, where have you got to?"

Frank presented himself at once, and the mate said impressively, "What sort of an officer do you think yourself, sneaking off below directly you see a slant, like any other waster? You'll keep watch up here with the pilot, while the captain and I go to get our suppers, and don't let me catch you shirking again."

Frank merely uttered the formula, "Very good, sir," and turned away rather relieved than otherwise, for he noted that the mate had recognised him as an officer, against his previous declaration that he was only a senior apprentice.

So he paced the broad expanse of the poop, looking round at the darkening, lowering sky and rising sea, and feeling a sense of responsibility coming back to him again to compensate him. Also the pilot spoke a few cheery words to him about his recent exploit, warming his heart anew, because praise from such men is of all the most valuable to a sailor.

Then came the mate, who said ungraciously, "Go and get your supper, and make haste up again. Don't sit there half the night."

Frank went, and found to his delight Mr. Wilson already at the table, and the two had a most delightful meal, hurried, it is true, but the food was good, and they were in full sympathy with each other on every point. Wilson, however, was inclined to be pessimistic, dwelling upon the obvious incapacity of the crew and the harshness of the skipper and mate. He had already come into conflict with the former, who, although a prime seaman, had the unfortunate belief that the way to treat young officers was to bully and discourage them, forgetting entirely his own first nervous essay as junior mate, so that, apart from the fact that he was a genial, gentlemanly young fellow, his heart went out to Frank, who, he felt, was going to be his brother in affliction, although of course they would see little of each other, being in different watches.

Having finished their meal, they both hastened on deck, to be met immediately by the thundered order of the skipper to get sail on the ship. "Now," thought Frank, "the fun begins." And it was even so. The utter incapacity and helplessness of the crew generally became at once a very real and pressing danger. They could not go aloft in most cases; those who did, always excepted the three prime seamen before mentioned, could do nothing when they got there but cling tenaciously to whatever rope came first, to do the smallest thing was beyond their power entirely.

But here, as so often happens, the boys came to the rescue. There were five of them, including Frank, who had been to sea at least a voyage, and three had received a comprehensive sea education in the *Conway*, the cadet-ship at Rock Ferry. So they were now called upon to exert all their youthful strength and skill in making up for the deficiencies of the men. The work, of course, took a shockingly long time to perform, for the wasters of the crew did not even know how to pull, being clumsy almost beyond belief, but still one by one the huge sails were spread, until the *Thurifer*, under whole topsails, foresail, and lower fore and aft sails, began to gain upon the tug, the wind blowing quite strongly from the west, with promise of a speedy increase.

The time had come to part, the ship being now in mid-Channel, abreast of Bardsey Island, with the deep bight of Cardigan Bay under her lee, the narrow strait between Carnsore and St. David's ahead of her, a gale imminent, and night coming on thick and black. But whatever any one felt he showed no sign, and the usual signal having been made to the tug, she eased astern in order to assist the crew to get in the mighty hawser. Indeed it is most probable that had she not done so they would have been unable to do it without losing a tremendous lot of ground. As it was, the job was got over fairly well, the tug dropped alongside and took off the pilot as previously arranged, and the *Thurifer* was left to herself and her crew.

No sooner were the yards trimmed and the hawser stowed away than the word was passed along for all hands to lay aft, while Frank was told to take the wheel. The skipper came to the break of the poop when they were all assembled and said, "Before the officers pick for watches I want to tell you fellows, all but the three sailormen among you, that if you think you're going to ship as A.B.'s aboard my vessel not knowing the first thing about your business, if you think you're going to obtain money under false pretences like that and have a good time, you've made the one mistake of your worthless lives. You are just a gang of low-down bummers, up to every dirty trick of loaferdom, and would see honest able men kill themselves doing your work, if you're allowed to. But you won't be. Until you pick up your work, and put all the guts into it you've got, I'm going to make this ship a floating hell for you, and don't you forget it. Now go ahead and pick your vermin, Mr. Vincent." And he turned on his heel and walked away.

The business of the selection was soon over, and the men were dismissed to begin, as inauspicious a voyage as could well be imagined. And whatever we may think of the behaviour of the skipper and mate, it must be remembered that the problem they had to face was a hard one—especially so under the present circumstances. But fortunately the gale increased in force very slowly, and held true to its point. Also the ship was splendidly staunch and strong, every item of her equipment being of the very best, so that they were able to carry sail until the morning, when the danger point was passed, and what had become an imperative necessity of shortening sail could be safely yielded to without jeopardising the safety of the ship.

But the toil and strain upon the handful of competents, especially the boys, was very great, for they had to do all the work that was hardest and most dangerous, in spite of the relentless driving exercised by the mate and bo'sun upon the wasters. Their lives were indeed made a burden to them, and doubtless in the eyes of all the others they deserved it, but landsfolk should be able to spare a grain or two of pity for them, seeing that they had never before realised the difference between a tramp steamer and a sailing ship.

As a plain fact, nobody on board could boast of having much of a good time during the first fortnight of the *Thurifer's* voyage. Nothing but sheer seamanship and dogged determination on the part of the skipper and mate brought her through gale after gale, which rose up against her, and tried to drive her back. So severe was the strain and the stress of iron discipline introduced by the skipper that Christmas passed unnoticed in the midst of the hard work of sail-handling and working up of the greenhorns, only the very slightest addition being made to the grub served out, and the very word Christmas being unmentioned in the after part of the ship.

And yet I feel sure that this iron time did Frank and the second mate good. It brought out all that was best in them, and the terrific training stiffened their muscles. Also, though they received no word of kindness or praise for the splendid manner in which they rose to the occasion, they got no active persecution, their services were far too valuable for that. And as Frank felt day by day that every boy in the half-deck was looking to him as their leader, he felt more and more of the bone and sinew of manhood developing within him, and a fine pride in himself came to help him live his life as it should be lived in spite of all drawbacks.

And then came the fine weather with its opportunities for the skipper and mate to work up the wastrels, an operation conducted with the utmost ruthlessness as regards their work, although being under the English flag there was no downright cruelty such as would have been dealt out unstintedly in an American vessel. But the effect of this working was most severe upon Frank. He was now recognised as third mate tacitly, although never called "Mr." or "Sir," and had to supervise the work which his watch were driven to do all day long, for except the good hands, no one forward had any watch below. And the bo'sun's services were far too valuable in the direction of the rigger work to make him just an overseer of labourers.

So Frank got no watch below in the daytime, he got no word of pleasant intercourse from anybody, the men he was compelled to drive hated him with a most virulent hatred, and he was fast degenerating into a mere machine. Worst of all for himself, he felt he got no opportunity at all to practise his navigation or add to his studies, and felt that all he had learnt in the past was slipping away from him. There was another point which he hardly admitted to himself, it seemed like some grim spectre threatening him; he was actually beginning to dislike his profession, which so short a time ago had seemed the one thing in the world to him.

Mr. Wilson, the second mate, was also in parlous case, even worse than Frank, for he had no such deep and enduring love of the sea as Frank had to console him. But having worked his way so painfully upward as far as his present position, it was a bitter reflection to him that he was in the hands of a man who not only had it in his power to destroy his career, but would do this diabolical act without compunction. There are occasions, of course, when to stop a man from going farther in so responsible a life as that of a sea-officer becomes a positive duty to a conscientious man; but when some infernal kink in the brain leads the man in power to abuse that power for the purpose of destroying the career of his junior, who with a little encouragement would become an entirely estimable officer, no words of mine could convey the horror and detestation that I feel at such an act. Most happily, with the passing away of the sailing ship that vile abuse of opportunity is becoming less and less frequent in its incidence, and I hope will soon finally disappear.

Under the incessant grind and constant supervision of the skipper, who, if he spared nobody on board, certainly did not spare himself, the noble *Thurifer* gradually worked down to the region of the "roaring forties" without any mishap, and this with a crew so drilled that the majority of them could not knot a ropeyarn, and could not go aloft and do something else besides hang on when they got there. It was a triumph, and Captain Forrest's grim face showed that he realised it to the full as he strode to and fro on his spacious quarter-deck, nothing escaping his keen eye. Yet it was strange that with these splendid qualities so manifest in him he could not, or would not, recognise merit in others, for even his chief officer and coadjutor was never admitted to any terms of intimacy with him. He apparently preferred to reign alone, unbendingly, an absolute monarch, who was self-satisfied, self-contained, self-centred, who could command, and did so supremely well, but had wilfully and deliberately crushed out of himself all the finer feelings of humanity, and apparently would have subjected all who came under him to the same stern rule of a loveless life.

CHAPTER XV
THE BITTER LESSON ENDS

Among his fellow-captains the master of the *Thurifer* was accounted a lucky man for his wonderfully smart passages and almost complete immunity from accident, the occasional loss of a spar now and then being merely incidental to the making of such passages, and hardly to be called accidents. This voyage, in spite of its inauspicious beginning, was no exception to the rule, for after getting out of the Channel and licking his scratch crew into shape, nothing ever seemed to go wrong again. Luck had but little to do with it, but consummate seamanship had, and the ability and determination which made his men admire while they hated him.

Poor Frank, who in spite of his high courage and dogged perseverance had drunk the bitter cup of unhappiness and loneliness to the dregs, could not help feeling that in one way, at any rate, the captain was rendering him a service, that is, by getting the ship as quickly to port as possible, for although hope was nearly dead within him, he could not help stealing over him now and then a shadow of anticipation that relief might come; but he did fear that it might come too late to save him from what he felt would be the irreparable harm of making him hate the profession he had loved so sincerely. He did not realise that even this cold neglect, overwork, and incessant fault-finding that he had been subjected to had been productive of benefit to others. He had been driven to devote himself during work hours, whenever possible, to assisting the boys to learn as much as he knew himself, and had fired them with emulation, so that they were all in a fair way of becoming good seamen much more rapidly than would otherwise have been the case.

At last, after a splendid passage of eighty-four days from Liverpool, the *Thurifer* was hove to off the Sandheads to receive her pilot from one of the beautiful brigs which ply about the entrance to the great Hooghly. With her usual good fortune the *Thurifer* had not even to wait for a tug, for the *Court-Hey*, at that time the acknowledged chief of the fine Calcutta tug-boats, came steaming past with a big outward-bounder, which she slipped just abreast of the *Thurifer*, then turned and hooked on to the latter vessel at once.

There is always in the breast of the most case-hardened old sailor a sense of prideful accomplishment upon the completion of a successful passage under sail, a feeling that has been most attenuated, if not entirely destroyed, by the advent of steam. And every man and boy on board the *Thurifer* seemed by common consent to have forgotten all their grievances in their elation at having made so fine a passage, with the exception of the two men primarily responsible for it, Captain Forrest and Mr. Vincent. Their grim faces never relaxed a line, their haughty unapproachable manner softened not in the least.

But Frank, for some reason that he was entirely unable to define, found himself for the first time during the voyage in almost boisterously high spirits, nor, although he found the captain's eye fixed upon him every now and then in sourest disapproval, did he feel at all inclined to curb them. He flew about his duties as if full of the joy of life, wondering why he felt so happy, and when the anchor rattled down at Garden Reach, he actually felt as if all his troubles were over.

When the decks were cleared up and the cry of "Supper" was raised, he went into his berth to find Mr. Wilson sitting in an attitude of deepest dejection, looking like a thoroughly beaten man from whom all hope had fled. Frank, somewhat alarmed, went up to him and inquired in the heartiest manner after his health, thinking he must be ill.

The young man, however, merely said, "No, my body is all right, but that demon of a skipper has broken my heart."

"Why, what has he been doing now?" eagerly inquired Frank.

"Oh, nothing fresh," groaned the poor fellow, "only he told me before the pilot and the fellow at the wheel that I wasn't worth a shilling a month, and that he wouldn't carry me for ballast, with a few other choice remarks of the same kind. Nothing worse than he has often said before, but coming to an anchor as we were, I felt sure that he intended to sack me here and give me a bad discharge. I've a good mind to jump overboard. I was so thundering happy when I heard I'd got this ship, and I've got on so splendidly before, that it's as if an earthquake had come into my life and broken it all up." And he let his head drop again and groaned aloud.

"Now, look here," said Frank after a pause, "I don't know what it is, but something tells me that our troubles are nearly over. I feel like a man who is waiting to be hung and has just heard that he has been pardoned. I don't know why or how I've got this feeling, but I'd like to give it to you, my dear man. But I do know this, that whatever happens to me in after life, I'll never abuse my position as this hateful beast has done, a perfect enemy of mankind I call him, all the worse because of his wonderful ability. Do cheer up, and remember that if the worst comes to the worst, and we have to go home with him again, we've both got good records up till the time we met him, and I don't believe he'll dare to malign us to the owner. Curse him," cried Frank in a sudden fury, "how dare he come into our lives and try and wreck them by means of his diabolical temper. He ought to be shot, and many a far better man has been shot for less, if only half what I've heard is true."

That night, for the first time since they had come together, these two young men were able to sit and talk for a long spell, comparing notes of their experiences and fighting their battles over again, but never a word more was uttered about the bane of both their lives.

When they turned in, Frank felt as if a crisis had arrived in his career, and, as he had done on a momentous occasion before, turned blindly to God and blurted out the desire of his soul. "Deliver me from this evil man," and with a swift after-thought, "and poor Wilson too." Then he sank peacefully and almost immediately to sleep.

Morning brought the mooring-boat and the allotted position off Prinsep's Ghaut. In the excitement of the work of mooring, unlike the process anywhere else in the world, Frank forgot all about his worries and his strangely unwarranted hopes. It was to him one of the most peculiar and, at the same time, interesting pieces of work that he had ever seen, the way in which the slender black men dived to the bed of the turbid river and hooked on ropes to the moorings which lay there; how skilfully they toiled in their huge launches to get the ship's cables attached to the mooring—chains ahead and astern, and how splendidly the ship rode when moored, unable to move in any direction but up and down.

It was a busy day, and there was no time for reflection until evening, when the steward came and called Mr. Wilson and Frank to supper, telling them that the captain and chief officer would not be there to the meal. It was wonderful how great was their sense of freedom, and when the steward had gone away on some trivial errand, Wilson lifted his cap and cried boisterously, "Good luck to them! may they never come back here any more!"

"Hush," said Frank, "we don't want anything reported to them when they return; you know what some of these stewards are. Let us go and have a smoke and a yarn on the poop, where we can sit now without fear of being made to feel as if we were stowaways."

And up they went, sat in the skipper's long chair and on the skylight settee, and talked until the bumping of the dinghy bringing the mate against the accommodation-ladder roused them from their long discussion of all things they knew anything about.

As they stood at the gangway to receive him, he said in quite a different tone from any they had ever before heard from him, "Good evening, gentlemen, glad to see you keeping such a good look-out. Come into the saloon, I've got some news for you."

They followed him with thumping hearts, wondering if their hopes were to be realised. As soon as they were seated, the mate said cheerfully, "The captain has just received the news that he has fallen heir to a great estate, which requires his attention at home as soon as he can get there, so he has resigned. And as the owners apparently think it isn't fair to the skipper of the barque *Coomallie*, which is lying higher up the river here, to promote me to this big ship over his head, I am exchanging with him to-morrow. I believe he is considered a very smart man. It's a pity, Wilson, that you hadn't got your mate's ticket, or you might have gone on here. As it is, the mate of the *Coomallie* is coming here, and I shall have to get a new one. That's all, good night." And turning abruptly from them he went into his cabin.

Wilson and Frank stared at each other for a few moments in almost stupid amazement, like men suddenly stricken imbecile; then, actuated by a common impulse, they both turned and made for the deck outside, which having reached, Wilson whispered hoarsely, "Frank, it can't possibly be true. Surely no such miracle has happened to save you and me from destruction."

Frank, who by this time had regained his composure, answered quietly, "I believe it *is* true. I've felt in my very bones lately that I was going to be set free from this man. My only fear was whether I did right in coming with him at all, since I knew what he was before we started. But I felt that I couldn't be far wrong if I did my duty, and I certainly never imagined that any man could be so evil-minded and cruel as he has turned out to be. I can only say, as I have had occasion to say before, 'Thank God for deliverance.'"

"And I'll say 'Amen' to that with all my soul," rejoined Wilson. "It means new life to me, for there can't be such another brute in the world of sailors as this one; or if there is, it's against all laws of chance that we should get him here."

Yes, it was true. Morning brought Captain Forrest and the new commander, Captain Sharpe, on board, when all hands were called aft and informed of the change by Captain Forrest in a cold, contemptuous fashion. He took no note of the palpable movement of relief which ran through the entire ship's company as the splendid news of his going entered their minds, but he could not help seeing the earnest look of pleased appreciation on every face when his successor stepped forward at the close of his little speech and said, "Well, my men, you've got a new skipper in me, and I hope and believe that we shall pull well together. It shan't be my fault if we don't, for I am proud to be appointed to so splendid a ship and such a good crew as you appear to be."

He stopped abruptly, having apparently no more to say, and a spontaneous joyous cheer went up from all of them. A cheer wherein was mingled immense relief and glad anticipation of better days in store. Captain Sharpe then went up to Wilson and Frank, and shaking hands heartily said, "I am very pleased to know you both, and especially you, young Brown. I know your friend Captain Burns in Lytham, and heard all about your wonderful work in bringing home the *Woden*; I'm proud to have you on board my ship."

Poor Frank was speechless, unable to say a word in reply, for a lump came up into his throat and nearly choked him. It was not necessary, however, for him to speak, for the captain patted him kindly upon the shoulder and passed on to say a cordial word to the apprentices, all of whose faces lighted up as he spoke to them. He was like a beam of sunshine breaking through the lowering clouds of a dark and gloomy day.

The retiring skipper and the mate collected their belongings, and left the ship without a word of farewell, consistently sullen and ugly until the last. Thank heaven we know them no more either, but we must not forget that there are more of the breed about, both afloat and ashore, who conceive that their mission in life is to make other people miserable, and who never cease their efforts for that fell end until death has mercy upon their victims and removes their oppressors.

That was indeed a momentous day for the crew of the *Thurifer*. For the new captain even improved upon closer acquaintance, and by the end of the first week not a man on board had any other opinion of him than that he must be about the best man in the world. I draw him from the life, gratefully, but not one touch of exaggeration is there about my description of him. He was a man of about forty-five years of age, with a handsome sunburnt face, a big fair beard, and a roguish blue eye. A prime seaman and navigator, he had yet been slow in getting up the ladder, more I think from native modesty and want of hardness in pushing himself forward, no matter who was pushed aside to make room for him, a trait only too characteristic of many successful men. But his chief charm was his innate kindliness and goodness of heart, breeding an intense desire within him to see everybody around him happy. Indeed a miserable face made him feel a sense of guilt, as if he were in some measure responsible for the unhappiness. Wilson and Frank literally adored him, and felt that they could cheerfully die for such a man.

One of his first acts was to institute a regular course of lessons in navigation and seamanship for the apprentices in the saloon, coupled with a standing invitation to a certain number of them each day to have dinner with him and his officers, no selection being made, but all enjoying his hospitality in rotation. Also he made great improvements in their dietary and accommodation, and visited their quarters every day, so as to keep them up to the mark of decent living, knowing full well that without such supervision boys on board ship invariably get slack and often lose all the habits of neatness and cleanliness instilled into them at home and at school. And all this he did not only from a sense of duty to his young charges, but from inclination, for he loved to act thus, and obeyed this the highest incentive to well-doing that man can have.

The loading of the *Thurifer* with jute for Dundee proceeded apace. It was a time of high freights and plentiful cargo, and all hands began to look forward with joy to the homeward passage. Mr. Wilson, of course, was busy in the hold supervising the stowing of the cargo, while Frank, now regarded as an officer indeed, was busy from dawn till dark with the bo'sun in attending to all the hundred and one details of the rigging and equipment which are necessary in order to prepare a great sailing-ship for her homeward passage, work which can nowhere be so well and expeditiously performed as in harbour. And in the evenings the captain would often remain on board, busy with some of his boys, while Wilson and Frank were able to go and visit friends ashore, whose acquaintance they would never have made under the old system.

Liberty day came and went without any disturbance whatever, the men all feeling so contented with the change that they voluntarily did what they could not have been driven to do, in fact they had all sworn not to go home in the ship with the other man. And I must interpolate one remark here, although it is slightly out of its turn; instead of being charged 2s. 4d. to the rupee, whose exchange value was then 1s. 5d., as they would have been under Captain Forrest, they were charged 1s. 6d., for Captain Sharpe disdained to rob his men even in strictly orthodox fashion, nor would he permit others to do so. There was only one cloud in the blue sky of content which enveloped the ship, and that was the uncertainty attendant upon the coming of the new mate. Everybody wondered much what manner of man he would be, knowing well how much of the comfort of a ship depends upon the character and ability of the first executive officer.

The day before she sailed the new officer came on board, and looked curiously about him as if he sought a sympathetic face. He would have had my sympathy had I been there, for I know of few situations more trying than his was. And it was well for him that he happened to strike a little community of really good fellows who wished to put him at his ease. They, that is, the captain and second and third mates, treated him exactly as they would have treated a man who had been in the ship for a long time. But he, poor fellow, actually mistook their kindly attitude for a tribute to his personality, a mistake he was never able to rectify afterwards. Because his personality was a kind to excite derision, not sympathy or respect. He was not able to take the smallest manœuvre without the stimulus of liquor, and he had brought on board with him a few bottles, of necessity few since his means were extremely limited, and before he had been in the saddle forty-eight hours everybody on board knew his weakness.

In this matter sailors are the keenest observers in the world. And when, in getting under weigh the next day, he stood on the forecastle-head and endeavoured to make up for his lack of ability by making a noise, the men under his command quietly ignored him and did the work they had been trained to do just as if he had not been there. Poor chap, his bemused brain took it all in but was unable to deal with it, and from thenceforth his position in the ship was a nominal one. I cannot here explain how such men come to the position of chief officer and sometimes captain, I only know that it is so, they do, and the fall they make is painful to witness.

But nothing now could affect the happiness of the *Thurifer's* crowd. The captain was such a real live man, so genuinely anxious for the welfare and happiness of everybody on board and so indefatigable in his attention to what he conceived his duty, that the fact of an incompetent chief officer having joined the ship was but a small detail in the general scheme of things.

No sooner had the ship got to sea than the skipper arranged a three-watch system, whereby Frank had the first watch from 8 P.M. till midnight, Mr. Wilson the middle watch, and the mate from 4 A.M. to 8 A.M., thus giving each of the officers a long spell of rest and recreation, as well as a chance to feel their power of independent command. And as the captain invariably rose about 4 A.M., he was able to keep his eye upon the mate and see that he did nothing wrong, but he never actively interfered. What he said to the mate in the privacy of his cabin no one but themselves ever knew, but it was doubtless something very stern and searching. Yet it had no effect whatever.

The man was hopelessly incompetent and growing worse, not better, every day. So that when at noon all the officers were grouped on the poop with their sextants getting the sun's meridian altitude, he was always the one to be out at even this, the simplest of all marine operations. For when you have, by moving the vernier on the arc of the instrument, brought the sun's lower limb in contact with the horizon and clamped it, you have only to turn the tangent screw gently as the sun rises until it rises no more, a sign that it is at its highest point or meridian for the day—it is noon at that particular spot. It is so simple, so easy, that any schoolboy could perform the operation with just a few minutes' tuition; but this poor bungler seldom if ever got a correct meridian altitude. And at the working up of the ship's noon position, while the agreement between the captain and Mr. Wilson and Frank was scarcely ever out more than a mile, it was the rarest thing for Mr. Carter to be within five miles of the correct position.

Still, as I said, this matter did not affect the general comfort of the ship or the happiness of the two junior officers, who both made splendid progress, the captain saying one day to Frank, "What a pity it is you weren't either a *Worcester* or a *Conway* boy, you would have been able to come as second mate next voyage. As it is, you'll have to make another trip as third before you can go up for your ticket."

"Then all I hope and pray is, Captain Sharpe," brightly responded Frank, "that it will be with you. I don't care a bit about the position as long as I am treated as you treat me; I am happier than I have ever been in my life before."

"That's all right, my lad, you deserve all you're getting," answered the captain. "I am always very pleased with you."

At which Frank turned away, his heart too full for utterance, and yet with a sense of shame that he should have allowed the transient evil of being under Captain Forrest to have almost made him hate the noble profession. In which I do not at all agree with him, knowing as I so well do what a hell of misery a bad captain can make of a ship.

So the *Thurifer* fared homeward, happily, uneventfully, her crew all now thoroughly trained and ready for any eventuality, a ship where there were no quarrels or discontents, where the work went as goes well-oiled machinery, dominated by the splendid personality of one man. Shall I be believed when I say Frank actually dreaded the arrival of the ship at her destination? I am afraid not, yet such was really the case. As each day saw her drawing nearer home, he had hard work to keep from feeling downhearted with the prospect of another ship or another skipper in view; he felt so fit and so happy, that the idea of again being bullied and worried as he had been on the passage out almost terrified him. So that in very truth he was what the old salts used to say the perfect sailor must be, wedded to his ship.

Indeed he grew to love her more and more every day, as the perfect weather they were having allowed them to paint, polish, varnish, and beautify her generally, even to the extent of granting a calm for two days, without more than an incipient swell, just to the southward of the Western Islands, so that they were able to paint her round outside quite close to the water's edge. Oh but they were proud men on board that ship, feeling that never did a homeward bound Sou'spainer come into port looking as their ship would look.

Nearer and nearer home they drew, still favoured by fortune with the brightest and best of weather, until they were met in the chops of the Channel by a heavy easterly wind, hardly a gale, but necessitating a good deal of stern carrying on in order to hold their own, since the bottom of the ship was of necessity foul, affecting her weatherly qualities very much. Now it so happened that just about this time Captain Sharpe was not at all well, not ill enough to lay up entirely, but compelled to take all the rest he could. And so he was not able to be with Mr. Carter in taking over the "gravy-eye" watch, as it is called—4 A.M.—when the tides of life run lowest, and some men find it positive agony to keep awake. There is little doubt that owing to the captain's constant supervision of him the mate had become utterly careless, so much so, that even the fact that he was left to himself to watch over the lives of thirty-four of his shipmates had no power to make him vigilant. At least that is the only construction I can put upon his behaviour upon this terrific occasion, the account of which I am now about to give.

It was about 4.15 *A.M.*, with a moderate gale blowing and the fine ship under topgallant sails, a tremendous press of canvas for the weight of wind, was standing across the mouth of the Channel on the starboard tack. As always with an easterly wind up there the weather was clear, but there being no moon it was fairly dark. Still there was ample range of sight for a sailor.

Suddenly a shout was heard from the forecastle, "A green light on the port bow, sir."

The mate emitted a sleepy roar in reply, but actually for several minutes did not trouble himself to go to leeward and look, although he must have known that by the rule of the road at sea it was his duty to give way to the other vessel in the event of their approaching too closely to each other, and at night it is impossible to be too careful with ships crossing. When he did go over and look, the crossing vessel seemed to leap out of the dark at him, she was so close.

Panic-stricken, he ordered the helm hard up, but as the *Thurifer* swung slowly off the wind, the officer in charge of the crossing ship having waited in agony for some sign that the other vessel was going to do the right thing and give way, until he could bear it no longer, hove his helm hard up also. The result was that the two ships, which might have gone clear had both kept their course, rushed at each other end on, and when the stranger hauled his wind again, it was too late, he had only time to present his broadside to the immense shock of the *Thurifer's* 4000 tons coming on at the rate of about eight miles an hour. There was an awful moment of suspense as men's hearts stood still, a tremendous crash, and the huge steel wedge of the *Thurifer's* bow shore its relentless way right through the strange vessel's middle, amid a gigantic chorus of crashing masts, rending metal, and human yells of terror.

CHAPTER XVI
CONCLUSION

There are, I think, few more terrible and majestic spectacles to be witnessed than a collision at sea between two large ships, and especially between two large sailing-ships. The moment before the shock the immense cobweb-like entanglement of masts, yards, sails and rigging is towering skyward in all its graceful beauty and scientific arrangement, making the uninstructed beholder marvel, not merely how it can support the tremendous stress put upon it by the vast sail area acted upon by the wind, but how it is held in its place at all against the incessant pitching and rolling of the hull upon which it is reared.

But when two vessels like that come crashing into one another with an impact of several thousands of tons, and the mighty top-hamper comes hurtling down in ghastly entanglement of ruin, the scene is even more terrifying than that of some gigantic forest-tree with wide-spreading branches being struck by lightning and falling in an avalanche of riven fragments of timber. It is, however, a sight that is seldom seen by an outsider, and as, moreover, it usually occurs at night, few indeed are the people who have even had the momentary glimpse of its terrors caught by the crew of either vessel in their agony.

In the impact of the *Thurifer* upon the stranger, not one of the usual horrors was wanting. In the first place the *Thurifer* appeared to rebound as if aghast at the deed she had done, but her impetus carried her on again, rending and tearing her gigantic way through the hull of her victim, which was literally cut in twain, and heeling away from her, settled down as the *Thurifer* passed through her.

Amid all the horror of the scene, two figures in fluttering white were noticed on the top of the forward house of the doomed ship as it came abreast of the main rigging of the *Thurifer*.

Some instinct, I suppose, prompted Mr. Wilson to leap with a rope from the *Thurifer's* rail on the house of the other ship, shouting as he did so, "Come on, Frank—women!"

Frank was close behind him at the time, and in a very tempest of energy the two succeeded in saving the two unfortunates, who were indeed the wife and daughter of the captain of the sinking vessel. And as they were hauled into the rigging of the *Thurifer* they sent up shriek after shriek for "husband" and "father" in Italian, and had to be forcibly restrained from leaping back into the whirling blackness of sea and wreck through which the *Thurifer* was relentlessly ploughing her way. At last, that is after two or three minutes of eternity, the *Thurifer* dragged clear, her upper gear a mass of entanglement, ropes, sails, and masts carried away and dangling most dangerously overhead, while beneath her keel the mass of ruin which had so recently been a splendid ship settled quietly down to a final resting-place on the sea-bed.

Now here was a case where the most superb seamanship was absolutely of no avail for any attempt to save life. The ship could not be handled, for her braces and running gear generally were in an apparently inextricable confusion, no one knew the extent of the damage done to the hull, although the carpenter, true to the instinct of that most valuable class of seafarer, regardless of the falling and dangling gear overhead, ran and sounded the well, finding that she was as yet making no water. The boats were mostly destroyed, and in any case the falling wreckage had made it an impossibility to get at them even had they remained intact. So Captain Sharpe did the only thing possible, called all hands aft to see if any were injured or lost, and found to his delight that every man answered to his name.

But Mr. Carter was missing! Is missing still. Whether in horror at the deed he had done he had jumped overboard, or whether he had been knocked overboard by a falling spar, no one will ever know; he was gone, and, if the truth must be told, no one could regret him very much. The unanimous opinion was, "Well, poor chap, if he made a mistake, and there isn't much doubt that he did, he's paid for it with all that man has to give, and may God have mercy upon his soul."

Now, while Captain Sharpe was outlining his plan of work to the men, who were all recovered from their fright and confident in the safety of the ship, one of the boys came up to him with the startling news that two men had just crept into their house looking like lunatics, as indeed they were temporarily. How they got there they could not explain, but the supposition is that when the *Thurifer* passed through their ship, they, feeling only the blind desire to save themselves, had sprung at the black side of their destroyer, had caught some gear hanging outboard, or perhaps the chain plates, as the iron bars to which the standing rigging is secured and which are bolted on the outside of the ship are called, and had climbed on board, hiding in some corner until their paroxysm of fear had passed away, when they had emerged and entered the first open door they saw, which happened to be that of the boys' house. But they completed the tale of the rescued, four in all, the other two being the late captain's wife and daughter, whom the steward was vainly trying to comfort in the captain's cabin.

Daylight was now beginning to struggle through the mist on the horizon, and the wind was falling fast. So that after giving a few general orders as to the clearing away of the gear aloft in order to enable the ship to be handled, and men to move about the decks without the imminent danger to life and limb of spars falling upon their heads, the captain and carpenter went forward to survey the damage done to the bows. In truth it was a grim spectacle. The ministering priest, torn from his beautiful attitude of blessing, hung dolefully head downward, battered out of all recognition and only held by a few wrenched and twisted bolts whose tenacity would not be denied, and the thurible, that emblem of beatific aspersion, was gone.

The huge bar of iron which held down the bowsprit, the bobstay, was still in place though bent and curiously twisted, and so was the sturdy steel bowsprit itself. The jibboom with its great complication of stays, guys, foot-ropes, sails, and downhaul was like a scene I witnessed once, where a man fishing from the end of a pier caught a conger-eel which he flung into the midst of his line by mistake and then attacked with his umbrella. It was just hideously hopeless, the sort of thing you want to cut off and let drift away as beyond the wit or skill of man to get disentangled.

The anchors, snugly stowed and firmly lashed to their respective bolts by the cat-tails, were all right but useless, for the hawse-pipes through which the cables should have led to secure the ship to them while they bit into the ground were torn and twisted beyond locating or use. And the stem, that splendid curvilinear girder of steel which had cleft the waves so proudly, it reminded now only of the battered, inhuman visage of an old prize-fighter, so curiously bent and broken did it appear. Lastly, and most serious of all, the two sides of the bows were stove in, two huge rents appeared there, into either of which you might have driven a cart, and into which the unresisted sea flowed gaily, resurging discoloured with coal-dust and laden with curious fragments, for the fore-peak, as that part of a ship is called, was now getting such a scouring out as it had never received since she was built.

But it will be asked, why did this fine ship not sink with such a tremendous wound in her most vulnerable part? Only because of that invaluable invention, the water-tight bulkhead. At a distance of some twenty feet from the stem or cutwater there is built into all such ships a barrier of steel plates at right angles to the line of the ship's keel, or right across the ship. And the general practice was to build them without any door, so that neglect could not vitiate the safety they promised. They were built quite perpendicular and flat, which I have always thought a mistake, a slight curve or angle from each side pointing forward would have made them so much safer when resisting the inrush of the water when the ship was head-reaching with a hole in her bows.

Now with the exception of any possible damage done to the bottom plates of the ship by the wreck as she bumped over it, the extent of the structural damage to the ship was fairly well defined, and as the bulkhead which kept the water out of the main hold was well shored up behind by the well-packed cargo of jute, and consequently there was little or no danger of its giving way under pressure of the head sea, Captain Sharpe's mind as far as the ship's safety was concerned was quite easy.

What, however, he could not rid himself of was the fear which all shipmasters must have when any accident to the vessel under their command occurs—would he be brought in as being to blame? It is here that so much injustice is done to the men of the sea. No allowance is made for possible accidents over which a man has no control; could have none, in the nature of the case, be he as careful and vigilant as a man may be, there being no discharge in this war. And if he be brought in to blame, in most cases he falls, like Lucifer, never to rise again. Too old for service as a junior officer in a tramp, he may get a precarious position in a line whose directors, trading upon their fellow-creatures' misfortunes, get skippers upon whom disgrace has come to command their vessels at a miserably inadequate salary, and keep them in terror of instant dismissal, making an immense merit of employing them at all. Pah! the whole business is vile, it should stink in the nostrils of all honest men.

However, Captain Sharpe was not the man to allow his work to be hindered by any premonition of coming disaster to himself, so he proceeded as vigorously as he possibly could, aided to the utmost by his good crew, in the work of getting his ship so far repaired aloft as to be manageable. This enormous task was made somewhat easier by the wind falling away to an almost perfect calm, during which many an anxious glance was cast around in the hope of espying some sign of life upon the floating wreckage. But never a glimpse did they see, and consequently the work being unhindered by the arduous job of getting boats out, by nightfall they had her again well under control.

True, she looked ragged and unkempt aloft, a sad, strange contrast to the beautifully-rigged and splendidly-kept ship she was before the collision, but the great thing, getting her dirigible again, was accomplished by sunset. In this work the two rescued men took active part, albeit they had to be spoken to in sign language almost exclusively. But all sailors know that at sea this disability is no bar to the employment of foreigners, it being no uncommon thing for an officer to find himself commanding a whole crew, none of the members of which can speak more than two or three words of English, and some no word at all.

When at last the *Thurifer* was moving through the water again to a light south-westerly breeze, Captain Sharpe went below, and calling the steward inquired after the well-being of his two unhappy and unwilling passengers. He was informed that they were now quite calm, and had taken a little food. So the good man went to their state-room and introduced himself to them, finding that the young woman spoke sufficient English to make herself understood. From her he learned that the sunken ship was the *Due Fratelli* of Genoa, bound from Peru to London with nitrate of soda, and that she had been one hundred and thirty days out when the calamity occurred.

More than that he could not ascertain, partly because the poor ladies were so overcome at the thought of all their woes and the anticipation of destitution in the future that they speedily became inarticulate with lamentation and sobbing, and such poor consolation as the captain was able to offer them was entirely unheeded. Moreover, he somehow could not help feeling that in a great measure they looked upon him as the author, or at least the proximate cause, of all their suffering. So after assuring them that every possible care should be taken of them, and that they should be landed as soon as possible, he left them to each other's sad company.

The vessel was now headed for Falmouth, and going at a fairly good rate, remembering her crippled condition, before the fresh breeze which had now sprung up. But the captain's mind was full of anxiety, knowing as he did that the bulkhead, which alone stood between them and foundering, was quite weak in itself; indeed, but for the backing of the close-packed jute it would not have been possible to sail the ship at all, for the sea rushing through those two enormous holes in the bows would have soon crushed it in. And nothing could be done to block those holes in any way, because of the great area of open, ragged ironwork they presented to the incoming sea. However, the distance being small, only some forty miles, and the wind as yet light, he hoped for the best, and carried all the available sail, which drove her heavily along at about four knots. Meanwhile every precaution was taken, in case of a sudden bursting-in of the saving bulkhead, to have the boats ready to get out at a minute's notice, and all the equipment they required or could carry put into them. And so that long, anxious night wore through, during which every man who slept did so ready to jump for his life at the call.

Fortunately the weather held good throughout the night, and at the first premonition of dawn the captain, sending Frank up on the main-topsail yard to have a keen look around, was intensely relieved to hear him shout, "Land right ahead, sir!" a shout that brought all hands on deck with a rush to realise the good news. Shortly afterwards they were spoken by a tailor's boat, the skipper of which, hearing the news, piled on all canvas he could carry for Falmouth, in order to warn a tug-boat of the job that awaited them. The day strengthened into beauty, and the great sun came out in all its autumn glory, flooding the heavens with gold, as the once splendid *Thurifer*, like some gallant warrior wounded, his armour dented and broken, his proud plumes drooping and bedabbled with blood, dragging himself wearily homeward from a stricken field, crept heavily towards the lovely entrance to Falmouth harbour.

The wind died away to a calm, the exquisite beauty of the shores, in all the splendour of their autumn tints, lay basking in the sun, under a cloudless sky; but most glorious sight of all to those hardly bestead ones was a grimy, fussy, gasping tug heading straight for them. So she came panting up alongside, full of importance, and lowering a boat put the pilot on board. There was no bargain, only a warning word from Captain Sharpe that his ship was in no danger, and that this towage was quite ordinary, having nothing in the nature of salvage about it.

Then the tug's hawser was passed, and the *Thurifer* began to move gently in towards the beautiful harbour of Falmouth. The sails were all furled as neatly as possible under the circumstances, and presently, under the eyes of the crews of the great crowd of shipping in the harbour (for Falmouth in those days had an immense vogue as a port for orders), the crippled but gallant *Thurifer* was towed to a berth alongside the wharf, where her arrival was greeted with thunderous cheers by the great crowd which had assembled to greet her on her triumphant emergence from one of the most terrible dangers of the sea. Then as soon as the shore warps were properly fast and the decks cleared up, the very welcome word was given, "That will do, men," and everybody retired to their respective portions of the ship's accommodation to rest and think over their wonderful escape.

Frank especially felt the need to be alone. He, of course, could not help recalling vividly his last home-coming, as wonderful in many ways as this, but certainly not fraught with such tremendous danger. And then he thought with a thankful heart of the splendid change wrought in his life during the homeward passage as compared with the sad time going out, and a feeling of conscious and entirely justifiable pride swelled his heart as he remembered that he had endured not unmanfully, and had been fully rewarded. It made his eyes moist and his face hot, and to ease his pent-up feelings he was fain to sit down and unburden his mind in a long letter home, such a letter as his parents had never received from him before.

But he had not been writing for more than an hour when he was called on deck to bid farewell to the two poor ladies, whose consul had come down with a closed carriage to convey them to an hotel. And as Frank, blushing and sheepish, came up to them, the younger, a girl of about his own age, flung her arms around his neck, and with her face flooded with tears kissed him passionately, uttering a very torrent of terms of endearment and thanks in choice Italian. Poor Frank was in a desperate plight, knowing not what to say or do, for he had not seen them since that awful night when he and Wilson had rescued them from going down with the ship. Then the elder lady kissed him gravely and sadly, murmuring blessings upon him in her beautiful language.

The young lady, however, controlling her feelings with difficulty at last, said in her pretty broken English, "My mater and myzelf pray God give you tousan, tousan blessing; we never forget you brave Engleesman save our life, an' also this good man here," turning to Wilson, who stood by almost as sheepish as Frank himself.

Then the consul came forward and made a most heartfelt and gracious speech, assuring the captain that apart from the calamity the bravery of his officers and his own kindness would certainly be warmly recognised by the King of Italy, adding at the same time his condolences upon the sad loss of the chief mate. Then the ladies were hastily conveyed to the carriage and driven away.

Captain Sharpe turned to his two young officers with a sad shake of his head and said: "Those two poor creatures are in evil case, for in addition to losing husband and father, I have reason to believe from what the consul tells me that they have lost everything in the world, as that was the skipper's first voyage in the ship, and he had spent all his savings before he got her, having been long out of a billet. I do hope the country will do something for them, but I'm afraid there is a black look-out ahead for them. And now about ourselves. I have wired the owner full particulars, and must await instructions. I think if the ship's bottom should be found intact that it is possible she may be patched up temporarily and towed round to Dundee, or even sail round, in which case there will be great saving. But we shall know in the morning some time. Mr. Wilson, will you call the crew aft, I want to say a few words to them."

Aft they came, looking full of eager expectation. "Men," said Captain Sharpe, "I have only praise for the splendid way in which you have done your duty under the most trying circumstances, and I wouldn't wish to have a better crew. Now the voyage as far as you are concerned is virtually over, and if you choose to take your discharge you must have it. But I hope that we may all be together for a little while yet, and that you will help me to take the bully old ship round to Dundee with the cargo. Anyhow, will you stay on until we know definitely what is going to be done? I will let you have what money you require on account of your wages, and of course you can go ashore at any time out of working hours, while the food shall be as good as I can get. What do you say?"

The men shuffled uneasily, as sailors under such conditions always do, from one foot to another, and looked helplessly at one another, until one of the Britons cleared his throat and said, "P'rhaps we'd better go forrard, sir, and talk it over, an' let you know in a few minutes."

"That's right," heartily responded the skipper, "do so." And away they all went.

They came back within five minutes, having decided to stay if the ship wanted them, and wisely, since but few hands are required in Falmouth. The captain was very pleased with their amenity to reason, and giving them each a sovereign on account, dismissed them to go ashore if they felt so inclined and taste the delights of Falmouth, although, to be exact, there was much more fun and profit to be found on board the ship, which was thronged with visitors all day long, most of whom were very generously minded towards men who had been through what even they could see were tremendous dangers.

In due time the owner arrived and also a representative of the underwriters, and after long consultation it was decided that as the ship had sustained no injury to her bottom she might be patched up as regards the bows, refitted aloft, and sailed for her original destination, Dundee. Which was immensely to the satisfaction of all hands, and especially Frank and the bo'sun, both enthusiasts in the "sailorising" side of their profession, because of the big job of rigging work they were now called upon to perform, all work of the most interesting character, and highly educational for most of the men as well. Few people ashore realise how a sailor enjoys a job of rigging work, if the conditions under which it is performed are at all bearable.

The repairs progressed apace, and Frank and Wilson both felt as thoroughly happy as ever they had been in their lives, especially as neither had received anything but good news from home. The only uneasy feeling they had was concerning their well-beloved skipper. He had yet to face the ordeal of the Board of Trade inquiry, an ordeal which is proverbially uncertain in its results, sometimes resulting in the grossest injustice being perpetrated upon a good man, sometimes allowing the worthless to escape scot free, but always, I believe, conducted with the most earnest desire to arrive at the truth. Unfortunately for the skipper, his suspense was prolonged by the fact that the Government department moved slowly, while his work went on very rapidly, so that the *Thurifer* was ready for sea before the inquiry could be held.

In three weeks from the time she entered Falmouth harbour she was towing out of it again completely fitted aloft, but temporarily patched as to her bows, and spreading her huge white wings, bore away grandly up Channel before a strong westerly breeze, a Channel pilot being on board, and all hands, including the two rescued Italian seamen, who had by this time learned enough English to swear by, highly pleased with themselves. Of course these latter were needed to give evidence about the running down of their ship, although it was evident that they could know nothing about it, they being by their own admission asleep at the time.

Now, by the perfectly marvellous combination of circumstances, remembering the time of the year, the *Thurifer* made a passage from Falmouth to Dundee without once having to shorten sail on account of wind. It was accomplished, too, in the remarkably short space of time of six days; and so persistently favourable was the weather that it was frequently remarked, both forrard and aft, that the ill-luck seemed to have expended itself upon the collision, for ever since then fortune had smiled upon them.

They were met by a tug outside the Tay, towed right in and docked at once, and Frank's first voyage as an officer was over. Never surely was there a heartier or kindlier paying-off than that. No one had any grudges to work off, no ill-feeling to suppress, and yet no one had done anything more than his duty. They could not separate, however, as the inquiry was yet to be held; but it came off within a few days, the unanimous verdict being, that in the absence through death of the officer of the watch, and the consensus of evidence as to the care and skill of Captain Sharpe, they could only bring the disaster in as the result of accident from some cause or causes unknown, adding many compliments, as a rider, to Captain Sharpe for his skilful handling of his ship after the collision.

And this closes my record of Frank's career as an apprentice. His next voyage ended with him in the position of second mate, but with that I have here nothing to do. If the fates are propitious I should like to go on and picture him as certificated officer and master, or skipper, in a subsequent volume; but at present I must leave him with you as having passed from boyhood to manhood with credit, and as having also, after a hard and trying apprenticeship, still retained his early love and enthusiasm for the sea.